Praise for *Evernight*:

'A story to devour, & then savour. *Evernight* is alive
with thrilling darkness and vivid magic'
Kiran Millwood Hargrave

'Darkly brilliant, wonderfully imagined . . . A fantastic
adventure with a cracking heroine at its helm'
Abi Elphinstone

'Ross MacKenzie is a wizard with words. *Evernight* is an
artfully spun story, vividly conjuring a complex and
convincing world of witches and magic unlike any other.
Gripping from the first line, this book will thrill and
delight in equal measure. A triumph of the imagination'
M.G. Leonard

'A darkly magical story set in a brilliantly realised, hugely
imaginative world that's perfect for fans of *Nevermoor*'
Anna James

'A wild and unique adventure full to the brim
with friendship and magic'
Peter Bunzl

'A refreshingly original, thoroughly bewitching read'
Catherine Doyle

FEAST OF THE EVERNIGHT

ROSS MACKENZIE

With illustrations by Amy Grimes

ANDERSEN PRESS

First published in 2021 by
Andersen Press Limited
20 Vauxhall Bridge Road, London, SW1V 2SA, UK
Vijverlaan 48, 3062 HL Rotterdam, Nederland
www.andersenpress.co.uk

2 4 6 8 10 9 7 5 3 1

British Library Cataloguing in Publication Data available.

ISBN 978 1 83913 047 2

Printed and bound in Great Britain by Clays Ltd, Elcograf S.p.A.

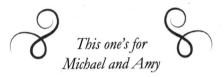

This one's for
Michael and Amy

Monsters

Sam Hushby's gun glistened silver in the light of the moon as he rode his horse along the rocky path from the city of Lake End to the Veil.

His new partner was waiting, just as the orders had said. Sam saw her from a fair distance, ghostly smoke drifting from the cigar in her mouth. When he drew closer, he heard her mutter a curse. By the time he pulled up alongside her she was shaking her head at the sight of him.

She sat high on an ironheart, a huge metal horse, and he could hear the whirr-click of its enchanted clockwork heart. They said that it could run for ever, the horse and the clockwork.

'Well look at you, boy,' she said, flicking the glowing butt of her cigar to the ground. 'All shined up like a new penny. How long you been outta the academy? A week?'

Sam tried to hide the flush in his cheeks. He knew he looked like the textbook rookie, perched on his flesh-and-blood horse; there were no scratches on his gun or his blade, no scuffs on his leather boots. The leather of his long coat was stiff and it creaked as he rode.

'Three days,' he mumbled. 'Arrived on the sunset steamer.' He snuck a glance at her. She was beautiful, in an angry kind of way. She shook her head again, tucked a curl of hair back behind her ear.

'What's your name again? Hushby?'

'Yeah. Sam Hushby.'

'Well, Sam, I'm Annalise. Annalise Francco. Now listen up: I didn't sign up to become a babysitter, you hear me? If I had wanted to be a nanny, I'd have gone to work for a rich northern family in King's Haven, like my mama wanted. You do as I say, and only as I say, and we'll get along just fine.'

Sam's face flushed. 'I ain't a child. And you can't be more'n twenty years old yourself.'

Annalise leaned forward in her saddle. 'I'm a deputy, third class. I'm your senior. And I've fired my gun at something with a heartbeat. Can you say that? You will address me as ma'am. Clear?'

'Yes, ma'am.'

She gave him another appraising look. 'You look frightened half to death, Hushby. Well, don't worry — you ain't gonna see too much action out here. Not the sort you're frightened of anyway.'

'But it's the Veil,' said Sam. 'I've heard . . .'

'You've heard the same stories every recruit's heard,' said Annalise. 'You've heard the war of the Old Gods ended here, right? That the Veil Forest sits on that ancient final battleground.' Her voice grew quiet and slow and deliberate. 'You've heard the trees grew up from the bones of the fallen, and that their whispering dead voices call out to all sorts of night creatures. You've heard the place is a-teemin' with monsters . . .' She gave a sudden, loud clap, and Sam almost fell off his horse, making Annalise snort with laughter and cry out, 'Ha! Well, if that's true, those monsters must be awful shy, because I ain't ever seen none of 'em. As far as I'm concerned, the only thing we need to look out for on this trail is bandits. The trees make perfect cover for thieves.'

Before them, the Veil was silent and dark, and the breeze coming from the forest seemed like the breath of a living thing.

'Come on,' said Annalise. 'We'd best get movin'.'

The edge of the forest was darker than the night and stretched as far as the eye could see, running alongside Giant's Foot Lake, which itself was so huge it reached beyond the horizon. Out in that vast darkness, Sam saw the flickering lamps on fishing boats.

The rangers rode in silence for a time, Sam listening to the click and whirr of the gears and cogs and machinery inside the shining body of Annalise's ironheart. The border of the Veil was marked by the white-hot flames of dragon-breath lamps. The warm breeze carried a sweet, damp scent from the thick forest.

'How long you been a southern ranger?' Sam asked.

'Since I was fifteen.'

'You like it?'

She laughed. 'Most of the time, yeah — when I'm not chasing shadows out here.'

Sam found himself glancing to his right, into the thick black tangle of branches and trunks and thorns. 'You said you've shot your gun at living things?'

Annalise shrugged. 'The occasional wolf. Shot a bear once — a real beast, he was too. Came a-chargin' out the shadows like an angry demon. I barely had time to—' Without warning, she stopped, listening intently.

Deep in the trees, something cracked.

Sam's eyes grew wide. 'What was that? Bandits?'

'Simmer down. Bandits work farther up the trail, away from the city. Probably just a fox caught the scent of your dirty diaper and came to investigate, is all.'

Another snap. This one closer.

Sam made to reach for his gun, but Annalise held up a hand.

'No. There's always the chance it's kids messin' around. Last thing we need is a rookie planting bullets in some nitwit who's entered the forest on a stupid dare. You stay here. If I need you, I'll call you.'

She climbed down effortlessly from the great metal horse, dropping six feet to the ground and landing with barely a sound. Then she walked towards the edge of the forest.

'Hey!' she called. 'Southern rangers. Is there someone in the forest?'

The sound of a snapping branch from somewhere else now, in the nearby thicket.

Sam shifted in his saddle. His heart was a wet hammer in his throat. He considered that maybe he should've just stayed in King's Haven and joined his dad's crab-fishing crew, like his parents had wanted.

Annalise's hand was hovering over the grip of her gun. She crept from the rocky trail into the first shadows of the forest. 'Stop messin' around, whoever's in there. Step into the open.'

The night was suddenly filled with a creaking groan, and several loud cracks. A tree toppled over, falling to the ground with a rushing crash, so near Annalise that she had to dive out of the way. She picked herself up, shaken and panting, and this time she did draw her gun.

'I think maybe I could use that help after all, rookie.'

Sam scrambled from his horse, half fell to the ground and made towards her, unholstering his gun with shaking hands.

'Wait! Annalise . . . ma'am . . . wait!'

But she had already moved deeper into the Veil, disappearing among the shadowy trees and vines and tangles of thorns.

Sam reached the fallen tree, scouted around. Saw nothing but the gloom of the night forest. 'Ma'am? Where are you?'

There was no answer. Sam cursed under his breath and took a few steps forward. 'Ranger? I've entered the Veil. Give me a signal to let me know you're all right!'

Blackness cloaked everything, coiled around him, squeezed him.

Cold fingers caressed his neck, and he gasped and spun around, gun drawn, to find that it had only been a hanging branch.

'Stop there!' That was Annalise. Was she talking to *Sam*?

'Ma'am? Ranger?'

'I said stop! Don't come any closer!'

'Annalise!'

'Sam?'

A gunshot sent him diving for cover. Then another, and another.

After that, silence.

Sam used a tree to drag himself up with one hand, the other still pointing the gun. His eyes flicked from one shadow to the next. He felt that he was trapped in every nightmare he'd ever had, that if he could only force himself to wake up, he'd be back in his warm bed in King's Haven.

He moved forward, staying low, darting from tree to tree. Here and there, the moonlight made it through the thick canopy of foliage and shattered in diamond splinters on the forest floor. The air was still as death, heavy with the earthy smells of the forest. And . . . something else.

Sam sniffed.

Blood. There was no mistaking it, that coppery smell. A strange sound began to drift into his ears; it was a wet sound, like slurping, or *sucking* . . .

Sam Hushby took a deep breath, and stepped out from behind the tree.

What he saw would haunt his thoughts for the rest of his life.

Annalise was sprawled on the floor, arms and legs splayed awkwardly. Her face lay in one of those splinters of fallen moonlight, deep brown eyes wide with shock, expression halfway between surprise and terror. She was dead. One side of her neck was ripped wide open. A hunched figure kneeled over her body. It was drinking her blood.

Later, Sam would not remember how long he stood and watched this gruesome sight. He was completely frozen with fear and horror. And then a spark flared in his heart, caught light, and he remembered that he was a southern ranger, and that he had a duty. He raised his gun, and his hand was shaking not only because he was frightened, but because he was angry.

'Stay very still,' he said, and he was amazed to find that his voice was strong and calm, 'and I won't shoot.'

At his words, the hunched creature stopped feeding. It went very still, the way some animals will go still when they feel that they are in grave danger.

'Now, I don't know if you can understand me,' Sam

went on, trying not to look at Annalise's face, 'but if you can, I want you to stand up very slowly and raise your hands. If you have a weapon, I want you to leave it on the ground.'

The thing did not move.

'Did you hear me?'

It turned its head.

An involuntary scream burst from Sam's throat.

A pale face stared at him from beneath a ragged black hood and a greasy curtain of dark hair. The face – that of a nightmarish young man – looked unfinished, puffy, like dough. The eyes were sunken, and the lips and surrounding waxy skin glistened with smears of fresh blood from Annalise's throat. The young man – not quite a boy, thought Sam – stood up in a slow, lumbering movement. Yet when he lunged, he moved with such quickness that Sam took a panicked step back and missed with a wild pistol shot.

The creature was upon Sam before he could regroup; it took Sam down with shocking force, knocking the gun from his hand, and began scratching and tearing at Sam's face with long, filthy fingernails. Frightened, desperate sounds escaped Sam's mouth, and he fought and kicked and pushed the creature off. He reached for his gun, grabbed it, fired, this time missing by just a whisker. The creature hissed at him and spun away, and Sam fired again, but the thing was lost to the forest shadows.

Sam shambled through the trees, stumbling back out to the trail, his breath coming in heaving gasps. He could taste his own blood, metallic as it ran from the deep scratches the attacker had left on his face. Sam's thoughts were a spinning blur. He rushed to his horse, hoisted himself into the saddle, and rode off towards the city as fast as he could manage.

An hour later, after Sam had raised the alarm and led a group of fellow rangers back to the forest, they found Annalise's ironheart standing on the trail. When they entered the Veil, however, Annalise's body was gone. The only sign she had been there at all was a spattering of blood on some rocks near the spot where she had been lying.

BETRAYAL

Back on the outskirts of the city of Lake End, Sam sat alone in an empty office in the ranger station and waited. The events of the night repeated over and over in his mind. He could not unsee the terrible image of Annalise sprawled on the woodland floor, could not wipe from his mind the wet, ravenous slurping sounds the creature had made as it feasted on her blood.

If he had been quicker off his horse . . . if he had got to her faster . . . would she still be alive? Or would he be dead now too?

The office door opened. Sam jumped up and stood to attention as Station Chief Barker entered the room, his big, bear-like body filling the doorway.

'Siddown, Hushby.'

Sam followed the order. Chief Barker walked around to the other side of the desk and sat on the chair, which creaked under his weight. He clasped his big hands and rested them on the desk. His grey eyes were ringed with dark shadows and deep crow's feet etched the skin near the corner of his eyelids.

'There was no attack.'

Sam stared blankly.

'Sir?'

Chief Barker shifted in his chair. 'Your partner . . . Ranger Annalise Francco . . . is a deserter. She has run away.'

Sam shook his head. 'No, sir. That's not what happened. Annalise loved being a ranger. She'd never run . . .'

'Maybe you didn't understand me,' said Barker, and his eyes flashed dangerously. 'Deputy Francco had been struggling for a while. She had talked about getting out of the ranger service once her seven-year contract was up. Obviously, she could not handle the thought of another two years, and took matters into her own hands. That is the story we will tell.'

'But, sir . . .' Sam could not take this in. 'She died in the line of duty. I saw her body myself – and the thing that killed her! We can't let her family think she upped and ran away! She's a hero!'

Chief Barker leaned over the desk.

'Hushby,' said Chief Barker, 'let me make this very clear: there was no monster. No attack. People round here have been livin' on their nerves since the Evernight came last year. Somethin' like your story could cause panic – and panic is the last thing we need, with tens of thousands of folks arriving here in Lake End for the Silver King's Evernight Feast in a couple of weeks.'

Sam glared at the chief. He knew that speaking up might land him in serious bother, but he was too exhausted and frightened to care very much. 'So you're just going to ignore what's happened, sir?'

A hesitation.

'There *is* another option,' said the chief. He pointed to Sam's face. 'Some nasty scratches you've got there, Hushby. Looks like fingernail marks. Would be awful easy to convince people that Annalise was the one who made those scratches on your face . . . in self-defence.'

Sam's head shot up. 'What?'

'You say somethin' attacked her, Hushby, and yet you can offer no proof. Now, the ranger in me hears about a missing young woman and sees you turning up with those scratches on your face, and to me it's more likely *you* attacked Deputy Francco and disposed of her body, than some phantom out there in the woods. I don't think a jury would take much convincin' at all. So, you have two options: either you go along with my story – that your partner ran away . . . or you speak up, and end your days dangling from a rope.'

Sam sat back in the chair. Beads of sweat were forming on his forehead. It felt like the chief had punched him in the guts. How had he ended up *here*? A few short hours ago he had been on horseback, making his way to start a shift patrolling the Veil, and now his partner was dead, and the chief ranger was threatening to pin the blame on him.

'Do we have an understanding?' asked Chief Barker.

Very slowly, Sam looked up from the floor. He nodded.

'Very good.' The chief stood up and wiped a speck from one of the buttons on his jacket. 'You've made the right choice, Hushby. For everyone's sake.' He clapped Sam on the shoulder with a heavy hand.

Not for everyone, Sam thought, as he watched Barker leave the room. *And sure not for Annalise.*

A TEST

Far away, beyond the furthest-reaching boundaries of the Silver Kingdom, north-west across the Pewter Sea, was Westerly Witch, the great city of the Witches. Most of the city was built upon a tree the size of a mountain — the Mother Tree — buildings and streets and alleyways crammed on countless criss-crossing platforms and rigs, and in the nooks and crannies and holes of the unimaginably huge trunk and branches.

Somewhere in the mid-levels of the city, in a sparse office waiting room, Larabelle Fox, Witch-in-training, sat fidgeting in her chair.

'Calm down,' said her friend Joe Littlefoot, a small, wiry boy with messy hair.

Lara swivelled around and fixed him with her large eyes. She had grown quite a bit taller in her time in Westerly Witch, and the dark brown skin of her face was dotted with a few pimples. 'Yeah, easy for you to say — you're not a Witch. You don't have to take the bleedin' exam!'

'Well, I wish I *was* a Witch,' said Joe, folding his arms. 'Then I'd pass the test and go back to the Silver Kingdom and take care of the king myself.' He gritted his teeth at the mere thought of the Silver King. A year ago, Mrs Hester, the head of the king's White Witches, had unleashed an ancient darkness known as the Evernight on the world. When things had spiralled out of control, the king and his army had run away, trapping the poor in the slums as they went, sacrificing the people there to the Evernight – Joe and his granny included. Joe had survived, but Granny had been too weak.

'Sorry,' said Lara. 'I didn't mean to make it sound like my problems are so much worse than yours. I know that's not true. I'm just really nervous. Hell's teeth, look!' She held out her hands, which were trembling badly.

'You know you're a good Witch,' he told her. 'You're one of them really annoying people who's good at everything. It's so irritating.'

Lara raised her eyebrows.

'It's true,' Joe went on. 'You've already passed all the other steps with distinction. Double Eight said you're naturally better at spell-making than him – and *he* passed. So stop worrying.'

From the office beyond the waiting room came a loud yelp and a low rumble. Putrid brown smoke poured out from under the door, sending Lara and Joe scurrying for the window, heaving and retching. The office door flew open, and a young man came staggering out, wide-eyed, the tip of his wand spewing the offensive smoke. He was closely followed by an examiner, a tall man with slick black hair who was scribbling madly in a notebook.

'I would advise you,' said the man, 'to go home and rethink your choice of career. There are plenty of jobs in Westerly Witch for those without the talent to obtain a licence to practise magic in the wider world.' He ripped the page out of his book and stuck it to the young man's back. It read:

Failed

The young man had stuffed his wand into his trousers in a desperate attempt to smother his failed spell, but this only resulted in the brown smoke puffing out of his trouser legs. 'But I want to travel!' he said, his bottom lip quivering. 'I want to go all over the world and find new potion ingredients and invent new spells.'

The tall man sniffed. 'And I want just one day to pass when I can go to work free of the dread that some eager-to-please student will turn me into a cabbage or make my office smell like a burst lavatory. But I fear neither of our dreams will come true. Good day.' And with that he pushed the young man out of his office onto the busy wooden walkway, and closed the door. Wiping his hands on his handkerchief, he turned to observe Lara and Joe.

'Miss Larabelle . . .' He flicked a page in his book and raised an eyebrow. '. . . Fox?'

Lara nodded.

'Come with me.'

He led her to his office and ushered her inside. Lara shot a glance back out to the waiting room where Joe gave her a thumbs-up, then the door closed, and she was alone.

'Take your place, please,' said the examiner. He indicated a workbench in the middle of the room, upon which sat a cauldron for mixing spells. Lara walked to the bench, her legs feeling shaky. There was still a faint whiff of whatever spell had gone so badly wrong for the previous candidate.

'Smells like the sewers under King's Haven in here,' said Lara. 'And I should know. I used to be a tosher, see. So was my mate Joe, out in the waiting room. We'd search through the muck down in the tunnels for lost treasure, and you wouldn't believe, mister, some of the stuff we found down . . .' The sentence withered away: she realised he was staring at her.

'You're rambling,' he said, and he noted something down. 'Don't ramble.'

'Right. Sorry. I'm just nervous.'

The examiner reached into his pocket, then opened out his hand. Lara peered at his palm. There, nestled among the folds and lines of the examiner's skin, was something tiny and dark and shining. A seed.

'I'm a little peckish,' the examiner said.

Lara looked up from the seed.

'You what?'

The examiner widened his eyes and flicked them towards the seed in his hand. 'I'm *hungry*, Miss Fox. I was wondering if you'd perhaps be able to help me remedy that.'

Lara looked first at the seed, then back to the examiner.

'Oh! Oh, I see! Right! Oh, yes, mister. I'll see what I can do. Right away.'

She took the seed from his hand with great care. He wanted her to grow a plant from this seed using magic, that much was clear.

'This is a tricky one,' said Lara, her heart speeding up.

'Of course it is,' said the examiner. 'You are applying for the licence to practise magic in the wider world. Magic can be dangerous, Miss Fox. We must ensure that we are not sending dunderheads out there with free rein to accidentally blow things up. We don't want any incidents, do we?'

'No. No we don't.'

'Then please proceed.'

Lara nodded. She had been training for moons for this moment, under the watchful eye of Bernie Whitecrow, the High Witch. 'You'll make a fine Witch, Lara,' Bernie had been telling her every day. Everyone seemed to think so: Bernie, Joe, and especially Double Eight – Lara's friend, who'd been one of the king's White Witches, before he escaped and helped Lara defeat the Evernight. He'd already

18

passed the exam and gone off to continue his studies in the field. Lara missed him dreadfully. It seemed the only person who did not really believe in Lara was Lara herself.

She looked at the cauldron, and at the book of witch paper, pencil and empty glass spell bottle on the desk next to it.

'Right. Here goes, I suppose.'

Taking up the quill, Lara tapped it thoughtfully on the end of her nose. She wanted to make this seed grow – to produce a tree bearing fruit – so what ingredients would go into a spell to make that happen? *Life*. That's the first word that came to mind. Now, what symbols might make a person think of life?

She touched the nib of the quill to the witch paper and drew, with a scritch-scratching sound, the shape of a heart. Next to the heart she drew a droplet of water, and after that a simple, shining sun. She drew a tree, and a leaf, and an apple. As she worked, her teeth worried her bottom lip and it came to her again just how wondrous the act of spell-making was. Spells were as unique as the people who made them. Every spell – every single spell that ever was – was one of a kind, woven from the imagination and the mind and the soul of the Witch who wrote it down.

Lara clutched the quill in her hands and studied her spell carefully, her eyes tracing every line of ink, every irregular stroke, trying to imagine as she did so the feel of tree bark, the tart taste of a crisp apple, the warmth of the afternoon sun on her skin. She imagined the feeling of raindrops on her face, the smell of the world after a rainstorm.

Hoping more than anything that her spell would work, she set the quill down, took up the witch paper and popped it into the flames inside the cauldron.

Next came the words that brought every spell to life. The Witch's Chant.

'Born of mind, born of fire,
Born of Mother Earth's desire,
Use it wisely, use it well,
My heart, my blood, my gift, my spell.'

Within the cauldron, the flames licked higher, and shifted through changes of colour. The paper curled and blackened, and from the fire shot sparks and fizzing pops of light. Then the crystalline, sweet melody of magic, ever-present for Witches, grew more intense, and Lara's newly made spell came drifting out of the cauldron in lazy, glowing tendrils of purple blue.

Lara grabbed the spell bottle, unstoppered it, and held it towards the spell, scooping up the glowing curls. Then she placed the stopper back on and examined the contents of the bottle. It looked like a good-enough spell; the colour was dazzling bright, and the way it fizzed and moved suggested that it was a lively one.

'There,' said Lara, holding the spell out towards the examiner.

He took it from her open palm, held it close to his face, and peered at the contents. He noted something down. Lara was trying to stay calm, but the nerves were eating up her insides like carnivorous insects. The examiner gave the tiny spell bottle a shake, and then, as the spell spun around in its glass home, he gave Lara a long, appraising look.

Her heart almost came to a stop as he reached into his jacket, brought out his wand, and proceeded to load her spell bottle into the metal revolver chamber. With a click, Lara's spell was live in the wand, glowing bright in the bottle. Next he took the seed and placed it on the floor.

'Are you ready, Miss Fox?' he asked her, and this time she sensed a softening in the hard edges of his voice.

Lara could not speak. She nodded.

'Very well,' he said. 'Best stand back, I think.'

As Lara stepped back, the examiner pointed his wand towards the floor, and pressed the trigger.

Lara's spell blazed in the chamber. With a crack, a short sharp jet of purple light blasted from the wand tip and hit the seed, which leaped high into the air. Lara gasped, and stepped further back, watching as the seed spun and arced and landed with a soft tick.

The seed vibrated. It began to glow, and as it glowed, it seemed to burn through the floor, disappearing with a hiss.

Lara stared at the smoking hole in the floorboards.

'Has it . . . did I? Have I failed?' she managed to say in a small voice as dry as a dead twig.

The examiner continued to gaze at the ground. He held up a finger to quiet Lara.

'Give it time, Miss Fox. Give it time.'

Out in the waiting room, Joe Littlefoot fidgeted with the books in an old bookcase. He wondered how Lara was doing. A year ago he'd seen her face the all-powerful darkness of the Evernight and an army of tattooed monsters, and yet she seemed more frightened of this test than she'd been of any of that other stuff. Joe knew Lara better than anyone, knew that despite her toughness and bravado and her uncanny ability to jut out her bottom lip and not give in during any argument, she was secretly worried that she would not make a very good Witch.

After all, her mother had been a great Witch, a member of the Doomsday Coven that had looked after the most powerful spell in the world for centuries. And despite the fact Lara had taken that spell and used it to defeat the Evernight, she had confided in Joe that she still did not entirely believe that she belonged among the Witches, or deserved the praise others gave her.

A rumble from the office interrupted his thoughts, and he stood up as the walls trembled. The shaking lasted for half a minute, and then there was quiet. After that, nothing happened for the longest time. Joe began to wonder if Lara's spell had gone wrong. He crept towards the door and was almost close enough to reach for the handle when it creaked open, and out came Lara with a face like thunder.

'So?' said Joe. 'How . . . did you? Is it good news?'

Lara glared at him. 'No. It's not good news at all.'

'Oh, Lara. Don't you think on it too much. You can always try again . . .'

'It's not good news,' repeated Lara. Then her frown vanished, and her face lit up with a huge smile. 'It's GREAT news. I passed!'

'You did? I knew you would!'

The examiner, still munching on the crisp apple he'd picked from the tree Lara had managed to grow in his office, signed his paperwork with a flourish.

'Larabelle Fox,' he said. 'I hereby declare, by the power of the High Witch and the Council of the Mother Tree, that you are licensed to practise magic anywhere in the world, provided you adhere to the laws of the Witches. Congratulations.'

Lara danced a jig, and Joe laughed and joined in, and soon they were shooed out of the examiner's office into the glorious summer morning among the branches and streets and platforms of the great Mother Tree.

Ginny Adder

The night after Ranger Annalise Francco met her terrible fate, a lonely shadow rode a horse along the trail between Giant's Foot Lake and the Veil Forest.

The shadow wore a long coat of fine black silken material, and her boots were heavy and worn. She wore a headscarf of midnight blue. Above, the sky was clear and awash with the milky light of the constellations, and the night was bursting with the scent of wild summer flowers. In the near distance, the lights of Lake End, the sprawling second city of the Empire, twinkled like stars.

'Whoa, girl, whoa.'

Ginny Adder stopped her horse and sat stock-still in the saddle, sniffing at the air. A short, stocky black woman with a big cloud of grey-white hair struggling to escape the headscarf, Ginny was old enough to remember this part of the world before the Silver Kingdom had swallowed it up. She groaned with effort when she dismounted, but when she touched down, her feet were light and silent on the dusty ground. She rubbed her horse's muzzle and it lowered its big head so that she could kiss it between the eyes.

'You stay here,' she said, and she turned and stared hard into the Veil, that tangled mass of trees and thickets and thorny tendrils. As she took her first steps towards the edge of the forest, Ginny Adder drew her wand, and double-checked the revolver chamber, where six spells were loaded and ready, glowing different colours in the dark.

Her wand half raised, Ginny pushed through the brush, the long grass reaching up to her waist, and then, with a look back at her horse, she ducked into the forest.

She'd been here before, of course; most folks stayed well clear of the Veil, but Ginny was a Witch; she knew the best spots to collect wild mushrooms and berries – and so long as you didn't stray too far in, the worst you were likely to encounter was a hungry wolf or maybe a fire-tail lizard. She knew the smells and the sounds, the feel of the air on her skin.

But tonight . . .

Tonight it was different.

Tonight, she could sense something rotten had been here, leaving a stain on reality. She could feel the aftershock of terrible magic.

Ginny spun the revolver of her wand so that the locator spell was loaded. When she pressed the trigger, a warm orange glow burst to life at the wand tip, and from the glow burst a hare made of orange light, leaping to the ground, nose twitching. The spell hare sat upright, and then spun away, hopping over fallen trees until it stopped and looked back.

'All right,' said Ginny. 'I'm comin'.' She moved between the trees, following the light of the spell hare deeper into the forest than she'd ever gone before. The trees were thick and gnarled and knotted, so closely packed together that their highest branches interlocked, blocking out all but the smallest glimpses of starry sky.

Wild eyes watched her from the darkness; she could feel them. Her hand shook a little, but the spell light held them back, and she pushed on, tripping on roots and snaring on thorns, until the spell hare stopped beneath a thorny tree and glowed blazing bright. This was the spot.

The body was still quite fresh, and the sight of it made Ginny's breath catch in her throat.

She kneeled beside it, reached for the ranger badge shining on the young woman's coat in the wand light.

'*Annalise Francco*,' Ginny read. She reached out and touched the place on the young ranger's neck where something had ripped and torn at the flesh. She stroked Annalise's cold face and closed her unseeing eyes with a gentle touch. 'You rest now, my dear. Be at peace. I'm gonna find who's doin' this. I'm gonna stop 'em.'

Ginny stood up, her knees groaning, and gazed down at the young woman's body one more time. She left Annalise and came back out of the Veil, happy to see her horse, to feel the warmth of its breath on her hand.

'Bad business, girl,' she said. 'Bad, bad business. I reckon we'll need help.'

Ginny reached into the saddlebag and brought out a sheet of witch paper and a quill and some ink. She wrote a hurried message, and when she was done, the paper folded itself up, becoming a paper bird, and flew off into the night.

JOE'S NEWS

Lara and Joe stood on the balcony of Lara's quarters in the crown of the great Mother Tree of Westerly Witch. From here they could see for miles across the Pewter Sea. The air was fresh and salty and, for Lara, filled with the twinkling sound of magic.

'I can still barely believe it, Joe. I'm a Witch. A proper Witch!' She paused, because the enormity of her achievement had begun to sink in, and it was wonderful and exciting, and more than a little frightening. 'Hey . . . everything all right, Joe? You seem a bit distracted.'

Joe was gazing out towards the horizon, his pale face serious.

'Mmm?' His eyes flickered to Lara, and then to his feet. 'I suppose now is as good a time as any to tell you. What with you passing the exam, I expect you'll be busy. You probably won't even notice.'

'Notice what?'

'Well . . . that I'll be gone.'

Lara blinked. 'Gone? What d'you mean *gone*?'

Joe took a big breath. 'I'm leavin', Lara. I'm going back to King's Haven.'

Lara swallowed down her first instinct, which was to knock him about the head.

'But you're safe here, Joe! King's Haven is a mess! The slum folk are rebelling! There's been fighting in the streets, killings . . . and that's not to mention the White Witches! The city is teeming with 'em. And they're not all nice like Double Eight, since they got their souls back. For the most part we don't know whose side they're on – except the ones that make up the bleedin' secret police! Those crooked White Witches are definitely on the king's side, and they're killers, the lot of 'em! You forgetting all that?'

'No, Lara, I'm not forgetting all that. Course I'm not. But you know as well as me that I don't belong here. I'm not a Witch.'

'That don't matter! We can keep you safe . . .'

'I don't want to be safe! I don't want to stand back and do nothing! Our king left the slum folk to die when the Painted arrived. Our people, Lara! Coves we knew growing up! My granny died because of him! And when the sky went dark, so many brave souls tried to fight the Evernight's Painted soldiers, and got a dark mark carved in their heads for their trouble. Turned to slaves.'

'I know, Joe, but . . .'

'But what? When it was all over, and the king came back,

29

he started rounding up everyone who was marked, hanging them as traitors. Traitors, Lara!' He was shaking with anger. 'How many of 'em are still stuck in King's Haven, hiding away?'

'We've been getting them out,' said Lara. 'Rob Nielsen's been smuggling them here, where they're safe.'

'Not enough of 'em,' said Joe.

'Just . . . just wait, Joe. Think about it. Please.'

'I have. It's all I've *been* thinking about. Maybe I can't go back to being a tosher. Maybe I can't be the person I was, but I belong in King's Haven. I know the streets and the sewers and everything else better than anyone, maybe except for you. I can help Rob get more of the marked folk to safety. And I can do other stuff too. It's already agreed.'

'How d'you mean?' said Lara, her hands on her hips.

'Bernie's asked me to help Rob with something,' said Joe defiantly.

Lara felt a surge of surprised interest. 'Really? What is it?'

'I can't tell you,' said Joe. 'I couldn't even if I wanted to, because I don't know myself yet! I only know it's something important and I'll find out more when I meet Rob.'

Lara gave him a piercing look, and she was surprised and a little ashamed to realise that she felt a tiny bit jealous that Joe and Bernie and Rob were in on some secret.

'I'm really glad you've found a place to belong, Lara. But my home is where we came from. The streets we grew up on. The sewers we hunted for treasure in together.

Our people are in danger, Lara. And I must go back and do what I can to help them. Do you understand?'

Lara did not answer at first. Hadn't she been prepared to give her own life in the fight to destroy the Evernight and to save her friends? She realised she was selfish to expect anything less of Joe.

'Course I understand. But that doesn't mean I have to like it.'

Joe smiled at her, then seemed to look past her, at something far off. 'Do you ever think about the way things used to be, back in King's Haven, before the Evernight?'

'All the time.'

'Me too. Sometimes I dream we're back there. They're great dreams, Lara; you and me, we're toshing in the sewers, and we don't have a care in the world. And my granny . . . Granny's waiting at home for us with a nice pot of rabbit stew . . .' His voice broke then, and Lara moved towards him, but he backed away and dabbed his eyes with his knuckles.

'When d'you leave?' she asked.

'Tonight.'

'You sure, Joe? Really sure?'

Before he could tell her that he was, a paper bird came arrowing through the branches, landed on Lara's shoulder and began pecking at her.

'Hell's teeth, all right!' She grabbed the bird, unfolded it and read the short message. 'Look at this. The High Witch wants to see me. It's urgent!'

BERNIE'S REQUEST

The High Witch's palace sat among the uppermost branches of the great Mother Tree, thousands of feet above sea level. The walls grew from the very fabric of the trunk, twisting and sprouting from the branches, and the musical whisper of magic at this height was intense and beautiful. The Blossom was in full flow, the many-coloured flowers blooming on the ends of every upper branch, breathing magic into the honey-sweet air.

The palace's tree-trunk-and-ivy doors swung open, and there stood Bernie Whitecrow, the High Witch, leader of all the free Witches in the world – at least those loyal to Westerly Witch. Bernie was middle-aged and apple-cheeked, with a short cropping of grey hair and fierce, shining eyes. She wore a long Witch's coat, and a crown of twisting branches on her head.

'Well, if it ain't my favourite fully-licensed Witch in all the world!'

Lara narrowed her eyes. 'You know I passed the exam?'

'Course I know. I'm the High Witch! You think I didn't have the feelers out? I knew you'd do well, my girl. Now, hurry on in, there's something urgent to discuss.'

Bernie led Lara through the palace, and as they walked the passageways, flowers bloomed on the walls. The perfume of the place was sweet and spiced, and the summer air was warm. Atop the palace was a balcony of creeping branches, and when Lara went to the edge and looked over, she could see the winding streets and rickety platforms of the city stretching down, down, down towards the crashing waves, multicoloured spell smoke drifting from the chimneys.

Bernie closed the balcony doors and thoroughly checked the branches above, as if making sure nobody else was about.

'Bernie? What's wrong?'

'I have some news for you, Lara.'

'What is it? Has something bad happened? Is it Rob? They haven't caught him in King's Haven?'

'No, it's not Rob. It's Double Eight.'

Lara took a sharp breath. It felt like a lead ball was forming in her stomach. 'What about him?'

Bernie waved a hand, and two bark chairs sprouted up from the balcony floor. They sat, and Lara was glad to be off her feet, because her legs had begun to shake.

'You know he went south?' said Bernie.

Lara gave a nod. 'Yeah. Lake End. I got a letter from

him a couple of weeks back. Sounded like he was really enjoying learning under . . . what's his name?'

'Sprout,' said Bernie. 'Krispin Sprout. A good Witch, Lara, very good indeed. It's always been the way to send young Witches out into the world to study under a mentor. That way they'll learn about life. They'll learn about people. A good Witch has to know about *people*. But as the Silver Kingdom has grown more and more aggressive towards us, we've had to change up where we place our youngsters – and shroud 'em in more secrecy than ever. Used to be, we'd send young 'uns to learn in King's Haven. But over the years Mrs Hester spread lies about us Westerly Witches, poisoned regular people against us, made them fear us. I sent Double Eight to Lake End because that poison hasn't taken hold in the south yet. Many of the people there still remember the way things used to be, before the Kingdom took over – even the secret police aren't all-powerful in Lake End. They've got the southern rangers to keep the law.' She stopped and stared at her fingernails. 'That's why I thought he'd be safe.'

Lara leaned forward on her chair. 'But Double Eight's not safe? Is that what you're saying?'

When Bernie looked up from her hands, the expression on her face frightened Lara. 'No, Lara. He's not safe. He's missing.'

Lara blinked. 'Missing?'

'Yes. For two weeks.'

Lara's breath was coming in shallow gasps. 'Two weeks? Bernie, why haven't you said anything?'

'Because you had your exam coming up and I wanted to know as much as I could first. Wanted to know the facts, such as they are, before I worried you.'

'And what did you find out?'

'Krispin Sprout is dead,' said Bernie. 'Murdered.'

Lara felt her throat tighten. 'Murdered?' she whispered. 'By *who*?'

Bernie looked old and tired. 'We don't know. There was dark magic involved, so it must have been a Witch that did it.'

Lara could not believe what she was hearing. There was a question on her lips, but she could barely bring herself to ask it, and when she spoke, her voice was very small. 'Do you think Double Eight is dead too?'

Bernie closed her eyes. 'Honestly, Lara, I don't know. I hope not. I very much hope not.'

The tears pooling in Lara's eyes split the brilliant daylight into streaks and shards across her vision. 'But why would anyone kill him?' Her voice faltered. 'He's the nicest, gentlest person in the world.'

'Before Sprout died,' said Bernie, 'he was investigating a series of other murders in Lake End, each one bearing the hallmarks of dark magic. Double Eight, as Sprout's apprentice, was helping with the investigation. Perhaps they got too close to the truth. Perhaps the killer acted to silence them.' She waved a hand. 'But that's just a theory, Lara.

Doesn't make it true. Double Eight may still be out there somewhere. I hope more than anything that he is.'

Lara stood and began to pace. Anger and frustration coursed through her like a storm-swollen river. 'What are we going to do? If he's alive surely we must find him?'

Still seated, Bernie said, 'I've already got one of my most trusted Witches down there. Her name is Ginny Adder. I'd intended to make her your mentor once you'd passed the exam. Now it makes perfect sense. Just today I had word from her of yet another murder. This time the victim was a southern ranger. Lara, I want you to travel to Lake End and help Ginny find out what's going on. In just ten days the king is holding a huge celebration to mark the anniversary of the day the Evernight ended. He's takin' credit for that, as you can probably imagine. Anyway, thousands from all over the Kingdom will be travelling to Lake End for a huge parade and feast, and we can't have all those people exposed to a crazed Witch. Will you do what I ask?'

Lara stopped pacing. She stared into Bernie Whitecrow's tired eyes and felt a fire rising in her chest. 'Course I will. I'll do anything to help find Double Eight.' Then the flames of the fire cooled. 'I just hope I won't let you down. Or him.'

'If I remember correctly, Lara, you are the girl who saved the world from the Evernight.'

'I know that, Bernie! But . . . well, what if that was just a fluke?'

'Hell's teeth!' scoffed Bernie. 'A fluke! If what you did

was a fluke, girl, I'm the queen of the fairies. In any case, I'm not asking you to lead the investigation. Ginny will be your mentor.'

Lara nodded. She went to the balcony's edge and stared out over the sea. Her heart was thundering, and a wicked storm of thoughts was battering her mind, showing her a hundred different terrible things that might have happened to her friend, and wondering about her new teacher. 'What's Ginny Adder like?'

'One of the finest Witches I've ever met, Lara. She's loyal, and tough – so, so tough; she's overcome terrible things. In another life, she might have been the High Witch. You couldn't be in better hands.' A pause. Then, 'There's one more thing, Lara.'

'Yeah?'

'It's difficult to even say the words . . . In a case such as Double Eight's disappearance, we must consider every possibility. Every single one.'

'I know, Bernie. I will.'

'And we must try not to let our feelings overrule our heads, yes?'

'Course,' said Lara.

Bernie stared at Lara from her seat. She narrowed her eyes very slightly. 'Good gal. Because there's one explanation for what's happened that's more terrible than the others.'

Lara swallowed hard and sat back down. 'What?'

Bernie rubbed at her temples as if trying to massage

away a headache. Then she looked right into Lara's eyes and said, 'It is possible, however unlikely, that Double Eight murdered Krispin Sprout himself, and is on the run.'

For the longest moment Lara could do nothing but stare at Bernie. It was like looking at a stranger. 'But that's mad!'

'I'm not *sayin'* that's what happened, Lara,' said Bernie. She tapped her head with a finger. 'But a Witch must be smart. A good Witch considers every detail. And you must be ready for others to doubt Double Eight along the way.'

'Why?' said Lara. 'Because he used to be a White Witch?'

Bernie nodded. 'To put it simply, yes. You've seen the White Witches who've run away from the Silver Kingdom and asked for shelter here. They're struggling to adapt. Until last year they were slaves for the king, and Mrs Hester had their souls locked away. They couldn't feel, couldn't dream. They were shells, Lara. Now all of a sudden, a whole world of magic and emotions has opened up to them. It's easy to see how such a change might send some of them over the edge. However much we don't want to admit it, Double Eight is at risk of that too. He always has been.'

Lara was still staring, the heat of her anger building behind her eyes. Bernie was the High Witch, and Lara knew she shouldn't question her, but she couldn't help it. 'How can you say that? This is *Double Eight* we're talking about. Do you really believe he could have lost his mind and killed a bunch of people, including his teacher?'

Bernie screwed up her face like she'd smelled something rotten. 'Course I don't! But until we find out the truth, we can't rule anything out. That's why you must go. You know Double Eight better than anyone. Find the truth.'

Lara clenched her fists. 'I will, Bernie. I'll find him. I'll bring him home.'

Bernie stood up too and took Lara's hands. 'That's the Lara I know,' she said with a smile. 'Now, come with me, there's something I want to give you.'

THE TRAVELLING TRUNK

Back inside the palace, Lara followed Bernie through the labyrinth of winding bark passageways, flowers blooming on the walls as they passed.

'You'll leave tomorrow night,' said Bernie. 'Course, you'll have to travel by conventional means, since the Witch gates are still all down.'

'Do you think we'll ever be able to get them back up and running?' said Lara.

Bernie shrugged. 'The surge of magic when you beat the Evernight fried the gates pretty good. Rob thinks we might need to build new ones. That would take a long time. Years.'

'So, I'll go by boat then?'

'Yes. Boat to King's Haven, with Joe. Rob will meet you, and together the three of you will travel south along the river network to Lake End.'

'Wait . . . Rob and Joe are coming too?'

'As far as Lake End, yes. When you get there, Rob and Joe have their own thing to do.'

'I really wish Joe would just stay here,' Lara said.

'We can't expect him to hang about for ever, Lara, even if we'd like him to. He's not a prisoner. He feels useless all the way out here. Who am I to stop him using his skills to help?'

'I suppose. But what will Joe and Rob be doing in Lake End?'

Bernie tapped the side of her nose. 'I'm sorry, but that's not information you need to know. I want your full attention on finding Double Eight and catching the murderer in Lake End – don't argue! I know you, Larabelle Fox. If you discover what Rob and Joe are doing, you'll find a way to get involved. It's your nature. You want to solve every problem you come across. But not this time. And don't think about askin' Joe, either, because even he won't find out what his mission is until Rob tells him.'

Lara folded her arms. 'I know. I already tried to get it out of him.' They reached a spiral staircase made from twisted branches and began to descend. Lara said, 'Bernie, how am I going to make it all the way to Lake End without the secret police catching on?'

'Ah,' said Bernie. 'There are a number of ship captains on our side. They help us smuggle spells and people – at great personal danger, I might add. One of 'em will take you south.'

They had reached the foot of the staircase. Bernie smiled, and opened a narrow door. 'And you'll have something else to help you stay inconspicuous.'

The chamber beyond was roughly cylindrical, and had

the appearance of the inside of a huge hollow tree. It was empty, except for a battered old travelling trunk in the middle of the floor. The trunk was plain and unremarkable, perhaps large enough for Lara to curl up inside, if she so desired.

It wasn't until Lara went close to the trunk that a most incredible thing happened. For almost a year, since her Witchhood had begun, she had heard the melodic whisper of magic at every waking moment. It was comforting, and warming, and she could not truly remember what life had sounded like before it had come. But now, as Lara approached the travelling trunk, it seemed that someone had suddenly snuffed out all the magic in the world. There was only a vast, empty silence. Lara grew cold. She shivered and stared at the trunk as if it was some frightful monster.

'It's all right,' said Bernie in a calm voice. 'The trunk is enchanted to conceal magic. It feels strange, I know – maybe even a bit scary the first couple of times you encounter it – but it has never failed me. Not once. You can stash your wand and cauldron and spells in there and no Witch alive will be able to sense them. Hell's teeth, you can hide in there yourself if need be!'

She brought out a small gold key and slid it into the lock. The lid opened with a click, revealing the black velvet-lined interior of a perfectly ordinary trunk. Then she closed the lid with a snap, locked the trunk, and brought out a second key, this one old and rusted, with one end in the shape of a bird's open wings. Bernie put this key in the lock, opened the lid, and Lara was astonished to be staring down into a deep shaft of darkness.

'There's a ladder!'

'There is,' said Bernie, and she approached the open trunk and climbed in, descending the ladder until she had faded into the dark. 'Come on!' Her voice drifted up into the warm perfumed air.

Lara edged to the trunk, peering in. She could see the bottom of the ladder some thirty feet down, and the glow of wandlight. With great care, she climbed into the trunk, and as she descended, she was taken back to her time as a tosher in King's Haven, when she'd sneak into the sewers every day and search beneath the city for lost treasure. Of course, at the bottom of this ladder there was no sewer tunnel. Instead, there was a door. And beyond the door, a room, low-ceilinged and crammed with shelves and boxes, all bursting with books and spell bottles. In the centre was an old writing desk and a wooden chair and, somehow, a warm fire burning in a simple hearth. Birds made of witch paper fluttered around between the shelves. One of them landed on Lara's shoulder and pecked at her ear, and she was filled with a sudden longing. She'd had a bird of her own once, an enchanted one made of gold and clockwork. Moonwing, she'd called him. He had been her companion, her guardian, but he had contained the most powerful spell in all the world – the Doomsday Spell – and Lara had been destined to find Moonwing, and use him to punch back the darkness of the Evernight.

She missed him.

Bernie sat down at the desk and Lara went to the shelves, stroking the spines of some of the old books. 'This is amazing.'

'It's a bit old and tatty now,' said Bernie. 'But it still works just fine – and I certainly don't have much use for it these days. It seems it's not the done thing for the High Witch to go off gallivanting on adventures.' She sighed, and added, 'Sadly.'

When Lara had left to prepare for her journey, Bernie sat back in her chair in the secret compartment of the trunk and rubbed wearily at her eyes. She looked at a framed picture on her desk, one from many years ago, in which she and her husband Magnus were smiling warmly. She reached out and touched his face. 'I hope I'm doing the right thing, Magnus. I hope I'm not asking too much of her. How I wish you were here to help me, my love.' A tear pattered onto the desk, and she wiped it away, and blinked, and took a deep breath. 'You're right, of course,' she told the picture of Magnus Whitecrow. 'I'm being a daft old crone. Larabelle Fox was born to be a great Witch. She'll be fine.'

But even as she spoke the words, Bernie sensed that dark things were brewing, and that she was sending a young girl who trusted her into the waiting grasp of danger.

OVER THE SEA

That night, by the glow of lamps filled with spell light, Lara gathered with a small group of friends on the harbour of Westerly Witch. The Blossom of the Mother Tree breathed strong, pure magic into the warm night air, filling the dark with a crystal lullaby.

Among the many vessels in the harbour was a fine steamship with slick black paint and a red funnel hooped with gold. Waiting on the ship's gangplank was Nel Pepper, a stout, imposing Witch with dark skin and sharp, curious eyes. Nel was a sailor, but she also captained an airship, and had, during the Evernight, swooped down to save Lara, Bernie and Double Eight from a great storm when they'd been cast adrift in the Pewter Sea.

''Bout time,' she said, observing the approaching group.

Bernie Whitecrow waved off her surliness. 'Good to see you too, Nel. You all set?'

Nel patted the ship. 'Aye.' Then she stared down at the

small, wiry frame of Joe Littlefoot. 'You sure 'bout this, boy? Sure you want to come?'

Joe gave her a long, serious look. 'I am.'

'As you wish. But remember, the Silver Kingdom is not like it was when you left. You'll be in constant danger. If the king's secret police find you working with Westerly Witches, they'll shoot you through the head. If you're lucky.'

'Leave him be, Nel,' said Bernie. 'The boy has work to do.'

Nel looked both interested and puzzled by this, but Lara knew that Bernie wouldn't say another word about Joe's mission – whatever it might be.

'Right.' Nel jerked a thumb towards the ship. 'Get aboard, then. But don't expect me to turn the boat round if you lose your nerve halfway to King's Haven.'

As Joe walked up the gangplank, Bernie called to him: 'Joe, you're welcome back in Westerly Witch any time you want.'

He turned and smiled. 'Yes, ma'am. Thank you for everything.'

Now only Lara and Bernie remained on the harbour wall. The High Witch reached into her long coat, brought out a tiny slip of witch paper and tossed it into the lamplit air, where it folded up and became a wasp and buzzed onto Lara's waiting hand.

'When you get to Lake End, send this to Ginny. She'll come and find you. You got all your magic stowed away in your new trunk?'

'Yes, ma'am.' Lara nodded towards the battered old trunk, which was sitting on the deck.

Bernie stared off towards the moon. 'I wish I was coming with you. It don't sit right with me, a-sendin' other folk off to do my work. I've never been one to sit around on my backside. And . . . I got a bad feelin' . . .'

'You comin' on board or not, girl?' Nel's voice boomed from the ship. 'We're burnin' coal here!'

'Mother Earth's marigolds, Nel!' yelled Bernie. 'Hold your horses!' She turned back to Lara, took both her hands and gave her a smile filled with such warmth that Lara felt she might burst into tears. 'You be careful out there, Larabelle Fox. You hear me? Keep your head down. Listen to Ginny. Find out what's happened to Double Eight.'

'I will, Bernie. I promise.' Lara hugged the High Witch, the woman who had brought her to Westerly Witch, had taught her so much, had, in fact, been the closest thing Lara had ever come to having a mother. But it was time to fly the nest. Bernie wiped her eyes and shooed Lara up the gangplank, and Lara and Joe were waving as the ship began to move off.

Lara's gaze remained fixed upon the High Witch as Nel steered the ship away towards the open sea. Even when Bernie had faded out of sight, Lara stayed rooted to the spot, marvelling at the size of the Mother Tree, breathing the sweet scent of the Blossom and watching the twinkling lights, her guts alive and churning with nerves and excitement at the adventures to come.

From another spot on the deck, Joe Littlefoot was also watching Westerly Witch. For a year the great Witch city had been a safe place. The Witches had made him feel welcome, and he was more thankful for that than he could ever put into words, but Westerly Witch was not his home. His home was King's Haven, and he missed every part of it. He missed the winding labyrinth of the slums, the shouts and yells of the people. He missed the smells – even the stench of the river at low tide on a hot day and the horse dung on the cobbled streets. He missed the smoky dragon breath as it burned in the streetlamps. He missed the fog. He missed the sewers, where he'd spent so much of his life.

Soon he would be back, and the thought of that, and of a secret mission with Rob Nielsen, caused a flutter of excitement and fear in his belly. What would the mission be, he wondered? And why, with all the powerful Witches at her disposal, had Bernie Whitecrow chosen *him*, an ordinary kid from the slums, to be the one to assist Rob?

Whatever lay ahead, he was sure it would be dangerous, but he didn't care much about danger. He only wanted revenge against the king for abandoning the slum folk during the Evernight. For causing Granny's death.

When he looked to the clear night sky, he imagined the

stars blinking out, the way they had when the Evernight swallowed up everything.

Then, shaking the vision away, Joe Littlefoot turned his collar to the spray of the sea and watched Westerly Witch disappearing into the dark, not sure if he'd ever see it again.

The Witch Hunter

The carriage was plain and black and instantly forgettable.

Its darkened glass windows reflected the warm light of the dragon-breath streetlamps as it rumbled through the twisting streets and alleyways of King's Haven. The hour was late, the summer air dank and heavy and warm, but the horses that pulled the carriage were ironhearts, charging on at a relentless pace.

Three men and a woman sat in the carriage. They were all dressed in long plain black coats with a silver skull pin on the breast pocket, and they did not speak as the ironhearts pulled them through the city.

Only one of them wore a hat. He was square-chinned and broad-chested, and his ham-sized hands sat folded in his lap. The hat was black and wide-brimmed, with a band of silver silk. He watched the streets passing. Quiet, tonight. But then again, they were away from the slums, where most of the rioting and marching and fighting had played out since the Evernight ended a year ago. Still, there were lots of coppers

50

on the streets – even if most of them wouldn't stand a chance if they came across one of the White Witches who'd run away from a life serving the king. That was gratitude, wasn't it? To turn against the very people who'd fed and raised and moulded you, the moment you got a sniff of a different life. Hags. They were all Hags. And that was where *he* came in.

The carriage turned a corner on to Pear Tree Lane, a wide, leafy street in an affluent part of the city lined on either side with tall terraced town houses. Here, as in many parts of King's Haven, strings of colourful flags were hung between the lamp-posts in preparation for the Evernight Anniversary Feast.

The driver brought the ironhearts to a stop at the steps of number seventy-three, and inside the carriage the man in the black hat said to the others, 'Wait until I'm inside and watch the door. If anyone tries to run, stop them.'

He opened the carriage and stepped down onto the cobbles of the darkened, deserted street. Most of the houses were in darkness too.

He was a big man, but he made no sound as he walked up the steps. He knocked on the door of number seventy-three.

A long moment later, the door creaked open, and a bleary-eyed servant girl stared up at him. It took her a moment to recognise the uniform, the skull pin on his coat and the silver-banded black hat, but when she did, her sleepy demeanour shattered, and she became suddenly wide-eyed and alert.

'Can . . . can I help you, sir?'

The man in the black hat smiled warmly. He tipped his hat to her. 'Good evening, young lady. I'm so sorry to bother the household at this late hour. I wonder . . . is this the residence of Doctor Henry Vanderbill?'

'Why, yes, sir. It is, sir.' She took a slow step away from him, and suddenly hid her hands behind her back. The man in the hat continued to smile, noting that the girl was trembling. A promising sign.

'May I *see* the doctor?'

'I don't know . . . That is, he's asleep, sir.'

The man in the black hat did not let his pleasant air falter. He pulled back one side of his coat just enough that the girl saw the handle of the wand he kept stowed in his belt. 'I'm afraid I'm going to have to ask you to wake the good doctor up.'

'Ivy?' The voice was gruff and sleep-soaked. 'What's the matter?'

The girl stepped aside so that the visitor was afforded a view down the hallway, where a tall, thin man with greying curly hair and heavy black eyebrows was standing at the foot of the staircase.

'Doctor Vanderbill?' said the man in the black hat.

For a moment the doctor did nothing but stare as if he were looking at some demon from his nightmares. Interestingly, his eyes flicked towards the maid. It seemed that he wanted to say something to her. Then he gathered his senses. 'Yes. Yes, I am Henry Vanderbill. What's this about?'

'My dear doctor, thank goodness,' said the man. 'I'm here to ask for your help. I need a consultation. I fear I am very ill.'

The doctor's shoulders were rigid. 'Sir, it's almost midnight. I'm afraid I must ask you to come back tomorrow morning. I shall be sure to clear my appointments and see you first thing.'

The man nodded. 'That's kind of you, doctor, but this really can't wait. I must see you now. It's quite urgent.' He tapped the skull pin on his breast pocket. 'And I'm sure you would never dream of turning away a patriot such as myself.'

The doctor's shoulders seemed to sag. He looked to the floor, and then he nodded to his maid. 'It's all right, Ivy. Please, go back to your room.'

The girl nodded and scurried away up the stairs, her arms tightly folded, hands still hidden away. The man in the black hat watched her until she was gone, and then he stepped in from the warm summer night and closed the front door.

'This way, please,' said the doctor, leading him through the house to a high-ceilinged room stacked with many books. There was a heavy oak desk, a leather couch, and a high bed, beside which sat a table scattered with shining medical instruments. The doctor lit two dragon-breath lamps in their wall sconces and sat in a chair on one side of the desk, while the visitor sat on the other.

'What seems to be the problem?' asked Doctor Vanderbill, folding his arms.

The man in the black hat clasped his huge hands in his lap once more. He smiled. 'Where are my manners? My name is Karl Younger. I'm pleased to meet you.'

'Yes,' said Doctor Vanderbill. 'I know who you are. Everyone does.'

Karl Younger let out a short, dry laugh. 'You flatter me, doctor.' His tone was most amiable. 'I take it, then, that you also know what I do?'

Vanderbill gave a single nod. 'You are the director of the king's secret police.'

Younger bowed his head. 'Quite right. But what do I *do*?'

Doctor Vanderbill was growing more agitated. 'I'm sorry,' he said, 'but did you wake me up in the middle of the night to have me take part in some sort of quiz? I have a surgery tomorrow.'

'Ah,' said Younger. 'Of course. I must get to the point. It is one of my flaws, or so I believe – I tend to talk and talk.' He stared with cold blue eyes, noticing beads of sweat gathering on the doctor's brow.

'You said you were ill?' Vanderbill prompted.

'Alas, I believe so.' Younger leaned forwards in the chair. 'I've been experiencing terrible pain.' He pressed a hand to the upper part of his stomach. 'Here.'

Vanderbill's eyes flicked to Younger's hand. 'I see. And what sort of pain is it?'

'How do you mean?' said Younger.

'Well, is it sharp? Dull? Does it come in waves?'

'Waves,' said Younger. 'Definitely waves. And it is a hot, searing pain. Do you think it is my heart?'

'I'm afraid it's too soon to tell anything like that,' said the doctor. 'But it does sound like it might need investigating. Tell me, how often do you experience this pain?'

Younger leaned further forwards in the chair. He placed his elbows on the desk. 'It's a very strange thing,' he said, his voice almost a whisper. 'The pain only strikes, you see, when I am in the company of a traitor.'

Silence – *absolute* silence – filled the room.

'And do you know something, Doctor Vanderbill?' he went on. 'I am feeling the pain right now.'

Silence once more. The sweat on Vanderbill's forehead was standing out in prominent beads. He swallowed hard. 'I'm not sure what you mean.'

Younger sat back. He was enjoying himself immensely. 'Oh, come now! Come, Doctor Vanderbill! You are an intelligent man.' He paused, reached down and brought out his wand, placing it on the desk. It was about the length of a man's forearm, made of polished dark wood, and fitted with a silver handle and a revolver chamber. In the chamber, he had loaded six spell bottles, and magic drifted and curled around inside each one. Doctor Vanderbill stared at those angry-looking spells, and Younger saw the terror creep into his eyes.

'Are you aware, Doctor Vanderbill, what my main duty is, as a member of the secret police?'

The doctor nodded. 'Yes, of course. It is your job to hunt down and execute White Witches who have run away from their old lives serving the king. Also, to unearth any Westerly Witches who may be living among us.'

'Hags,' corrected Younger. 'Any Witch not on our side is a Hag. Traitors. Poison.' A small, chilling smile began in the corners of his mouth. 'My colleagues have given me a nickname. I am quite proud of it. They call me the Witch Hunter. I have a quite uncanny ability to track down runaways, you see. Call it a gift.' At this he sat back in the chair and gave the doctor a long, appraising look. 'There is a runaway White Witch in this house, doctor— Sit. Down.'

The doctor had begun to stand, but he froze, and did as Younger ordered. 'That's absurd!'

'You have been helping her,' said Younger. 'You have disguised her as a maid. Not only that, you have allowed Westerly Witches to use your home as a meeting place, *and* you have sheltered the marked here too.'

Doctor Vanderbill's mouth was trembling. He looked like he might burst into tears. 'It's not true!'

'Doctor, she answered the door to me just now. I could *sense* the magic crackling at her fingertips. Most interesting. Now, I could hit you with a spell that will make you tell the truth, or torture you until you break, but I am not going to

56

do either of those things. Not yet. I am going to give you a chance. I'm sure you know the penalty for conspiring with runaways or Hags is death, yes?'

The doctor nodded. He seemed to have lost his voice.

'Well, I am here to give you a chance at life. You are not a Hag. You were never a White Witch. For all I know, you might have been enchanted or forced to help the Westerly Witches against your will. It happens sometimes. Do you want to live, doctor? Are Hags and runaway traitors and marked folk really worth *dying* for? Or would you like a second chance?'

Still Doctor Vanderbill did not speak. He stared at the wand on the table and chewed so hard on his lip that he drew blood. At last, he said in a tortured voice, 'Tell me what you mean by *second chance.*'

'Not now. Oh, please, not now!'

Ivy Robin, the housemaid, sat on the bed in her small room at the top of the house, staring at her trembling hands. Bright sparks and currents of magic were leaping between her fingertips. She closed her eyes, tried to breathe slowly. 'Calm down,' she told herself. 'Just calm down. The doctor will sort this out.'

The sparks at her fingertips faded away, thank goodness. Oh, what a mess everything had become since the Evernight! Until then, Ivy had used a wand like every other White Witch she'd ever heard of, but after she'd got her soul back, the magic in her had started to get out of control, to leap from her body without a wand or spell bottle. She felt like a freak. An oddity.

Presently, Ivy got up and crept to the window, chancing a peek between the curtains. A black coach and shining ironhearts waited down on the street. More secret police no doubt.

Hell's teeth, she was in a pickle this time. And so was poor Doctor Vanderbill. He was a good man. After the Evernight, she had run away from her position among the king's White Witches, and the doctor was the one who'd taken her in. It had all seemed so much to bear back then, suddenly being able to feel all the wild magic in the world. And all those free thoughts and dreams! Ivy had thought she was going to burst. And sometimes the magic *did* burst from her! But Doctor Vanderbill had helped her. Slowly, she was learning how to live, how to be a proper person who laughed and thought and felt. She had made great progress.

And yet . . .

Sparks and currents leaped between her fingertips again, and she shut her eyes tight and tried to be calm. It was always worse whenever she was angry, or frightened. It seemed that a great force gathered in her like a storm on those occasions.

She breathed deeply, thinking of the sound of running water, which always seemed to calm her, and the sparks died away as she pushed back the intense force inside.

She prayed the man in the black hat had indeed come to the house because he was feeling ill, and not for any other reason. But if that were the case, why had he brought others with him? She swallowed. Did he, the man in the black hat, know that Ivy was a Witch? Had he come for her? Had he sensed, or seen, the sparks dancing at her fingertips when she'd answered the door?

She stood up, went to the mirror on the wall, reached out, through the glass, and brought out her wand. The revolver chamber was empty. She reached in again, for the spells she'd stowed there in case of emergency, and she carefully loaded them into the wand, cursing under her breath, shaking the magic sparks away from her trembling fingers. It took a few tries to load the wand. She stepped back, imagined her reflection was an enemy, and aimed the wand. Her arms dropped to her sides and her shoulders sagged. She was hopeless with a wand. If it came to it, she'd never be able to use it to fight her way out.

The sound of a tinkling bell made her start.

Doctor Vanderbill was calling from the examination room. Her heart quickened, and it seemed that her ribcage was shrinking, squeezing the air out of her.

Ivy stood up and tucked the wand into her housecoat. Then she hurried from her little room, down and down and down the stairs to the ground floor, and along the narrow passage to Doctor Vanderbill's examination room. Fear was bubbling in her stomach as she knocked on the door. Magic sparks fizzed at her fingertips. She thrust her hands into her housecoat pockets.

'Come.'

The examination room was dim; the doctor had lit only two of the lamps and their faint glow had not chased all the darkness from the corners. The doctor sat alone at his desk. There was no sign of the man in the black hat.

'You rang, doctor?'

Doctor Vanderbill looked waxy and shaken, older somehow, as he sat at his desk. A tremulous smile crossed his lips, and then a tortured, sorrowful expression took hold of his features. Suddenly his face changed; his eyes widened to great circles and he yelled, 'Get out, Ivy! Run!'

A flash, and a whip-crack, and a scorpion tail of blazing red light plunged into Doctor Vanderbill's chest, through his back, through the chair. He made a terrible gargling sound, and stared at the tail of the death spell still sticking from his chest. His eyes found Ivy, and they filled with tears.

Ivy had been frozen, but her senses came crashing back. 'Doctor!'

She took a step towards him, reached out, but the blazing spell made a thrumming sound, and the doctor screamed. Ivy watched, not able to move, not even able to scream, as Doctor Vanderbill's skin turned to ash and fell away, leaving only a smouldering skeleton sitting in the chair.

The door clicked softly shut, and from one of the darkened corners stepped the man in the black hat. He held out his wand, bright, angry spells coiling in their bottles in the revolver chamber.

'Hello, Ivy.'

'The doctor!' said Ivy, her eyes streaming. 'You killed Doctor Vanderbill!'

He nodded. 'Quite so. It didn't have to be, though. He had a choice. He chose poorly. He chose you. Though why anyone would do that is beyond me.'

Ivy was still very frightened, but the fear was mixing with searing anger, and the desire to hurt this man. She could feel the magic in her, pushing to get out, and the more she held it back the greater the pressure became.

'You were a White Witch,' said the man. 'I was, too. But we chose very different paths. I . . . well, I chose to stay loyal to the king, to the Silver Kingdom. But you? You chased your foolish dreams of freedom. Your fate was sealed the day you made that choice, just like every other traitorous Hag I've killed these past months.'

Ivy was shaking, not with fear, but with effort. The magic in her was boiling up, churning and spitting and pushing. It gathered behind her eyes, and in her fingertips, and the musical sound of it fractured into a million screams.

'I ran away,' she said, 'because I was frightened of what I might do. Who I might hurt. *You* are going to get hurt, mister, if you don't leave me be.'

The man in the black hat looked first incredulous, and then amused. 'I'm Karl Younger,' he said. 'The Witch Hunter.' He raised his wand, pointed the tip at her. 'You're just another Hag who deserves to die.'

Ivy's body was burning up inside, the magic rumbling and crashing. She looked at what was left of dear Doctor Vanderbill, and she knew that her only chance of getting out of the house alive was to let go. She threw back her head and screamed.

When the house exploded, the magical blast was so powerful it wiped out three houses on either side and tore a deep enough crater in the street to expose the sewer tunnel beneath. As the dust was beginning to settle, Ivy staggered out of the thick cloud, tripping on rubble and debris.

She stared at the devastation and dropped to her knees. How many people had been hurt? Oh, how sorry she was about that. But what had she been supposed to do? Just let Younger kill her? Do nothing as he put her down like a rabid dog?

The shrill scream of coppers' alarm whistles echoed in the warm city night, and she knew they would be here soon. Ivy struggled up, weak, trembling, her housecoat smoking and ragged, and stumbled off into the night.

Somewhere among the rubble, Karl Younger's eyes cracked open. The scent of fire and smoke and dust stuffed his nose, made him cough and splutter. A good agent was always prepared, and he was the best agent there was. He always kept a powerful shield spell loaded in a chamber of his wand, and he had fired it just in time as that . . . that *freak* had let rip with her wild magic. He wondered, as he lay in the dark, how many layers of rubble sat on top of him, how long he'd have to wait in this magic cocoon before they discovered him.

There would, at least, be plenty of time to think. To digest. To plan.

This Hag . . . *Ivy* . . . had power beyond anything he'd ever encountered. He had faced strong Hags before, of course, but nothing like this. When every White Witch had been reunited with their soul, the full world of magic had been opened to them, and, as is always the case in nature, some of them proved to be strong, others weak. This girl reminded him of the history books he'd read.

If you were going to hunt Hags, it made sense to find out as much about them as possible, didn't it? Younger had read all about them, and discovered that, long ago, in the golden age of magic, there were stories of vastly powerful witches who could use magic without wands. They had been rare even back then, or so the books had told him. This girl, the runaway, seemed to be a throwback to those ancient times. A curiosity. If she ever learned how to control her strength, she'd be unthinkably powerful.

Despite the fact he was under many tonnes of brick,

despite the fact he had been taken by surprise, despite the fact she had got away this time, Karl Younger smiled. He thanked Lady Light for providing this challenge. How he loved a good hunt. And the hunt was most certainly on.

A Close Shave

The Pewter Sea was kind, and the steamship made good time; four days after leaving Westerly Witch, Lara and Joe arrived in King's Haven. Around the time Karl Younger was interrogating poor Doctor Vanderbill, Lara and Joe bade Nel Pepper and her crew goodbye and stepped from the gangplank onto the lamp-lit docks. Lara was exhausted and stiff from the journey, but when she stepped down onto solid ground, she smiled, and thought, *I'm home.*

She had not set foot in the city for almost a year. She breathed deeply; the smells of the docks – the heat of the fire whisky and salt-tang of the seaweed and blueshell crab – swirled around with the smells of the street – the horses and coal smoke and sewers – creating a concoction of aromas that could never be replicated. She had grown up on these streets, learned to be independent here, become the greatest tosher in all of King's Haven, the best at finding lost treasures in the miles of sewer tunnels beneath the city.

King's Haven felt different now, though. There was

tension in the air; it thrummed on your skin. She had heard all about the trouble in the slums, and of course there was the matter of the secret police, swaggering around like they owned the place, with free rein to arrest anyone who looked at them the wrong way, hunting runaway White Witches and poor marked folk.

There was another change too, but this one, only a Witch would notice.

It was the sound of magic.

When Lara had lived here, the White Witches had been soulless and their magic tame and colourless. Back then, the sound of magic had been almost non-existent. These days it was a constant crystal whisper in the air: since the Witches had been reunited with their souls, the entire world of magic had been unlocked.

King's Haven had become a dangerous powder keg; some White Witches had stayed loyal to the king, while many had run away in search of free lives. And all were coming to terms with the newly found powers that their returning souls had brought, testing dangerous and unstable wild enchantments.

'I can't believe I'm back.' Joe stood at Lara's side, and she could see from the misty look in his eyes that he had been waiting for this moment for a long time. 'I'm really back.'

'Try not to attract attention,' said Lara. 'The streets are crawling with coppers and secret police.' She stopped, and tapped at his arm, gesturing to a pair of coppers patrolling the docks, the shining buttons on their starched uniforms twinkling in the lamplight. 'Act natural.'

'What does that even mean?'

'It means don't act like we're lugging around an enchanted trunk full of illegal magic. Hell's teeth, be calm! They're coming this way!'

The two coppers, a man with a round fat belly and a woman with shocking red hair, had examined someone else's papers and waved them on. They were now walking towards Lara and Joe.

'You two,' said the woman. 'Hold it.'

Lara and Joe glanced at each other, stopped, and put down the travelling trunk.

'Is something wrong?' In Lara's past life as a tosher and occasional thief she'd had many run-ins with coppers. She fancied she knew how to talk to them. Even so, a cold finger of panic was creeping down her spine and she hoped it didn't show in her face.

'Papers,' said the man, holding out a fat hand.

'Yeah. Course.' Lara nodded to Joe and reached into her coat pocket, pulling out and handing over a folded sheet of paper. Joe did the same. The coppers stared carefully at the identification document, and then at the two youngsters.

Eventually, the woman said, 'Fine. Be on your way.'

'Yes, officer. Thank you, officer,' said Lara, taking back her papers.

They picked up the trunk and turned to leave, relief surging through them. Then another voice said, 'Stop!'

Lara's heart almost froze. A woman in a long black coat had joined the coppers. She wore a silver skull pin in her breast pocket. An agent of the secret police.

'Can . . . can we help you, officer?'

The agent's eyes flicked to the travelling trunk. 'What's in there?'

'Oh,' said Lara, fighting the urge to turn and run. 'Nothing important. Just clothes. We're travelling south to visit an aunt.'

The agent came nearer. When she moved within a couple of paces of the trunk, she drew a sharp breath and put her hand to her chest. Lara knew at once what was happening: the agent was, of course, a Witch, and the enchantments placed upon the trunk were taking effect on her. The agent moved her head around with great concentration, listening intently for a sound she could no longer hear – the sound of magic. In moments she had become pale and shaken.

'Are you all right, officer?' Lara asked with false concern.

The secret police officer took a faltering step back, and another, and with the second step Lara assumed she'd moved out of the reach of the trunk's enchantment, for a look of great relief came across her face, and the colour returned to her cheeks. For a long moment she stayed still, regaining her composure. Then she frowned, and Lara could tell she was trying to work something out. The agent's gaze travelled first to Lara, and then Joe, and lastly the trunk.

Lara tried to hide her worry. She wondered if the trunk had perhaps not been a good idea. Bernie claimed it had never failed her, but Bernie had never had to use it to avoid secret police before. Maybe it was not such a good hiding place from Witches at all . . .

BOOM!

Lara dropped to her knees on the dock. She felt as if the air had been sucked from her lungs. It seemed that everything slowed almost to a stop. A great hand of pressure pushed down upon her, and the sound of magic in the air, usually musical, was a screaming roar. She reached out and grabbed Joe's hand, felt his trembling grip squeeze back. Then the magical roar died away, and the sounds of screaming and yelling came flooding over her.

The agent had fallen too. Lara helped the woman up, but noticed the agent's attention was no longer on her, or Joe, or the travelling trunk. Instead her eyes were wide and fastened on the sky.

Lara followed the agent's gaze, saw a gigantic plume of glowing spell smoke rolling out over the night sky on the far side of the city. The distant sound of coppers' alarm whistles began to gather in the air, and the secret police agent, forgetting all about Lara and Joe, sprinted off into the night.

With all eyes turned to the sky, and the relative quiet of the night shattered by whatever had just happened a few miles away, Lara and Joe grabbed the travelling trunk and scurried off into the tangle of streets.

A Familiar Place

Twenty minutes later, near the centre of the city, away from the never-ending bustle of the docks and the raucous night-time happenings of the slums, Lara and Joe carried the travelling trunk down a quiet alleyway at the back of the great opera house, stopping atop a narrow stone staircase leading to a small basement door.

'What d'you suppose might cause an explosion of magic like that?' said Lara. She held out her arm, rolled up her sleeve, showing Joe that the hairs on her arm were standing on end and her skin was all gooseflesh. 'Hell's teeth, I can still feel it! My skin is tingling and there's a strange taste in my mouth.'

'I wonder if something went wrong in one of the White Witch factories,' Joe said. 'You know, because they can all use wild magic now. Some experiment might have got out of control.'

'Maybe. Whatever it was, I've never felt anything like it.' In the distance, coppers' whistles and fire alarm bells sounded as the authorities rushed to respond. Lara said, 'We'll get in out of the way and send a message to Rob. Come on.'

They each grabbed an end of the trunk and carried it down the stone steps to the small green door.

'Just like the old days,' said Joe with a smile. 'You think the way in still works?'

'Let's find out.' In her time as a tosher, Lara had made her home in the opera house. The place was huge, and Lara had settled in one of its forgotten corners. Now she put her end of the trunk down, placed her hands flat against the door, and pushed. 'They haven't fixed it. The door frame is so loose in the brick you can open it just by . . . pushin' the door . . . sideways . . .' She grunted with effort and a flurry of paint flakes fell to the ground in the darkness as the door budged and the lock came free. Lara pushed it open, allowing herself a smile of satisfaction. 'Haven't lost my touch. C'mon.'

Joe laughed. 'Yeah, but you could just use magic to get in now anyway. You're a qualified Witch, remember.'

Lara chuckled. 'I guess. It'll take a while to get used to that, I suppose. Anyway, feels right doing it this way . . . like I used to every day.'

Inside was a small square room, empty but for a couple of old crates, the walls grimy under a coating of coal dust. The smell of damp was strong. They carried the trunk through a warren of red-carpeted passageways, up staircase after staircase, until an old wooden door groaned open to reveal a large cluttered attic room illuminated by the cold light of the moon, which fell through a series of dusty skylights in silver bars.

Lara had grown accustomed to the effects of the trunk now; at first the absence of magic around it had made her feel quite ill, but she had learned to grit her teeth and bear it. Once in the attic, Lara took out the special key Bernie had given her, opened the trunk, and lifted the lid to reveal the deep shaft of darkness. Lara climbed in first, then Joe, and soon they were in the secret room deep in the trunk.

Lara sat at Bernie's old desk, took a sheet of witch paper and scrawled a message to Rob. When she was satisfied, the witch paper came to life; with a series of crisp folds it took the shape of a bird and fluttered up and out of the trunk. Lara and Joe followed, finding the bird flying all about the attic.

'Help me with this, will you, Joe?' said Lara, approaching one of the skylights. 'The handle is stiff.'

Together they managed to open the skylight enough so that the paper bird could shoot out into the dark.

'What now?' said Joe.

Lara shrugged. 'Guess we just have to wait.' She went back into the trunk and fetched her wand and a brown paper package in which Nel Pepper had packed them a chicken and vegetable pie. Next, Lara took a tiny spell bottle, loaded it into the revolver chamber of her wand and pulled the trigger. Warm light spilled from the wand tip, pushing back the gloom of the old attic, illuminating the many props and costumes and pieces of set that were hidden away up there like fragments of a forgotten memory.

They sat cross-legged on the floor and dug into supper.

'This is good,' said Joe through a mouthful of pie.

Lara nodded, wiping her mouth. 'So, you really don't know what sort of mission you'll be going on with Rob?'

He stopped chewing, swallowed. 'I swear I don't. Bernie wouldn't tell me. She knew you'd ask me about it . . . and she knew I couldn't keep a secret from you.'

Lara couldn't help smiling a little. 'Well, she was right about that, wasn't she? You can never keep your trap shut about anything.'

Joe opened his mouth to argue, and then thought better of it. 'Anyway, whatever Rob has in store, I just hope I don't let him down.'

'You won't, Joe. You've never let anyone down. You might not be a Witch, but you're brave, and street-smart, and you know things that can't be taught.'

'Thanks.' A bit of a pause followed, and she could tell he was building up to something. At last he said, 'How about you?'

'How about me what?'

Joe helped himself to another slice of pie. 'Well, how are you feelin' about going all the way to Lake End?'

Lara chewed on the question. 'Fine, I guess.'

'Aren't you nervous about meeting your mentor?'

'A little. Bernie says she's a good cove, though. And being nervous don't matter. I just want to find Double Eight. I keep thinkin' about him, wonderin' if he's hurt, or –' she couldn't bring herself to say the word – 'or worse.'

'Yeah,' said Joe. 'Me too. And then there's a part of me . . .' He stopped, gathered his words. 'Well, it must have crossed your mind, there's a chance Double Eight might be the killer.'

She almost spat out a mouthful of chicken. 'Not you too, Joe! Bernie's already been spouting this nonsense.'

'Come on, Lara. We both know where he came from.'

Lara was staring at her oldest friend like he had suddenly sprouted another nose. 'What do you mean by *that*?'

'You know what I mean. He used to be a White Witch.'

'And that makes him guilty, does it?' said Lara, feeling her face flush with anger.

'It makes him unpredictable,' said Joe. 'You've seen the state of some of the poor runaway White Witches who ended up in Westerly Witch.'

'I know,' said Lara. 'Bernie's already been through that with me too. It's horrible: the damage that vile Mrs Hester did to them, stealing their souls when they were just babies, making 'em slaves for the king, none of that will heal quick.

But it also don't make Double Eight a killer. You know him better than that, Joe!'

Joe shrugged. 'What if it all got too much for him? What if he flipped?'

'I think *you've* flipped,' said Lara. 'He'd never do what you're saying.'

'How can you be sure?'

'Same way I can be sure you'd never turn bad. I know you. Friends are supposed to believe in each other, Joe. I thought Granny taught you better than that.'

A hesitation. Joe went to speak, and then fell silent and stared at Lara with a look of great hurt. He stood up. 'I'm going to lie down for a bit. I'm tired.'

She watched him go, knowing she'd gone too far using Granny against him in an argument. 'Joe . . .'

He cut her off. 'I'll see you when Rob arrives.' He buttoned himself into a sleeping bag from the travelling trunk and lay in silence.

Lara moved across the old attic, recognising every trinket she came across, and found her old bed – a wooden sleigh upon which she'd once arranged a comfortable nest of covers and blankets. It was exactly as she remembered, as if she'd only left that morning, and as she climbed beneath the dusty sheets and looked up through the skylight towards the stars, a rush of memories came to her, of her old life as a tosher, of the feeling, as she set off down into the tunnels, that anything might be possible. And of the pure exhilaration of finding a treasure, when all the world melted around her and her heart seemed to beat in time with the flow of the water.

But that was all gone now. The world had changed. She, Lara, had changed. Feeling sorry that she'd upset Joe, she closed her eyes and tried to get some sleep.

Rook's Plan

As Lara and Joe were talking in the dusty attic of the opera house, Ivy Robin was stumbling through King's Haven's streets, madly trying to get away from the scene of destruction she'd left.

Clothes torn, heart thudding like an angry fist against her insides, she moved through the warm summer night, away from the wide tree-lined streets where the toffs lived, towards the narrow, suffocating maze of the slums. Here, crowds of frightened and curious people had gathered in doorways and street corners, chattering about the blast under the honey-glow of the streetlamps.

Images of poor Doctor Vanderbill flashed in Ivy's mind, of his wide, unseeing eyes, of the shocked look for ever etched on his face by that awful agent's death spell. Her thoughts were cluttered, her mind a fog of anger and fear and sorrow. Somewhere deep inside her, something wild and powerful stirred once more – the same force that had spilled out of her when that damned Karl Younger killed the doctor. A few blazing, spidery currents of magic danced at her fingertips.

She could not stay out here on the streets.

Lately, the doctor had trusted Ivy enough to bestow upon her the responsibility of delivering messages to a Westerly Witch contact. Sometimes the Westerly Witches would use his house as a place to shelter runaways before sending them across the sea to the great Witch city. The contact was a woman Ivy knew only as 'Rook'. She could only pray to Mother Earth that Rook would take pity on her now.

But who would want to help a monster?

A flurry of alarm whistles sounded. Ivy ducked out of sight into an empty doorway, watching from the shadows as a swarm of coppers hurried past, no doubt towards the smoking crater she'd left in a city street a couple of miles away. Her hands gripped the stone doorposts, and a series of sparks jumped from her fingers and fell to the ground in a tiny shower of light. The feeling of being watched made her look away from the coppers – now some way up the street – into the wide, beautiful eyes of a little girl standing on the fringes of one of the gatherings of people.

Ivy froze. She had seen, hadn't she? This little girl had seen the magic in Ivy's hands. If she cried out, or pointed, or drew any attention to Ivy, then who knew what might happen. The thought of another fight, of another explosion, of hurting more innocent people, made her shiver. Trembling with fear, she raised a finger to her lips in a *shhh* gesture.

A few tiny currents of magic leaped from the end of her finger like miniature lightning bolts.

The little girl smiled, nodded.

Ivy closed her eyes in relief, put her hand to her heart and made a small bow towards the girl. Then she flashed out of the doorway and scurried on between tall tenements that became more crooked and cramped with every street.

'The slums are a different world,' the good doctor had once told her, and she saw that he had been right; where the more civilised parts of the city had been buzzing with rumour and chattering from those awakened by the explosion, the slums proved to be alive in a different way, with the raucous sounds of arguments and laughter and fiddle music, with street fights and drunks. It seemed that most of the people here were either oblivious to what was going on in the rest of the city or did not give two hoots. The perfume of slum air was many-layered, a heady mixture of dung and mud, of dragon oil and roasting chestnuts and pea soup.

Ivy's breathing was ragged, the strength leaving her quickly. She hurried along an alleyway and through a square-sided court as quickly as she could, bouncing off of the walls, clutching at bannisters and pipes and doorways to stay upright, until, at last, she found herself, miraculously, at the crooked doorway of a tiny basement flat on Needle Street. She barely had enough strength to knock on the door.

The door edged open, and there stood Rook. A tall,

broad-shouldered woman with cropped white-blonde hair. She wore a shocked expression, her small watery eyes looking Ivy up and down.

'Hell's teeth! What's happened to you? Are you all right? Where's Doctor Vanderbill?'

At this Ivy could no longer hold back. She burst into tears and collapsed on the poor woman, who dragged her inside, sat her by the warm stove and splashed cold water on her face.

'He's dead,' Ivy managed to say. 'Doctor Vanderbill is *dead.*'

Rook's eyes stretched even wider. 'What? How?'

'Younger came to the house.'

Mention of that name caused Rook to take a sharp breath. 'Karl Younger?'

'He came for *me*,' said Ivy. 'But I suppose the poor doctor wasn't ready to give me up. He stood up for me and Younger . . . murdered him in front of my eyes!'

She began to cry again, while Rook poured them both a drink.

'And how did you get away?' There was perhaps a hint of suspicion in Rook's voice.

'I . . . I blew up half the street.'

Rook gawped at her. '*You* caused that big thunderclap I heard earlier? How? Is Karl Younger dead?' There was some hope in her voice then.

'I don't know. He might have made it out. As for how I

did it . . . Ever since Mrs Hester disappeared, since I got my soul back, there's been this . . . power inside me.'

Rook nodded. 'Wild magic.'

'Yes. But . . .' Ivy searched for the words. 'Are you a Westerly Witch, Rook?'

'No. I'm not any sort of Witch. But I'm on their side. And I've been around them enough to know a thing or two about their ways.'

Ivy went on. 'You've heard of the sound of magic, then? All Witches can hear it. Doctor Vanderbill once told me that some Witches believe that sound is the voices of our ancestors singing to us. I don't know about that, but it surely is pretty to hear. At least, most of the time it is. You see, sometimes, when I'm angry or frightened – and sometimes for no reason at all as far as I can tell – that lovely fragile music becomes a terrible scream in my head, and this white-hot force builds up in me. Doctor Vanderbill was trying to help me control it better.' She stopped, wiped her eyes, and there it was again – that hum of power coursing through her, building, the crystal music of magic becoming more intense. 'Seeing the poor doctor dead, I got so terrified and furious that the scream became louder than ever. I wanted to hurt Younger, I admit it. So, I let it all out. But I didn't mean to hurt anyone else!'

She brought a fist down on the table and sparks of magic went zinging off around the room, causing pots and pans to fall clanging from their hooks on the wall, and making Rook's cat – a fat tortoiseshell that had been curled up by the fire – spring up and run crying to the shadows.

Rook was now looking at Ivy as if she were some dangerous animal that had escaped from a cage. Her eyes flicked downwards to Ivy's hands. 'You can't stay here.'

'What? Oh, please!' Ivy brought her hands together as if in prayer. A few sparks jumped at her fingertips. 'I'm sorry about the mess. Look, I'll clean it.' She got up and began collecting the scattered pans.

'Leave them,' said Rook. 'Look at me.' Ivy did. 'It's too dangerous – both for you and the folk who live around these parts. If Younger is alive, he'll come hunting for you. If he's dead, someone else will come in his place. When that happens, only Mother Earth can help anyone who gets caught in the crossfire. Do you know how many people are crammed into these buildings? If you get out of control here, I shudder to think how many you might hurt. Do you want that?'

'Of course not. I'm not a monster! But where will I go?'

Rook let the question roll around her brain for a long moment, then bobbed her head up and down in agreement to a thought that was forming in her head. 'We must get you out of the city. The doctor thought very highly of you, and I will not see you fall into the hands of the king.'

Ivy's head was swirling. 'But how? Where?'

'You leave that to me.'

CORNERED

'Lara? Lara?'

It had been a dreamless sleep, deep and empty, until the voice brought her up through the dark like a wriggling fish on a hook. Lara blinked, shaking her groggy head. A huge figure was standing over her, and the sight of it made her sit bolt upright.

'Easy, Lara! It's me! It's Rob!'

A flare of light erupted from the end of his wand, and she saw him properly, a mountain with a beard. He wore a long overcoat and his eyes twinkled like black jewels.

'Rob! Oh Rob, it's brilliant to see you!' Lara leaped up, taking his hand.

'Rob!' Joe was awake too, crowding the big man, smiling and laughing in delight at seeing him.

'I'm very glad to see you two as well,' said Rob. 'But we'll have to save the pleasantries until we deal with *that*.' He pointed to the place on the wooden sleigh where Lara had draped her long coat. A bright, turquoise-green light was radiating from one of the pockets.

'It's not one of my spells,' she whispered. 'They're all safe in the trunk.'

'Then what is it?' said Joe.

Rob crept around the sleigh, the old floor creaking under him, and reached into the pocket of Lara's coat. He brought out his hand and opened it, and there, nestling in his big palm, was a spell bottle the size of a thimble. The spell inside twined and spun at terrific speed, its greenish glow dazzling in the dimness of the attic.

'What is it?' asked Joe again.

Lara lowered her head towards the spell, trying to listen. 'There's no sound of magic coming off it. I thought magic always had a sound.'

'Not always,' said Rob. The turquoise spell lit him from beneath, casting deep shadows around his worried eyes. 'This here is a tracer spell. Someone must've planted it on you.'

Lara's chest tightened. 'The agent at the docks – the one who stopped us, Joe! She must've slipped that in my pocket when I helped her up after the explosion. Oh how could I have been so bleedin' stupid to think we'd get away just like that?'

'No point worrying about that now,' said Rob. His voice was low and calm. 'A tracer is usually hidden much better than this one. Whoever placed it must have been in a hurry. But it's done its job – the way that spell is a-fizzin' around, I reckon whoever planted it is closing in. They might even be in the building.'

Rob was correct. The secret police were not inside the building just yet, but a dozen or so had gathered outside the main entrance, flanked by their shining ironhearts and black carriages. One of them– the agent who'd first spotted Lara and Joe at the docks and planted the tracer spell in Lara's pocket – was holding out her wand, and from the wand tip looped a rope of spell light. On the end of this rope, straining and sniffing, was a small terrier, also formed from spell light. It had caught the scent of the tracer spell and led the agents here, to the opera house.

The sound of trundling wheels brought another black carriage into the street. Two great ironhearts pulled up on the cobbles, the door flew open, and out from the carriage stepped the tall figure of Karl Younger, the Witch Hunter. Usually, his appearance was flawless, not a crease in his clothes or a hair out of place. But this had not been an ordinary night. The incident at Doctor Vanderbill's house had left him bruised and tattered. And very, very angry. He stood stock-still for a moment, then sniffed at the warm summer breeze. He approached the agent with the spell dog.

'What's happening, Hackett?'

Hackett, still straining to keep the sniffing spell dog under control, said, 'I was on duty at the docks earlier, Director. Spotted a girl and boy coming off one of the boats. They seemed suspicious.'

'How so?'

'Well . . . they were peering about, sir, as if to check nobody was looking at them. They had a trunk – weird it was, sir. Can't quite put my finger on it. When I approached them, they were all on edge – especially when I asked about that trunk. Before I could properly investigate, that great explosion went off and then . . . well, it was all hands on deck, sir, wasn't it? But I slipped a tracer spell in the girl's pocket before I left.'

Younger nodded. 'A wise move.'

'Thank you, Director. There was something about that girl, sir, and her friend, and especially that trunk, that I can't quite explain.'

'Indeed, Hackett?'

'Yes, sir. Well, ever since the Evernight, I've been hearing magic every waking moment. I expect you have too. But when I was near that girl . . . near the *trunk*, sir, it was like all the sound of magic went away. Inside my head became deathly silent. And I thought, *Well, that isn't right.* I thought . . . *What if they're Hags?*'

'An interesting theory,' said Younger.

'Director?'

'Yes, Hackett?'

'Well, if I may, sir, it seems to me that you don't bother yourself with every tracer spell that goes off around the city. What's so special about this one?'

Younger considered this. 'Tonight, I saw a young lady destroy a street using nothing but the pure magic in her veins. I was buried under thirty feet of rubble, and she got away. In short, Hackett, I have not had a good night, and I would very much like to *hurt* someone. If, as luck would have it, you happen to have uncovered a couple of Hags, so much the better. Hand over the tracer.'

Hackett released the trigger of her wand, and at once the spell dog and its leash disappeared. She spun the revolver chamber of her wand, removed one of the bottles, and handed it to Karl Younger, who loaded it into an empty chamber in his own wand.

When Younger pulled the trigger, the cold blue-green of the tracer spell exploded outwards, forming a thick rope of spell light, and on the end of the leash, a huge glowing hound appeared, wide-shouldered, stocky and muscular, its gums pulled back over drool-spattered fangs, its hackles up. The hound put its nose to the cobbles, picked up a scent, and began to emit a low, rumbling growl. Then it strained at the spell-light leash, pulling at Younger, who let it lead him around the enormous old building to a narrow alleyway at the rear of the place, filled with rubbish bins and shapes in the shadows that might have been people asleep under blankets.

The spell-light hound dragged Younger down a steep set of steps to a small green door, stood up on its hind legs and scratched at the surface, growling and whining and fussing. Younger indicated the door. 'Open it.'

A dozen or so secret police agents had followed him, and they lined up behind him on the stairs, still and quiet as shadows. One of them descended the steps, brushed past Younger, and, keeping the ghostly silence in place, pulled the trigger of his wand and fired a spell at the door, turning it to ash that scattered in the warm night breeze.

The small, low-ceilinged room beyond lay in thick blackness, but no one cast a light spell; the secret police were trained to work in the dark, to see in other ways, and the dim light of the spell dog was plenty to go by.

At once the spell dog was off again, yanking at the leash, pulling Younger into the labyrinth of empty opera house passageways. Past kitchens and costume stores and offices they went, through a system of stairways and corridors, breathing dust and fresh paint and varnish, up and up and up, until at last they came to a door at the very top of the place, in a long-forgotten, cobwebbed corner.

The hound was straining so much that Younger's arm ached. He released the trigger on his wand, and suddenly the spell dog became a cloud of glowing particles and faded to nothing.

Younger gathered his agents, looking around their

ashen faces. They stood around the little attic door, wands drawn, angry red death spells glowing in the chambers.

Younger closed his fist and gave a single nod.

The largest of the agents stepped forward and caved in the door with a single kick. Then Younger and his team rushed into the attic.

THE HUNT BEGINS

'All clear, Director Younger.'

'Clear here, too, Director Younger.'

'And here.'

'No sign of them anywhere, Director.'

The attic was rambling and crammed with props and various costumes and pieces of broken set – plenty of places to hide – but a thorough search had seen the agents come up empty-handed.

Karl Younger stood by a wooden sleigh, which someone had turned into a makeshift bed. In his hands was a small coat he'd discovered hanging on one end of the sleigh. In the pocket of that coat, he'd found the tracer spell. He crouched, touched the blankets. 'Still warm. They're here somewhere.'

'Maybe they knew we were coming,' said one of the agents.

'Director Younger? Sir?'

Younger's attention turned towards the door, where Hackett – the agent who'd planted the tracer spell – was standing beside a travelling trunk. At first glance the trunk seemed unremarkable, a forgotten prop, perhaps, like most everything else in the attic. Yet as he neared it, Younger felt that he had crossed a threshold, that he was standing in a vacuum where the ever-present force of magic was absent.

It was a deeply troubling sensation – and Karl Younger was not an easily troubled man.

'It's the trunk I was telling you about, Director Younger,' said Hackett, her face pale. 'The one from the docks. You can feel that, can't you? It's not right.'

Younger did not answer. The silence near the box – the absence of both the sound and feel of magic for several feet around it, had his full attention. He took three steps back. On the third step, he crossed back over that strange border, and the feeling of magic rippled over his skin once more, crackling in his veins. The sound of it came back too, melodic and crystalline.

His eyes fixed on the travelling trunk, Younger took a slow step forward. Sure enough, magic died away in an instant, leaving silent emptiness. Younger's mind burned with curiosity and an unsettling sense of the unknown. Slowly, he reached out a hand, his wand ready to strike, and touched the lid of the trunk. It was smooth and cold. Nothing else. Then his fingers reached for the handle, wrapped around it . . .

Younger opened the trunk.

It was deep and lined with midnight blue velvet.

And it was empty.

As Karl Younger stared down into the trunk, he felt a flush of anger rise from his toes. But he did not let it show, because anger was weakness, wasn't it? Anger let other people see that there were cracks in your armour.

He closed the lid softly. 'Take this trunk back to Snaptooth Street. I want to examine it properly.'

The agents in the cluttered attic glanced around at each other. The place was hushed.

'Well?' said Younger. 'What's wrong with you? You two!' he snapped his fingers, pointing at the two nearest agents, whose names escaped him. 'Take the trunk outside, put it on a carriage and have the driver take it back to the headquarters.'

Neither of the agents in question had the appetite to try Younger's patience any further. After a momentary hesitation they came forward. Younger saw them slow when they crossed the threshold into the magical vacuum, saw the unease settle deep in their bones. He beckoned them forward. When they bent to lift the trunk, one at each end, Younger half expected that it might stay rooted to the ground, enchanted, but they seemed to lift it easily enough. He watched them out the door and away into the dim passageway, and when they were gone, he turned to the others.

'They must be in the building somewhere. There's no way they had time to get out. Search every inch of the place. Wake up the caretaker and have him show you every passageway, cellar and hidden corner.'

The remaining agents, ten of them, hurried from the attic.

'And check the roof!' Younger shouted after them.

When he was alone, he took a slow walk around the attic, letting his thoughts form freely. Well, this had turned out to be an interesting night, hadn't it? First the run-in with the little Hag at the good doctor's house, and now this. Younger picked up a replica of a human skull that had been gathering dust on top of a wardrobe. He held it up and stared into the empty sockets. Not so long ago, there had been about as much life in himself as there was in this skull. Before the Evernight, before Younger got his soul back, everything had been shrouded in a mist devoid of feeling. It had not been living, really. Only existing. Eat, sleep, spell, repeat. Every day the same. Every moment controlled by Mrs Hester.

But she was gone now. When the Evernight had first ended, and his soul had found him, Younger had been so frightened. All those feelings. All that anger. The inescapable, maddening din of magic in his ears, stabbing at his thoughts like shards of glass. The power of wild magic in his veins . . .

At first, he had wished for Mrs Hester to come back and take his soul again, to be numb.

And then, searching for a purpose, he had joined the secret police, becoming director of the entire operation. The first time he'd hunted down a runaway White Witch,

94

executed her, watched the life leave her eyes . . . he had felt alive, truly alive, for the first time.

Karl Younger had found his calling.

Presently, he gave the skull a thin, cold smile. He realised that a part of him was glad – actually happy – that tonight's runaway Hag had evaded him. Just as he had been glad when he'd opened that trunk and found no Westerly Witches hiding inside. The two strands were connected, he could feel that in his soul. And he would pull the threads together and make a nice tight knot around their necks. The thought of that heightened his senses, made his skin tingle and the hairs on his arms bristle. This was going to be a fine hunt.

Younger placed the skull back in its spot and left the forgotten attic, feeling wide awake and alive.

THE MEMORY MOTH

'Hurry up. I don't like this.'

'Oh, and I do? Don't push! I'll break my neck on these old stairs!'

These were the grumblings of the two secret police agents charged with carrying the trunk through the many passageways of the opera house. They were tough men, and prided themselves on it, but the strange enchantment on this old trunk was preventing them from using their wands to light the way, and so the darkness and creeping shadows of the corridors pressed in on them, and their toughness melted away in the heat of their wild imaginations.

'Sshh!' said the first. They were still, listening.

'What?' said the second. 'You hear something?'

'I don't know. I thought I did. Probably nothing.'

'Yeah. Probably nothing,' said the second, though he did not believe it. 'Say, what do you suppose is wrong with this trunk?'

'I don't like to think about it.'

A pause. They were shuffling along again, their feet soft on the thick carpet, their noses picking up the smell of fresh lacquer from some nearby workshop.

'Do you think it's cursed?' said the second. 'By the Hags?'

'Don't say that! Don't even think it!'

A bang somewhere far off in the dark made them both jump and drop the trunk down on the carpet with a heavy, muffled thud. Then there was only stillness and darkness, and the sound of their ragged, frightened breathing.

'Just look at us,' said the first agent. 'Look at what this thing's done to us! We're officers of the king's secret police for pity's sake! We've come up against Hags and runaways, and brought them down before.'

'You're right,' said the second. 'It's absurd to be frightened of a simple old trunk. Only . . . let's step away from it, just for a moment, eh?'

A pause. 'OK. Only for a moment, though.'

They stepped back, one step . . . two . . . three . . . on the fourth step they crossed the threshold, and the crystal sound of all the magic in the city air came rushing around and through them, as comforting as a warm hug.

'That's better,' said the first man, spell light spilling from the tip of his wand, glinting on the gilt frames of the many paintings hanging on the walls. They closed their eyes and let the magic replenish their spirits, and then, only when they thought they might have heard someone coming and were frightened that Karl Younger would find them idling, did they busy themselves with carrying the trunk again.

This time they made it all the way out to the alleyway, and then the street by the main entrance where the coaches waited, the ironhearts motionless, reflecting the flicker of the streetlamps.

With great haste they secured the trunk in the luggage rack upon the roof of a carriage, jumped down, and were glad to be free of it.

'Take this back to HQ,' the first told the driver. 'And be mindful of it, Merryholme! There's something terrible inside. It's making my blood freeze just to be near it.'

Mr Merryholme, high on his driver's seat on the coach and grasping the reins, was not a Witch, so he had no idea what they were talking about and looked down at them like they were strange, foreign creatures.

'Well, what are you gawping at, Merryholme?' exclaimed the second agent. 'Director Younger wants this item back in Snaptooth Street at once! Go!'

At the mere mention of Younger's name, Merryholme's expression changed. He snapped the reins, and the eyes of the ironhearts lit up, glowing blue-green. Their enchanted clockwork innards whirred and ticked and spun. Merryholme snapped the reins again, and this time the metal horses set off down the street at a brisk trot.

When the carriage was out of sight, the two agents heaved sighs of relief.

'I never want to see that thing again,' said the first.

'Too right,' said the second. 'Come on – we'd best get back inside and help with the search.'

Mr Merryholme lashed his whip, urging the ironhearts on through the theatre district, away from the opera house. This part of King's Haven was mostly made up of theatres and offices and studios. It was deserted – a world away from the simmering jungle of the slums, and unaffected by the chaos that Ivy Robin had left in the toffs' residential district a few miles to the east.

The ironhearts galloped at tremendous speed, rounding cobbled corners so quickly that the wheels of one side of the coach would leave the ground, and then crash back down. Merryholme smiled to himself as he went – without a coach full of secret police agents, all pale and watchful and disapproving, he was having quite the time whipping along.

But he did not know – how could he? – that disaster was about to strike him.

Behind him, on the luggage rack on the roof of the coach, the lid of the trunk slowly opened.

Merryholme did not notice; the sound of the ironhearts' hooves on the ground and the wind in his ears made sure of that. And his eyes were fixed on the street ahead, so he was not aware of the huge bearded man climbing up impossibly from the depths of the travelling trunk. Rob Nielsen stood up, bent at the knees to find his balance atop the fast-moving coach, and was across the roof in two strides, standing directly behind the driver, his knees level with Merryholme's head. He took his wand from his coat, pointed it at the driver, and tapped him on the shoulder.

Merryholme jumped in fright, giving the reins an unintentional jerk, causing the ironhearts to rock the carriage. When he looked over his shoulder and saw the spell bottles glowing in Rob's wand, then glanced up into Rob Nielsen's wild red beard and twinkling black eyes, his face fell. Rob mouthed at him to stop the coach, and Merryholme nodded and did as he was told.

The cobbled street was wide and silent, lined with sleeping fashion boutiques and coffee houses and purveyors of fine tobacco and clay pipes. As Merryholme raised his shaking hands, the only sound was his shallow breathing, and the clockwork whirr-click of the ironhearts.

'I ain't armed,' he said. 'And I promise you, there ain't so much as a bronze coin on this coach. Oh, please don't harm me, sir. I'm only a driver. I've got a family waitin' at home.'

'I'm not after money,' answered Rob. 'And I won't hurt you, so long as you do what I say. Be a good man and climb slowly down from the coach. Keep your hands where I can see 'em!'

Again, Mr Merryholme did as Rob told him, climbing down from his seat and hopping from the step onto the cobbles. 'Are you planning on taking the coach?' he said. 'Because if you are, the secret police'll come after you.'

Rob laughed. 'Oh, I think I'll be seeing them again soon regardless!'

'And you're not frightened? You must be insane!'

'Look,' said Rob, 'I wish I could hang about all night chatting, but I have places to be. So . . .' He spun the revolver of his wand so that a purple-blue spell blazed bright in the chamber, and he pointed the wand at the driver.

Merryholme backed away a step, hands up. 'Please! You promised!'

'Hold still, man!' Rob pulled the trigger. From the end of his wand blossomed a single, glowing moth, silver-blue, fluttering in that scatterbrained way moths tend to do. The driver watched, bewitched, as the moth approached him and circled his head, leaving a tiny trail of spell smoke in the warm night air. The moth landed on the tip of the driver's ear, and he stood still, his eyes sliding sideward as if he was trying to look at his own head.

'What's . . . what's it doing?' The moth crawled down his ear, into his ear canal, and a moment later the driver's face became blank and expressionless. He looked up at Rob Nielsen, who had sat down upon the driver's seat on the coach.

'Oh, hello,' said Mr Merryholme in a friendly sort of tone. He frowned. 'I'm a little embarrassed. I seem to have clean forgot what we were talking about.'

'It isn't important,' said Rob. 'I stopped to ask directions, is all. You've been very helpful.'

Merryholme raised his eyebrows. 'Have I? Oh. Good.'

Rob took up the reins, but before he snapped them, he stared back down at the driver.

'You won't remember our meeting. After I leave, you'll forget all about me.'

'Yes,' said the driver. 'I will.'

'Good man.' Rob lashed the reins, and the ironhearts leaped to life, thundering away down the street and out of sight, leaving Mr Merryholme alone. His every thought was shrouded in fog. What was he doing out at this hour? He felt like he'd had a few pints of beer too many. Wasn't he supposed to be on duty tonight? Had they given him the night off? It didn't sound likely. But ... he took a deep breath of the night-time city air, humid and bursting with the smell of the river and horses, and, in this leafy part of King's Haven, the flowering trees.

Oh well. He'd better get home before the hour grew much later. As he walked back through the streets to his humble little house, Merryholme could not shake the feeling that he had forgotten something very important.

STARBIRD

Ivy Robin peeked out from under a black shawl at the unfamiliar sights of the early-hour slums. Rook had an iron grip on Ivy's hand and was pulling her along so that she could not stop and gawp at the drunks spilling out of pubs, arguing and fighting and then making up and laughing and singing songs. She heard shrieking laughter, babies crying, and dogs barking. She smelled roasting chestnuts, and the air was sticky and full of summer heat and sweat and the gentle song of magic.

'Where are we going?'

'Quiet,' snapped Rook. 'Keep your head down. If Younger is after you that means every agent in the city is on the lookout. Head down, you hear me?'

As they moved, Ivy lost count of the streets and alleyways and courts. There were so many people, all crammed in tiny, stinking dwellings. She had never seen this part of King's Haven; it made her old dormitory back in the White Witch district seem quite luxurious, and that was something she never thought she'd say.

The sulphurous seaweed smell of the river grew stronger, and they came at last to a place where the river Anchor flowed through the slums. It was quite narrow at this point, maybe only a hundred feet across, with a crumbling stone bridge joining the two banks. And here, down a series of steps, they came upon a wooden jetty where twenty or so small boats and canoes were moored.

'That's it,' said Rook. 'This way. Watch your step.'

The shouting and music of the night-time slums was muffled and faraway down here, replaced mostly by the lap of the gently flowing water mixed with the ever-present lullaby of magic.

'This one.' Rook was surprisingly nimble; she hopped into one of the moored canoes with graceful ease, then turned and offered Ivy a hand. 'Come on, gal. Quick.'

'I've never been on the water,' said Ivy. 'I can't swim.'

'Well, Mother Earth permitting, you won't need to swim tonight. Get in, and be quick about it – the water's a safer way for us to get to where we're going.'

Ivy took her hand and, feeling shockingly clumsy, stepped aboard the canoe. At once she was uncomfortable with the way the vessel moved beneath her, and she grasped the sides tight.

Rook slipped the mooring rope off the wooden post, took up the paddle and manoeuvred the canoe out into the water with expert ease, being careful to keep close to the steep banks, where the light of the dragon-breath streetlamps struggled to reach and the shadows were deepest.

'Keep down,' Rook told her, and Ivy hugged the sides of the canoe and watched the city drift past. The river grew wider, the buildings taller and grander, and the steep banks turned into brick waterways. In the slums they didn't see many other boats at all, mostly just those moored, but as the river widened, they passed barges and large cargo boats heading south through the network of rivers.

'Damn,' said Rook.

'What? What is it?'

Rook brought the canoe to as much of a stop as she could, right in the shadow of the steep bank walls. '*Shoosh*, gal. Get down! There's a copper patrol boat passing.'

Ivy felt her tongue stick to the roof of her mouth and her stomach lurch. 'Will they see us?'

'If you don't shut up, they'll hear us first! Get down!'

Ivy did as she was told, ducking into the canoe, peeking out across the river. There were several boats, including a residential barge and a larger merchant ship. But the only one she was interested in at this moment was a small steam vessel powering through the middle of the river.

'Do you think they're looking for me?'

Rook gave her another scolding look. She shook her head. 'I don't think so. There's regular patrols in these waters – mostly they're only interested in the larger boats;

that's where runaway White Witches are most likely to be stowing away or smuggling spells.'

From the shadows, Ivy watched the police boat pull up alongside the merchant vessel, and several coppers stepped aboard. There was a conversation between the coppers and one of the women on board – the captain, most likely. She showed the coppers some papers, and then gestured around the ship, and the coppers began to nosey about. When they had all disappeared inside the boat, Rook gave a sigh of relief and set about paddling once more, this time with more speed and purpose, and Ivy watched the larger boats shrink into the distance and, at last, drop out of sight.

The river grew narrower again, and the buildings changed once more, this time from grand offices and houses to warehouses and factories belching smoke into the night air.

'How deep is it?' asked Ivy, her fingers brushing the black water.

'Hundreds of feet in the middle,' said Rook. 'They say there's monsters in there. I'd watch my fingers if I was you.'

Sounds of the surrounding docks built up in the air, clangs of metal tools, the hum of engines, shouts, yells, horses, cranes, and soon they were paddling between a multitude of moored vessels. Rook brought the canoe closer and closer to one of the boats.

'Watch out,' said Ivy. 'We're going to crash!'

Breathless with effort, Rook said, 'Of course we are, girl. We have to let him know we're here somehow!'

Ivy braced for impact, but when the canoe came up against the metal hull of the boat in question, it only bounced off with a loud and echoing *THUNK*.

A moment later they heard footsteps up on deck, and a man's craggy face appeared over the edge of the boat, lit harshly by the dragon-breath lamp in his hand. He peered down into the dark shadows.

'Rook? That you?'

'Well who else would it be?!' she said.

He grunted and disappeared, returning a moment later. 'Come on up.'

A rope ladder unfurled down the side of the boat, and Rook helped Ivy climb. It wasn't easy; the rope swung around and tried, it seemed, to throw her off. By the time she reached the gunwale and the man pulled her aboard, her hands were blistered and sore.

'That's it. I got you. Please, get out of sight.' He indicated a doorway in the metal structure of the boat, and on unsteady legs she made it through, stopping in the mouth of the passageway and looking back to see the man helping Rook aboard.

'Come inside. Both of you.'

He led them down a ladder and along another passageway to a cramped hold where they sat around a wooden table while he prepared three cups of strong coffee. It was warming, and sweetened with lots of sugar, and Ivy sipped it gratefully.

The man stared from one to the other. 'So? You going

to explain what in the world is a-goin' on, Rook? Your message didn't exactly tell a detailed story.'

'I'm sorry,' said Rook. 'It was an emergency. Ivy, this is John Starbird. John, meet Ivy. I'll spare you any more pleasantries and get right to the point. Ivy is a runaway White Witch.'

'That much I guessed,' said Starbird. 'But what's this in your message about Doctor Vanderbill?'

'You knew the doctor?' said Ivy, unable to keep quiet.

Starbird nodded. 'Of course. Anyone taking up against the Kingdom knows him. He's a good man. Helped a lot of runaways and marked folks escape King's Haven.'

'He *was* a good man,' said Ivy, and a tear dropped from her eye to the table.

Aghast, Starbird looked to Rook for confirmation.

'I'm afraid it's true,' she said. 'The good doctor is dead.'

'But how?'

'Karl Younger came a-callin' earlier tonight. He was after Ivy here. As you can probably imagine, the doctor was not about to give her up.'

'Younger killed him right in front of me.' Ivy was shaking, and tears rolled down and fell from her jaw. That searing pressure was building up inside her again, the magic coursing through her veins. 'It happened so quick; there was nothing I could do . . .' A spark of magic fizzed from one of her fingertips, bouncing off the metal structure of the boat with a loud *PING!*

Starbird moved slowly away from Ivy, as if she were carrying some deadly disease.

'It's all right,' she said, closing her eyes, breathing deeply. Magic sparks jumped a few times between her fingers and then faded. 'I'm not going to explode. It seems to have calmed down a bit since the doctor's house.'

Starbird was staring. 'What happened? How did you get away?'

'You hear that explosion earlier?' asked Rook.

'*Hear it?* It nearly knocked me off my feet!'

Rook leaned forward, took another sip of steaming coffee. 'Our young friend here was responsible.'

John Starbird's gaze turned to Ivy, and she explained as best she could what had happened, how she'd lost control and the magic in her had spilled out. When she was done, he was leaning away from her as if she might explode again. 'Don't worry,' she said. 'It's not going to happen now. I've never let it all out like that before. I think it might take some time to build up again. Doctor Vanderbill was trying to help me understand it more, but . . . that's all finished now.'

Starbird stood up and began to pace. 'It's fine,' he said to himself. 'It's all going to be fine, Starbird. The most wanted woman in the entire Kingdom is aboard your boat, but it's fine. It'll all be fine.'

'Oh, for pity's sake, sit down,' said Rook. 'We had nowhere else to go. I'm not asking you to keep her here. I know Rob

Nielsen is coming to see you tonight. He can decide what to do with her.'

He sat and swept the long greying hair from his face. 'Yeah. Yeah, that's a fine idea. Rob'll know just what to do.'

'Don't I get a say?' said Ivy.

Rook and Starbird exchanged incredulous looks. 'I beg your pardon?'

'I don't mean to sound ungrateful,' said Ivy. 'But you're both talking about me as if I'm not here. Shouldn't I get a say in what happens to me and where I go? And who is this Rob Nielsen anyway?'

'That would be me.'

He stood in the doorway, an enormous man in a long overcoat, peering down at them from the wilds of a huge red beard. There was a wand in his hand, and he was pointing it at Ivy.

SETTING OFF

'I understand why you're all looking at me like that,' said Ivy.

Rob Nielsen had brought two children with him, introduced to Ivy as Lara and Joe, so the hold had become quite crammed, and every pair of eyes was upon her. 'Like I'm some unstable spell that's about to go off. But that isn't true. At least, I don't think it is.'

Rob had seemed most troubled by her story. 'This changes everything,' he said, rubbing at his temples with his eyes squeezed shut. 'We'll have to take you south with us.'

'South? I don't want to go south!'

'With all due respect, young lady,' said Rob in a quiet, dangerous voice, 'you don't have much of a choice. You can't stay in King's Haven, not after tonight. And there's this power of yours to think about. We can't risk the lives of innocents should you go off again. You don't want to hurt anyone, do you?'

Ivy stared fiercely at him. 'Of course I don't! That's why I was with the doctor to begin with. Look, if I have to leave King's Haven, can't I go to Westerly Witch? Doctor Vanderbill told me you've been smuggling White Witches there for ages, that it's safe there.'

Rob stroked the end of his beard. 'If I had my way, that's exactly what would happen. But it's not that simple. We don't have a boat ready to go. Next one isn't due to leave for a couple of days, and we can't send it early because the latest group of runaways and marked folks are depending on it to get them out of the city. After the explosion, Younger will have every copper and secret police agent in King's Haven on the lookout for you, so we can't risk you a-waitin' it out. You see why you must come with us?'

Ivy glanced around the table again, at the faces of these strangers, and thought that they were all looking at her like she was a ticking bomb.

All except the girl, Lara. She was smiling sadly, and she said, 'We're not a bad bunch, miss.'

'Oh, I don't think you are,' said Ivy. 'But I've had quite a night and it's all a bit much.'

'Starbird,' said Rob, 'how soon can we leave?'

Starbird got to his feet and gave Rob a lazy salute and an easy smile. 'All fuelled up, boss. Ready to go, soon as you say the word.'

They bid farewell to Rook, who paddled her canoe back up the river and was lost to the shadows. Starbird slipped anchor, and the boat's engines rumbled and growled as it cut through the black surface of the water.

Four hours later, Lara and Joe were hanging back near the stern of the boat, looking on from a doorway as Ivy stood out on deck and watched the world pass. The surrounding landscape had changed drastically as the boat steamed downriver, from the buildings of King's Haven to a rolling patchwork of farmland and fields, and now to mountain and forest. The first rays of morning sun had blushed the eastern sky over the mountain peaks.

'Should we speak to her?' Joe asked, nodding towards Ivy.

'I reckon we should,' said Lara. 'Poor thing's all alone and frightened.'

They came out of the doorway slowly and took great care in approaching her.

Ivy, not taking her eyes from the surrounding landscape, said, 'I've never been out of the city before.' She took a deep, deep breath. 'Smell that fresh air! I can feel it cleaning out my lungs.'

Lara nodded. 'I know how that feels. I lived all my life in King's Haven until just a year ago. Joe, too. We only left when the Evernight came.'

Ivy turned to look at them. She was in her mid-teens, tall and skinny and pale, with sharp cheekbones and black hair cut very short. Her piercing blue eyes studied Lara with great interest. 'I overheard Rob Nielsen speaking with Rook and Starbird earlier. Is it really true you're the one who beat the Evernight?'

'I had a little help,' said Lara.

'And Mrs Hester? You got rid of her too? Broke the spell she had over us White Witches?'

'Now, *that* I definitely didn't do alone. Joe here had a big part to play.'

Ivy looked at Joe, who seemed to shrink back. 'So both of you,' she went on, 'helped me get my soul back?'

Lara and Joe looked at each other. 'I suppose so,' said Lara.

'Then I owe you a great debt. Because of what you did, I'm whole. I can feel, and dream, and live a proper life.'

'But it must be so much to deal with all at once,' said Lara. 'I can hardly imagine. It must be like living life in black and white, and then all of a sudden there's colour everywhere. When we first heard we'd helped reunite all you White Witches with your souls, we thought it could only be a good thing. But it's been overwhelming for some. I've seen it. Poor coves hiding in Westerly Witch, afraid to step outside.'

Ivy's blue eyes examined her own hands. As if on cue, a single spark of magic leaped from the tip of her right index finger and streaked off into the air. Ivy noticed the look on Lara's face and said, 'I'm a freak, aren't I?'

'What? I never said that.'

'But it's true. You're a Witch, and so is that Rob Nielsen,

and even you both look at me like I'm something from another world. This thing that happens to me, the magic that spills out, you ever seen it before?'

Lara paused. 'Well, no, but—'

'There you go, see? I should be better off as an exhibit in one of those awful freak shows that travel all about the Kingdom.' Ivy was quiet for a moment, and Lara said nothing. Then Ivy stared back out towards the surrounding mountains. 'Why are we going south?'

Lara explained about Double Eight and the murders in Lake End, and that Rob and Joe had a secret mission, too.

'You don't think your friend's guilty?' Ivy asked.

'Course not!'

'But you,' said Ivy, nodding to Joe. 'You have doubts? You think he did it?'

Lara tried to catch Joe's eye, but he wouldn't look at her. 'I'm not saying he's *definitely* guilty. I just don't think we can rule it out. He used to be a . . .'

'What?' said Ivy. 'A White Witch like me?'

'I didn't mean it like that.'

'Is there another way to mean it?'

Before Joe could dig his hole any deeper, Rob Nielsen's voice called him from somewhere inside the boat. Taking his chance, Joe scrambled away.

'He's a strange one,' said Ivy, watching after him.

'You don't know the half of it,' Lara replied. 'He ain't had it easy, you know. When the Evernight came to King's

Haven, and the slum folk were left to face the Painted Men alone, Joe lost his granny.'

'That's horrible. Is he all alone then?'

Lara smiled. 'No. He has his friends. And you're not alone neither, you hear me?'

Ivy smiled – truly smiled – for the first time since Lara had met her. The smile lit up her face. Then it was gone, replaced by puzzlement. 'What do you think Joe and Rob Nielsen's mission is?'

Lara stared off in the direction Joe had run. 'I haven't the foggiest idea.'

THE HOUSE CALL

Behind enormous stone walls, in the part of the White Witch district that had been turned into secret police headquarters – Snaptooth Street – Director Karl Younger stepped from a carriage, his mood as dark as the night sky, and entered a large brick warehouse.

The search for the owners of the trunk – suspected Westerly Witches – had been unsuccessful. His agents had combed every part of the opera house, every single inch, and come up empty. The only explanation, the only possible solution that his mind could accept, was that these missing people were somehow *inside* that trunk. This troubled him greatly, because not only had he let them escape, but, if he was correct, he had given them a free pass into his HQ. And what if that is what they had been after all along? What if this was all some grand terrorist scheme cooked up by the Hags?

Karl Younger's mood did not improve when he inquired at the warehouse desk about the whereabouts of the trunk. The puzzled clerk explained that no such item had arrived.

'Check again.'

The clerk gave him a fearful nod. 'Yes, Director Younger. Right away.' He disappeared through a door, into the great storage warehouses in which the secret police locked away confiscated items. He returned a few minutes later. 'I'm sorry, Director, but I've checked again and we haven't received any such thing tonight. In fact, nothing new has arrived since yesterday.'

Younger became aware of a bubbling, heavy feeling in the pit of his stomach. Anger. No one had ever evaded him in such a way. In a few moments he was out in the warmth of the summer night, and soon his carriage was in the city proper once more. In the east, the sky was marbled with pink and blue; before long the sun would be a burning ruby over the Pewter Sea. Already the city's earliest risers were at work, no doubt gossiping about the cause of last night's explosion. The smell of fresh bread drifted from a multitude of bakers' ovens, and the shouts of the newspaper sellers echoed along the alleyways and courts. Here and there a tosher scurried into open drain covers and disappeared into the subterranean labyrinth of the sewers.

Younger's carriage swept into a long residential street on a steep slope. The houses here were small redbrick terraces, the sort occupied by the working classes. Near the crest of the hill, the carriage came to a stop. The driver opened the door, and Younger stepped down onto the worn cobbles and approached a narrow front door. He knocked with a gloved hand and waited, brushing a speck from the sleeve of his long black coat.

Footsteps. The rattle of a lock.

The door swung open, revealing a small, slender man with greying curly hair. The expression on his face was dopey at first – the look of someone still floating on the edge of sleep – but when he realised that Karl Younger was standing on his doorstep, he straightened up and became very alert.

'Director Younger, sir? It's an honour! What brings you here?'

Karl Younger smiled. It was a warm smile, one that he had practised many times.

'Mr Merryholme. How relieved I am to find you safe and well.'

A sleepy call drifted down from somewhere upstairs. 'Harry? Who is it?'

'Nothing to worry about, Mags,' replied Mr Merryholme. 'Go back to sleep, love.' He turned back to the door, and Younger could see that the colour had left his face. 'Would you like to come in, sir? Have a cuppa?'

Another smile. 'No. Thank you.'

'You mentioned, sir, you was glad to see me safe. Why might that be?'

'Well, when I heard you'd disappeared on duty earlier tonight, Mr Merryholme, I was deeply concerned.'

'Disappeared, sir? On duty, sir?'

Karl Younger's keen eyes were locked on Merryholme's confused face.

'Yes. On Duty, Mr Merryholme. Driving my search party to the opera house. Surely you remember?'

Merryholme's face contorted in a jumbled mix of puzzlement and concentration. 'I, uh . . . I can't remember, as it happens, sir. Come to think of it . . . I can't remember anything at all about last night. You say I was at the opera house?'

Younger continued to stare, unblinking. Either Merryholme was an exceedingly talented liar, or he genuinely could not remember. 'Yes. We were on the trail of an unknown number of suspects. Possibly Westerly Witches. We came across a trunk with . . . peculiar properties. You were charged with taking the trunk back to Snaptooth Street. But you never arrived. The carriage you were driving is missing. And here I find you, back at home. The trunk is very important. So, Mr Merryholme, I ask you: where is it?'

Merryholme shook his head. 'I . . . I haven't a clue, Director Younger, I swear it! I . . .' he screwed up his eyes, thumped his forehead with the palm of his open hand. 'There's something . . . *something* I'm not remembering. It's . . . it's all missing.'

What Younger did next, he did quickly, with power and

precision. With one hand he grabbed Merryholme by the throat, dragged him sideways and then pushed him back against the red brick of the terraced house. Merryholme tried to shout out, but Younger squeezed his throat, pushed him back further and touched the index finger of his free hand to his lips. 'Not a sound, Mr Merryholme.' Then, with that free hand, he reached into his long coat and brought out his wand. There was one spell in the barrel, a spell he'd crafted himself. It burned and spat in violent swirls of deep orange inside the spell bottle. Still grasping Merryholme's throat, he raised the tip of his wand towards his ear and pulled the trigger.

The spell bottle flared burned orange, and from the end of the wand came a ribbon of glowing spell smoke. The end of the ribbon curled around Merryholme's ear, took the form of a cockroach and began burrowing into his ear canal.

Merryholme's eyes were wide and wild with fear and shock and pain, his head shaking, his face purple-red. Then, when the cockroach had scrambled and scratched all the way in, attached to the wand by that glowing ribbon, Merryholme's body relaxed. His arms fell to his side, his eyes were glassy, and he stopped struggling. At this, Karl Younger released his grip, stepped back and waited for the spell to do the rest.

The sounds of the waking city seemed suddenly very far away as the glowing cockroach climbed back out of Merryholme's ear. He stood stock-still, his eyes glassy, as

Younger reached out a hand, allowing the spell cockroach to scuttle up his arm, his shoulder, his neck, and to burrow into his own ear.

The pain was sharp, and hot, but Younger did not flinch. He watched as a lost memory, one that had been buried deep in Merryholme's mind by the magic of some unknown assailant, formed around him.

He was beside Merryholme, on the driver's seat of the carriage, heading away from the opera house at great speed through the wide, deserted streets of the theatre district. To Younger's surprise, Merryholme was smiling – laughing, in fact – as he snapped the reins, driving the metal horses ever faster.

And then came the moment someone tapped Merryholme on the shoulder, and he turned and found that he was in trouble.

As the ironhearts came to a stop, Younger twisted around in his seat. He smiled, because the man standing on the roof of the carriage could not see him. But Younger could see the man, see his huge frame, his wild red beard and hair, his small shining black eyes.

'Got you,' said Younger.

He then watched with interest as the red-bearded man – a Westerly Witch, by the look of his wand – buried Merryholme's memory deep, and drove off with the coach and the trunk.

When the last of the memory faded, Karl Younger

found himself back outside the little terraced house at the crest of the hill. Merryholme blinked, seeming to come fully back to the present, and took a step forward, his hands pressed together in prayer.

'Oh, Director Younger, I'm so sorry. I didn't know . . . the memory was gone, I swear . . . but you saw, didn't you? It weren't my fault. There was nothing I could have done against a Hag like that. Please don't sack me, Director Younger. I've got mouths to feed!'

And there it was again, that warm smile Younger had come to use so well. 'Relax, Mr Merryholme. I'm not going to fire you.' He reached into his coat, brought out a spell bottle in which a green spell swirled, and loaded it into the revolver chamber of the wand.

'Thank you, sir. Thank you, Director Younger. Some folk say you're cold, y'know, that you don't have a heart like a normal man. But I'll tell 'em, Director! I'll tell everyone you're a good cove . . . What's that for?'

Younger had touched the tip of his wand to Merryholme's hand. When he pulled the trigger, a large spider blossomed from the wand tip, made from emerald spell smoke.

The spell spider bit Merryholme on the wrist.

'*Aaoow!* What was that? I don't under—'

Merryholme clutched at his chest with one hand, his throat with the other. He made a series of rasping attempts to take a breath, but his airways had closed up like clenched fists. Foam formed in the corners of his mouth, and his face turned purple, then blue. His eyes rolled back in his head as he slid down the red brick wall of his terraced house and collapsed, dead on the cobbles.

'Harry? Harry? What was that?'

Harry Merryholme did not answer his wife's calls.

Karl Younger calmly stowed his wand away. He walked back to his coach, climbed in, and sat back as the driver snapped the reins, guiding the ironhearts towards the White Witch district.

Younger had seen the face of the man who'd stolen the trunk. The man who'd escaped him. That thought burned in his mind. Two escapes in one night. Nobody had escaped him before. Nobody. And now this? First the servant girl, then the red-bearded man. And there was the business with the boy and girl who'd brought that strange travelling trunk to King's Haven. Hags? That felt correct. Something in the pit of his stomach told him that they were connected, that he stood on the edge of a very dangerous place.

He cracked his knuckles, and watched the first golden rays of the morning sun fall between the buildings. He would need to speak to the Silver King. But first, he would send an order to every copper and secret police agent in the city and beyond. He'd shut down any chance for the red-bearded Hag and whoever else might be involved in this mess to escape.

By the time his coach had returned to Snaptooth Street, Younger had already composed his order. No one was to leave King's Haven. All coaches, trains and ships were to stay put. All airship flights grounded.

He gave the message to a clerk, and five minutes later, thousands of paper birds were flying out in great flocks, carrying Karl Younger's order far and wide.

DISCOVERED

'I still don't like it. It isn't right.' Ivy shivered as she climbed out of the travelling trunk into the relative warmth of the ship's hold. She stepped away from it, beyond the magical border, and Lara could see the relief on her face when she heard the sound of magic again, mixing with the loud hum of the steamer's engines. 'Being in that thing reminds me of what it was like as one of Mrs Hester's White Witches. No sense of wild magic. Being *numb*.' She glanced to Joe. 'Is it true what they say? About Mrs Hester keeping all of our souls in a mirror?'

'Yeah. It's true. All in little cages, aching to be reunited with their bodies. It was horrible.'

'But you smashed the mirror? Doctor Vanderbill told me the story.'

'I did,' said Joe. 'Pushed it out the window of Mrs Hester's tower in the palace in King's Haven. But not before she stabbed me and left me for dead.'

'So what happened?'

'The souls.' Joes eyes filled with a faraway look as he remembered. 'The souls came out of the mirror, and healed me, and carried me across the city to Lara and Double Eight.'

'I wonder,' said Lara, 'if Ivy's soul was one of the ones that saved you, Joe?'

Joe smiled. 'Maybe. Wouldn't that be a thing, eh?'

'And what happened after that?' said Ivy. 'The doctor told me nobody knows for sure except the people who were there to see it – and that's you!' Her eyes were wide with wonder and excitement, and sparks of magic danced at her fingertips.

'Well,' said Lara, eyeing the sparks nervously, 'the moment the mirror smashed, Mrs Hester changed before our eyes, grew so old she was barely more'n a living skeleton. All the youth she stole from innocent folk across the generations finally caught up with her. I don't reckon she'd have lasted long after that night. Probably turned to dust and scattered in the wind.'

There was an awful metallic crunch, and a series of rattles and pops, and finally something that sounded like *PEEEEWWOOOOOOO*. Lara and her friends rushed up on deck, where they were met with a fog of acrid black smoke belching from the steamer's funnel, and a hail of curse words from John Starbird. He stomped past and disappeared down into the belly of the vessel. When he reappeared some minutes later, his face was smeared with engine oil and his expression was like thunder.

'Well?' said Rob.

'Oil leak,' said Starbird, wiping his hands on a rag.

Rob looked to the sky. 'I thought you said this bucket of rusty rivets is the fastest steamer on the whole riverway!'

'Shush!' Starbird put a finger to his lips. 'Don't you let her hear you talkin' 'bout her like that. She *is* the fastest steamer on the riverway. She's just a little . . . temperamental sometimes, is all.' He patted the boat lovingly.

'She picked the wrong time to be temperamental, John,' said Rob through gritted teeth. 'We need to get south fast.'

'I hear you,' said Starbird. 'It ain't a big leak. Won't take more than an hour to fix. There's an old mining town not far from here. I'll dock us there and set to work and have her good as new.'

Starbird knew these waterways as well as he knew himself, and less than a half hour later the old steamer limped around a bend in the crystal-green river to find a small harbour, and a railway bridge crossing the river. 'This here is the town of Cobalt,' he told his passengers. 'The locals mostly work in the coal mine in the mountain across the river there. They aren't too keen on strangers, and most of 'em carry guns because, as you can see, we're in the middle of the mountains where there are coyotes and wolves and bears, so I'd thank everybody to stay aboard and refrain from riling the townsfolk.'

'We need more supplies,' said Rob. 'We didn't account for having Ivy with us on the trip.'

'Didn't account for your appetite, more like,' said Starbird under his breath.

Rob ignored this. 'There isn't enough food to last us until Lake End, so I'll take a quick walk ashore – but everyone else stays on board.'

Starbird brought the shuddering steamer into the harbour and cut off the engine. When they were docked, Rob set off into the steep, narrow streets of the little town, unaware that all hell was about to break loose.

The big, rickety window of Sheriff Clive Hooper's office looked right onto the entrance to Cobalt harbour. He could see everything, and that's how he liked it. He knew everyone's business in this town, knew enough secrets to ensure that nobody ever crossed him. It was new folks he had to be wary of, because new folks weren't under his thumb yet. And new folks, on the very rare occasion that they *did* come to town, always arrived through the harbour.

He sat back in his chair, took a swig from his stained coffee cup, and picked up the folded paper on his desk again – an urgent message from Director Younger himself, alerting officers across the land to the threat of a dangerous fugitive. A Hag – maybe even a group of Hags – had escaped King's Haven and was to be intercepted and taken alive if possible. Ha! Taken alive! That made Hooper chuckle. Any Hag unlucky enough to cross his path would find themselves chewing on a bullet. They were filthy creatures, unnatural. Every breath a Hag took was stolen air.

Hooper unfolded the note again, and as he did so, the enchanted witch paper breathed inky spell smoke into the room. The smoke twined and tumbled and took the shape of a head, a man's head, with a great bushy beard and fierce black eyes. Hooper sneered and patted his belly thoughtfully. He was awful glad that this Hag was someone else's problem; Cobalt, after all, was the sort of town people ran from, not towards.

Then, halfway through another swig, Hooper almost choked.

With coffee dripping all down his smooth chin, he put the cup back on his desk, jumped out of his chair and dashed to the window. His small watery eyes grew wide in disbelief.

There, in Hooper's town, walking from the harbour as if he had not a care in the world, was the fugitive Hag.

Hooper felt his stone-cold surprise become heated anger, rising from his stomach and spreading up under his starched collar and into his face. He would not tolerate a Hag in his town. He would catch him and hang him and remind everyone that Cobalt was Hag-free and would be as long as he was in charge.

His hand went to the revolver nestled in the holster by his hip, and he traced the shape of the handle with his finger. Maybe there would be a reward, he thought, for being the one to bring the Hag to justice. That would be a welcome bonus.

His mind made up, he left his office, went out to the main room of the station, and addressed the on-duty deputy.

'Tom, go round-up a posse.'

Tom, the deputy, looked up at Hooper from behind his newspaper. 'Everything all right, Sheriff?'

'No,' said Hooper, 'everything is not all right, Tom. That's why I want you to round up a posse. There's a Hag in town, and we're going to deal with him the way a Hag deserves. Now go, get out of here.'

Rob Nielsen was walking back towards the harbour, thoroughly enjoying one of the many smoked fish he'd just bought, when he turned a corner and knew at once he was in for trouble.

The street was empty, save for six men and two women, who stood shoulder to shoulder, blocking his path. The man in the centre of this barricade was the sheriff; Rob could see his gold badge glistening in the light of the fine morning. He was tall and rangy and red-faced. Rob could tell from the way the sheriff was glaring at him that these people knew what he was.

'Everything all right?' he asked, trying to sound casual.

The sheriff reached into his jacket, brought out a folded piece of paper, and opened it. Spell smoke drifted into the warm air, and Rob's heart sank as he saw his own face appear in the smoke.

'Now, I don't want any trouble,' he said. 'And I don't want to hurt nobody. We don't have to do this, sheriff. If you just let me get to my boat, I'll be gone and you can get back to your business. I just need to get to the harbour there—' he made to point, and as his hand moved, the sheriff and his companions all drew their guns.

'Don't. Move,' the sheriff called. 'Not another inch.'

Rob looked down their line. From what he could see, the posse comprised of the sheriff and three deputies, and the rest were locals. He had no doubt that they were here to kill him.

'All right. All right. I'm not a-movin'.'

The sheriff nodded. 'Good. On your knees.'

Rob did not move. 'Don't do this, sheriff. I don't want to hurt you or these other people, but I will do what I must to get outta here.'

The sheriff sneered. 'The arrogance of you Hags never ceases to amaze me.' He waved his gun from left to right. 'Last I checked, there were eight of us and one of you. Now I'm gonna say this one more time, boy. Get on your knees.'

Rob sighed. His wand, fully loaded, was hidden as always in a special pouch up the sleeve of his long coat. All it took was one tug, and the wand fell into his waiting hand. Before the posse even realised what was happening, Rob pulled the trigger, activating the defence spell he always kept loaded.

With a flash of purple light, a great grizzly bear made of

swirling spell smoke stood between Rob and his assailants. The posse yelled out and began firing at it as if it was a living thing, and the spell bear soaked up the bullets. Then it reared up, three metres tall on its hind legs, roared, brought its front paws back down like thunder, and charged.

Ivy Steps Up

Lara sat with Joe and Ivy on deck, playing cards, while they waited for Starbird to finish repairing the ship.

'Another hand to me,' said Joe, smiling at them in such a way that made Lara want to get out her wand and turn him into a lizard. 'That's four games in a row!'

'You're good at this,' said Ivy.

Lara scoffed. 'He's a card shark, is what he is. Back in our toshing days he used to take money off anyone soft enough to play him. He hasn't lost his touch, I'll give him that.'

'And you're still as sore a loser as ever,' Joe said, chuckling.

Lara was about to swear at him when she heard a commotion from somewhere in the town. There were yells and screams and bangs, like gunshots, and then what sounded like the roar of some great animal.

They all stood up and hurried to the edge of the boat to get a better view.

'I wonder if it's a bear,' said Joe, excitement in his voice.

'Starbird said they get bears here. Maybe one of 'em wandered down off the mountain.'

But Lara wasn't so sure. She had a bad feeling bubbling in her belly, and when she saw Rob running down the dock towards the boat, her heart skipped a beat.

'It's Rob! Who's that chasing him?'

They heard the zip of stray bullets from the chasing gang.

'Hell's teeth!' screamed Lara, bringing out her wand. 'Get the boat started!'

'I'm trying!' called Starbird from somewhere below deck.

Rob came tearing over the gangplank and onto the steamer, his big feet skidding on the deck. 'Get us outta here, Starbird! Now!'

The engine coughed, sputtered, and wheezed to life.

Rob fired a warning spell at the posse, making them scatter momentarily. But they soon regrouped, and the leader, a lanky sheriff with a red face, returned fire with his pistol, bullets pinging off the gunwale inches from Lara.

'Go! They're almost here!'

The boat moved off and pulled away. Horrified, Lara saw a great many folks running to the docks, boarding vessels of their own, and smoke billowed from funnels as these boats cast off from the dock.

'They're chasing!' Lara yelled.

'What happened back there?' said Joe.

Rob ignored the question and glared at the chasing boats. 'We need more speed!'

'She hasn't got any more!' came Starbird's call from the wheelhouse. 'I wasn't done with the repairs!'

'They're catching us up!' Joe said, and he was right enough; the chasing boats were faster than the steamer and gaining on them by the minute. Soon a hail of bullets started to hit the boat, pinging and zinging as they rebounded off the metal.

Lara and her friends ducked down behind the gunwale.

'We're penned in!' said Rob, loading his wand again, reaching up, firing blind spells over the edge of the steamer. Lara went for her own wand and realised with dawning horror that it was still packed away in the travelling trunk. There was a loud *PING* as a bullet bounced off the gunwale by her head, making her throw herself to the deck. 'We have to do something!'

'Like what?' growled Rob. He reloaded, poked his head above the gunwale and ducked back down again, away from a fresh spray of bullets. 'We're sitting ducks!'

PING!

 PING PING PING!

 BANG!

Bullets everywhere. Sparks. Yelling. Ivy could not move for fear. Her body was ice, her blood frozen in her veins. She was going to die on this boat with a group of well-meaning strangers. How had it come to this? Just over a day ago she had been in the care of Doctor Vanderbill, and optimistic about what the future might hold. Now the doctor was dead, and with him, it seemed, her dreams of a peaceful life.

The fear and anger and injustice welled up, lit the fire in her again, and there was that gathering storm of magic in her brow, behind her eyes, at her fingertips, sparking and jumping in small blazing currents.

Among the chaotic scramble, Ivy caught sight of Joe, huddled in a corner, fear etched on his face, and Lara with him, and she wished that she could know friendship like that. But it was too late, wasn't it?

No. It wasn't too late. It wasn't over yet. She would not let the doctor's death be for nothing. That awesome power, that wild, untamed magic, rose up like a tide, intensifying with every heartbeat, until the pressure in her was so great she knew there was no holding it back. Clambering to her feet as the steamer shuddered, she saw that the river was taking them through a ravine, and there were high rock walls on either side.

An idea cut through her fear.

'What are you doing, Ivy?'

'Get down, girl!'

'Ivy, you'll be shot!'

But she paid no attention. As bullets whizzed past her, she closed her eyes and reached out a hand, pointing at one side of the ravine. When the pressure of her magic became so white hot that she thought she'd burn up, Ivy opened her eyes and channelled every bit of her strength through her arm, her fingers, and out towards the rock.

A bolt of blue lightning leaped from her hand. The heat of it was searing and intense. It hit the rock wall, causing a landslide of stone to roar down into the river, spraying water, shaking the steamer with large waves. When it was done, the bullets stopped coming. The collapsed ravine had completely blocked the narrow stretch of river, forming a dam between the steamer and the chasing boats.

Knowing they were safe for now, Ivy lowered her hands and turned to face the others. They had come out from the shelter of the gunwale and were all staring at her like she was an angry dragon.

'It's all right,' she said. 'They can't get us now.'

Then she collapsed.

A Transaction

'How did they know to come after you?' Joe asked.

Ivy was asleep in a cabin, and Lara and the others had gathered on deck and were chewing over what had happened back in Cobalt.

'The sheriff had a paper,' said Rob. 'Had my picture on it. Seems I'm a wanted man.'

'We're all wanted, after what just happened,' said Joe. He was quiet for a moment, and then added, 'How did Ivy do that? How did she make an entire cliff collapse into the water without so much as a wand to help?'

Rob shook his head. 'I've never seen anything like it. I wish Doctor Vanderbill had told me about her. Then I could have got her away safely to Westerly Witch long before now.'

The steamer made a metallic belching sound, and acrid black smoke came rolling from the funnel. Next moment, Starbird hurried out of the cabin.

'I told you she wasn't ready. Her engine won't last much longer if we don't fix her up.'

Rob approached him, placed a big hand on his shoulder. 'John, there's something we need to discuss. After what happened in Cobalt, they'll be a-lookin' for this steamer. We have to ditch her.'

By the look on his face, it seemed that Starbird would have preferred being shot to hearing those words. 'Ditch her? We can't do that! I won't!'

Rob shook him a little. 'Every copper in the Kingdom is going to be on the lookout for this boat. She might as well have a great big target painted on her hull.'

Starbird looked like his heart had been ripped in two. 'But she's *my ship*.' He was almost whispering. 'We been through so much together. I can't just let her go.'

'We'll get her back,' said Rob. 'I give my word. One day we'll get her back. But, John, there are bigger things going on. We need to get to Lake End before the Evernight Feast, and we need you to get us there. Will you do it?'

Starbird looked dazed, as if someone had punched his lights out. He gave a slow nod, and then, without another word, he turned and went back to the wheel.

Lara cupped a hand to her mouth. 'Well, now we know,' she whispered to Joe, 'that whatever you're going to be doing in Lake End involves the Evernight celebrations.'

Joe met her eye, excitement and realisation dawning on his face, and nodded.

*

An hour later, another cargo vessel came into sight a little way up the river; it was smaller than Starbird's steamer, but more modern, with a slick black paint job and gleaming red paddles. As they came closer, Rob gave the word to Starbird, who signalled to the other boat, and it slowed and stopped alongside.

From the wheelhouse came a wiry old man wearing a heavy wax jacket.

'Are you in trouble?' he asked, pointing a crooked finger at the black smoke belching from the steamer's funnel.

'In a manner of speaking, we are,' said Rob. From his pocket he pulled a small bag, and he opened it and brought out a handful of gold coins. Lara's eyes widened, and she and Joe shared a look of awe; in their toshing days, finding just one golden coin like that would have fed and watered them for weeks.

It seemed the gold had caught the old man's attention too, for he leaned on the side of his boat, his long silver eyebrows raised. 'I'd be happy to help, of course.'

'Very kind of you,' said Rob, smiling under his great red beard. 'Now let's get down to business. How much do you want for that fine little boat of yours?'

King's Orders

Behind the high walls of the White Witch district in King's Haven, in a large building of grey stone, the Department of Magical Experimentation worked tirelessly to discover new ways of using magic to strengthen the Silver Kingdom.

Deep in the basement of this place, in a room so secret that only a handful of people in the entire world knew of its existence, Karl Younger sat in a sealed chamber in a cloud of spell smoke, breathing deep, speaking with a swirling, three-dimensional image in the smoke: the Silver King. Swaddled under layers of shimmering silk and dripping with jewellery, his watery eyes seemed to be for ever popping out of their sockets with the constant fear that someone might try to assassinate him, and an ever-present sheen of sweat glistened on his waxy skin.

A thousand miles away, in the southern city of Lake End, the Silver King sat in a similar chamber deep in the bowels of his Red Fortress. In his chamber, the king spoke to a smoke version of Karl Younger. This method of communication was very new, and very dangerous; more than ten minutes in the chamber could do great damage to the lungs.

'You think they're coming here?' said the king, a hint of panic in his voice. 'To Lake End?'

'I've consulted the finest seers we have, Your Majesty, and while the signs are sketchy at best, they do point to Lake End, and to the runaway White Witch girl being with the Hags. It would make sense – you'll be hosting the Evernight memorial celebrations. Welcoming everyone to the feast. If the Westerly Witches are up to something, what better time for them to strike than that?'

'I will not have them spoil this moment,' said the king. 'The Evernight Feast is supposed to remind my people of how I led them out of the darkness. It is supposed to make them rejoice in my greatness, and the greatness of the Kingdom.'

'And it will, Your Majesty.'

'Half the army is here for the parade,' said the king, babbling now. 'The navy too. They'll protect me. Yes. But it might not be enough. I want you here, Younger. I need my best man on this.'

'I wouldn't have it any other way, sir.'

'Good. Get here as quickly as you can. Now . . . about this girl. The runaway. Ivy Robin. You say she's with them?'

'We believe so, Your Majesty. She's . . . a very interesting one.'

'Did she really blow up an entire street?'

'She did.'

The Silver King pressed the tips of his fingers together. 'She could be a great weapon for us.'

'Perhaps. But, Your Majesty, I was there in Vanderbill's house when Ivy Robin unleashed her magic. I do not believe she meant to do the damage she did. I think she lost control. If she is unstable, she could be a great danger to us.'

'Then we will teach her,' said the king. '*You* will teach her.' He coughed and hacked and thumped his fat chest as the spell smoke burned his lungs. 'Nearly out of time. Bring the girl in alive, Younger. She could be the weapon we've been waiting for. Just imagine what she might be able to do with proper training. When we finally invade Westerly Witch, she could win the battle for us.' He coughed again, and then stood up. 'Must go. Get here quick as you can.'

'Yes, Your Majesty.'

Karl Younger left his seat, wound a lever on the wall, and breathed the cold, fresh air as the chamber door clicked open. He left the room without speaking to the White Witches who'd been monitoring the chamber. When he was out in the corridor, he stopped, and leaned back against the cool stone wall, gritting his teeth. The king wanted the girl alive. This was not good news, not for Karl Younger. The king's attention span was notoriously short. If he, Younger, delivered Ivy Robin to the king, and she fulfilled even a tenth of her potential, then soon Karl Younger would be thrown aside and forgotten about. He would not let that happen. He had not clawed his way up the ranks only to give it to some upstart Hag with anger issues. No. And he would certainly not train his own replacement! Bringing Ivy Robin in alive was not an option. She'd have to die.

And if there was one thing Karl Younger was better at than anyone else, it was killing.

Hurried footsteps approached, and a young secret police agent skidded down the corridor. 'Director Younger, sir! I have news of the fugitive!'

Younger straightened up. 'Well?'

'We've had an urgent message from the sheriff in Cobalt, sir.'

'*Where?*'

'It's a mining town quite far from here, Director. Had to look it up on a map myself. The sheriff sighted the Hag and tried to apprehend him.'

'Let me guess,' said a weary Younger, 'the sheriff failed?'

'Yes, sir. From what we can make out, sir, the runaway was there too. The one who blew up the street.'

Younger licked his lips. 'You're sure?'

'It sounds like it, Director. She brought down tonnes of rock from a ravine to block the river and get away. And she didn't use a wand.'

Younger's heart rate had picked up. 'Tell them to ready an airship. I want to see for myself.'

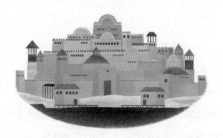

LAKE END

The sun was low in the sky when Lara and her companions finally reached Lake End.

At first they saw it from afar when the river widened, the tallest buildings and the reddish towers and spires visible through a haze of southern heat. Atop it all was a grand red stone castle, with enormously tall walls and ramparts.

'That's the Red Fortress,' said Rob, and Lara noticed that his eyes were intensely focused on the building. 'The king will be holed up in there.' He spat out the word king like it was something truly disgusting, like a slug.

When the lake opened before them, vast as a sea and turquoise blue, the full grandeur of the place became clear.

Lara's home city of King's Haven was huge and rambling, made of grey stone and brick and spread out over a great distance. Lake End was concentrated within a much smaller area, but the red clay buildings were enormously tall. A dark forest of strange, thorny-looking trees surrounded Giant's Foot Lake.

The port sat front and centre of the city, and on each side were golden sands stretching for miles upon miles. Upon these sands, massive campsites had been set up for the arriving soldiers set to march in the king's Evernight parade. Black tents stood in row after row, thousands of them, and smoke drifted from campfires in lazy black coils. The air was hot, and the lake packed with jostling fishing boats and spice merchants' ships. Overhead, royal airships were black dots against the sapphire sky. Near the army campsites, an entire armada of hulking naval ships floated proudly by the shore.

Lara stared on in wonder, every part of her itching to explore the streets and alleyways of this strange new place. She found her old tosher brain switching on, wondering what glittering treasures might lie in the sewers.

Starbird docked the new steamer in the port, grumbling under his breath about how it wasn't a patch on his own boat.

'Send your message to Ginny Adder,' said Rob. 'Tell her we're here.'

Lara did as he asked, and barely an hour after the message had soared out across the sky, the hunched figure of a woman on a fine black horse came along the dock and halted beside the steamer.

'Rob Nielsen?' she said, high on her horse's back. She was short and broad and wore a long coat of fine black silken material. Her hair was bursting out in silver springs from beneath a pretty headscarf. Her skin was darkest brown, her complexion weathered, her expression serious and stern.

Lara, usually outgoing and confident, felt herself shrink back a little. When she spoke, her voice sounded like it belonged to someone else, someone timid. 'Ginny?'

The woman nodded, looked around the boat. 'And you'll be Lara?'

'Yes, ma'am.'

'Very good. Come with me.'

Lara's eyes flicked around at her friends. 'What? Right now?'

'No,' said Ginny. 'Let's do a nice bit of sunbathing first, eh? Of course right now, girl! There's a killer to catch!'

'Oh. Right. Course. I'll just get my stuff.' She turned to Joe, who made a 'Good luck with this one' sort of face. 'Help me with my trunk, will you, Joe?'

'Ain't no need for any trunk,' said Ginny.

Lara blinked. 'But it has my stuff in it!'

'And how d'you suppose we get a trunk all the way to my camp, eh? Float it along behind us and advertise the fact we're Witches? In case you haven't heard, this city is a-crawlin' with secret police and coppers for the Evernight Feast.'

'I know. But this trunk is special. Bernie gave it to me.'

Ginny raised her eyebrows. 'You surely aren't talking about that old travelling trunk of hers?'

148

'Yes, actually,' said Lara, becoming a little annoyed. 'Why? What's wrong with it?'

Ginny let out a sharp laugh. 'She had that old thing back when we was fending off Kingdom attacks on the Witch colonies down here in the south! Grab your kit, girl. Come with me and see some real magic.'

Lara rushed into the boat, opened the trunk and went down the ladder to the secret room. She gathered some clothes, her wand and spell-making kit, stuffed them into a canvas bag and was back on deck in minutes, the keys to the trunk stowed safely in her pocket. 'Thanks for getting me here safely,' she told Starbird. 'And you, Rob. We'd have been in real trouble back in the opera house if it wasn't for you.' Then she turned to Ivy. 'Rob can be a bit of a grump sometimes, but his heart's in the right place. You'll be well served if you listen to him.'

'I will,' said Ivy. 'Good luck, Lara.'

Last up was Joe. 'All the best, Lara. You get back here in one piece, yeah?'

She smiled, but deep down she was worried about him. Joe had been safe and sound in Westerly Witch for so long, and now here he was, out in the world again, about to go on a dangerous mission doing goodness knows what, and she, Lara, would not be there to help him. 'Same to you, Joe. Be careful. See you soon.'

'And, Lara . . . I hope you find Double Eight. I hope he's all right.'

'Thank you.' She hugged him, turned away and walked up the gangplank to the dock, where Ginny gave her a hand up onto the back of her horse.

'Hold on, girl.'

Lara wrapped her arms around the old Witch's thick waist, breathing in the strong smell of lavender, and Ginny urged the horse on.

'Goodbye,' called Lara, as the horse took her away from the boat, and from her friends, weaving between the crowds of sailors and workers and ironhearts. 'Goodbye, Joe!'

Lara was relieved to know there was solid ground beneath her feet again instead of water. The roads in Lake End were narrower than in King's Haven, flat and covered in fine red dust, and the people were generally much darker-skinned than in the north. They wore different clothes too, mostly dresses and trousers and loose shirts of light, colourful cotton. The smells were new and exciting. There were stalls selling street food, cooks frying curried shrimp and noodles over leaping naked flames. The smells from restaurants and coffee houses were fragrant, perfumed with cinnamon and seaweed and exotic spice. There were some ironhearts here too, just like in King's Haven, but mostly the horses were flesh and blood. It seemed every lamp-post, every window ledge and awning, was festooned with many-coloured flags and paper chains in preparation for the feast.

Along the winding streets Ginny's horse galloped, through archways and short tunnels, beyond the city walls to the western shore of the lake, where the land was flat and they found meadows of long yellow grass and patches of woodland. It was in one of these meadows, in the shade of a cluster of large thorny trees bearing purple berries, that Ginny brought them to a halt. 'Here we are.'

Lara looked around in confusion. 'Are we?' Then it dawned on her. 'A hidden camp?'

Ginny dismounted, reached into her coat and brought out her wand. The handle was carved in the shape of an eagle's claw. She helped Lara down. 'Give us your hand, that's it.' Lara did as she asked. Ginny touched the tip of her wand to Lara's hand. 'Look again.'

Lara did, and she saw.

The camp sat beneath the trees, a small, shabby tent and a fire. On the fire sat a cauldron, and around it were a few simple wooden stools. As they entered camp, a familiar feeling came over Lara. The sound of magic in the air vanished, leaving a silent void. It was the same feeling she got from being near Bernie's enchanted travelling trunk.

'Ah. I see why you told me not to bring the trunk. This whole place covers up magic.' She went to the tent, looked within and found that, despite its tiny exterior, its inside had been magically expanded to become an enormous space furnished with rugs, two comfortable-looking beds and a pair of deep armchairs. She muttered 'Hell's teeth!' because, as used to magic as she was becoming, it still had the ability to surprise and delight her.

'It's not a difficult spell when you get the hang of it,' said Ginny, patting the dust from a plump cushion. 'I travel around a lot, y'see. Didn't used to bother so much with fancy beds and such, but I like to be comfortable in my old age. C'mon. Let's eat.'

Ginny made steaming hot smoked fish and potatoes for dinner under a burning orange evening sky. As Lara ate, she could sense Ginny's eyes boring holes in her, as if she were trying to look inside Lara's head. 'Is something the matter?'

Ginny put down her now-empty plate, pursed her lips. 'Bernie thinks very highly of you.'

'She does?'

'Oh, yes. Indeed she does. And after what you did last year, facing down the Evernight, I can understand why. But don't expect any special treatment from me, you hear? You've come south to learn, and to work.'

'Of course,' said Lara. 'The last thing I'd ever want is special treatment. And just so you know, ma'am, I didn't face the Evernight all by myself. I had help from my friends – and Double Eight was one of 'em.'

Ginny said nothing. Her eyes lingered on Lara a long moment. She picked a fishbone from between her teeth, then reached into one of what appeared to be a hundred pockets inside her silken coat, and brought out a small wooden carving and a sharp lock knife, and commenced whittling away the wood. The carving was of a small boy, maybe four or five years old, with a huge mop of curly hair.

He was running, and though his face had only been roughly cut, Lara could tell he was laughing.

'That's nice. Who is it?'

Ginny did not answer the question. Her eyes stayed fixed on the carving as her hands worked expertly, scraping away layer after fine layer. 'What can you tell me about this Double Eight?' she said at last.

'Well . . . what do you want to know?'

'What sort of person is he? What words come to mind when you think of him?' The point of Ginny's lock knife was busy, her gaze fastened on the carving.

Lara thought for a moment. 'Brave. And loyal.'

'He was a White Witch, yes?'

'Yes,' said Lara. 'But he was never under Mrs Hester's full control. She was starting to lose her power over some White Witches by the time he was born, so when she took his soul, she didn't get all of it. I met him the day the Evernight came to King's Haven. He never left my side after that, stuck beside me until the job was done and the Evernight was gone.'

'Did you ever catch a glimpse of another side of him?' Ginny asked.

'Like what?'

'Did he have a temper? Did he ever mention dark magic when he was speaking to you?'

'No!' A pause. 'You think he committed these murders, don't you?'

Ginny stopped carving. 'You don't?'

153

'No. He'd never do that!'

'I'd thank you to take the word "never" and throw it away. You won't have any use for it in my company. And you won't learn nothing until you open your mind to every possibility.'

'But Double Eight isn't a killer.'

Ginny put the carving away in her coat, folded up the lock knife and pointed the handle at Lara. 'Maybe he is and maybe he isn't. From what I can tell, the murders started in Lake End a couple of months back – and Double Eight was already here in Lake End studying then.'

'That doesn't mean he's guilty,' said Lara.

'Well, thank you so much for explaining that to me, girl,' said Ginny, fixing Lara with a sharp stare.

'Sorry. I just meant . . .'

'I know what you meant. Listen, I don't take pleasure in causing you heartache, girl, believe me. But you are here to help me find answers, and so you must know the truth right from the beginning. It seems to me that there are two likely explanations for Double Eight's vanishing. The first is that the killer got him too, and nobody's found the body yet. The second is that Double Eight is still alive, and he's the one doing the killing. Neither option is very palatable, I know, but we must gather the facts and let them guide us. Now, you've had a long journey, and we need to be up with the sun, so I want you to do up these dishes and then get some rest.'

'Yes, ma'am,' said Lara. But she knew she wouldn't get a wink of sleep. It seemed that everyone believed Double Eight was the killer. First Bernie, then Joe, and now Ginny Adder. Somehow, Lara would prove them wrong. Bernie and Ginny had told her to keep an open mind. She would do that. Of course she would. But keeping an open mind, so far as she knew, did not mean that she should ignore her gut. Lara's gut was telling her that Double Eight was innocent. It was also telling her he was still alive. It would be up to Lara to prove both. Unfortunately, at the minute, she did not have a clue how she was going to do that.

THE MISSION

As Lara and Ginny were arriving at the hidden camp
outside the city, Rob Nielsen was making his way back up to
the deck of the steamer in Lake End Port.

'Well?' he said, squinting his eyes at the glare of the
southern sun. 'What do you think?'

Joe, Ivy and Starbird had been playing cards around a
makeshift crate table while they waited. When they turned
and looked at Rob, none of them spoke. Joe dropped his
hand of cards and they went fluttering off across the deck.
Starbird swept his hair out of his eyes to get a better look.
Ivy was confused.

The reason for this reaction was simple. With the entire
Kingdom seemingly on the lookout for a huge, red-bearded
Witch with long wild hair, Rob had reluctantly realised that
he would have to change his appearance. So, half an hour
ago, he had disappeared into the boat with a razor in his
hand and commenced to chop off his hair and beard.
Presently, he stood in the sun clean-shaven, his face livid

red from the scrape of the razor and his hair hellishly uneven, sticking up in a cow's lick at the back of his skull.

'You look . . .' Joe began, searching for the words. 'You look . . .'

'I look like a potato,' said Rob glumly.

'Well,' said Joe, 'there are worse vegetables to take after. A turnip, for instance. Or a crabcumber. I've always thought the crabcumber must be the ugliest vegetable there is. My granny used to make a mean crabcumber soup, right enough—'

'That's plenty, Joe,' said Rob.

'Right. Sorry.'

'It's strange to say it,' said Starbird, still staring at Rob's smooth jaw in fascination, 'but I never actually thought of you having a face under all that beard.'

Rob jutted out his substantial chin. 'Do you think anyone will recognise me?'

Joe shook his head. 'I don't think your own mum would recognise you.'

'Good. We all set to go?'

'Yup.' Joe pointed to a few bulging canvas bags by the gangplank. 'All packed up.'

'I'll wait here, as agreed,' said Starbird. 'I'll have her ready to go should we need to make a quick getaway.'

'I can guarantee that we will,' said Rob with a grim smile.

'What in the name of Mother Earth's marigolds are you going to get up to, Rob?' Starbird asked.

'You know I can't say. Just you be ready to leave in a hurry when we get back.'

'Are you sure you want me to come along?' said Ivy. 'What if I draw attention to you?'

'Karl Younger is after you,' said Rob. 'Where we're going, he'll never find you. I can keep you safe. Now let's go.'

'This is it?' said Joe. 'This is the safe house? *This*?'

They had come through the city, through the riot of colour and noise and heat and scent, through open markets selling fresh shining fish and tomatoes the size of Rob's head, to the quiet, shady backstreets, where clothes hung drying on lines fastened between the high apartment buildings, and beneath these, lines of coffee houses and taverns buzzed with activity.

Rob had led them into one of the buildings, up four floors of a steep, narrow staircase to a grey front door with peeling paint. 'Not quite,' he said. He took a key from his pocket, unlocked the door and let them in.

The apartment was worse even than Joe had feared from his first impression of the dirty front door. It seemed, from the lack of furniture and the damp on the walls, that nobody had lived here for quite some time. The bare floorboards were warped and creaky, and the walls were stained with patches of dark, furry mould. The air was oppressively humid and heavy with the smell of damp.

'I've been in sewers nicer than this,' Joe said.

'I don't mean to be rude,' Ivy added, 'but where are we meant to sleep? Or sit? Or cook? There's no furniture.'

Rob shook his head. 'Oh, ye of little faith. Come with me.'

They went to one of the bedrooms; you could see the marks a heavy bed had once made on the floor. Now there was nothing at all. Except . . .

There was a painting on the wall, hanging at a jaunty angle in a dirty frame. It was an oil painting of a little cottage on a clifftop overlooking the sea. Rob straightened the painting, leaned on the wall beside it and said, 'Well? What do you see?'

'Um. A painting?'

'Yes. But what is it a painting of?'

Joe and Ivy shared a perplexed look. 'Are you feeling all right, Rob? You're not in shock from shaving that beard off, are you?'

'Just answer the question,' said Rob.

'Fine. It's a painting of a house.'

Rob smiled, tapped the canvas with his finger. 'Right. And would you say the house in the painting looks . . . *safe*?'

Silence.

Joe stared at Rob. Then at the painting. He took a slow step towards it, his eyes focusing on the little stone cottage atop the cliff. He could almost taste the salty air, feel the sea breeze on his face. 'You don't mean . . . that's the safe house?'

'In the painting?' Ivy's voice was soft and breathless. She reached up, towards the thick globs of dried paint on the canvas, but before she could touch them, a spark of magic jumped from her finger and into the painting. She drew her hand away. 'We're going in there?'

'It's perfectly safe,' said Rob. 'Trust me. Take my hands.'

They did, Joe on one side, Ivy the other. Rob could feel the sparks of magic jumping from Ivy's hand into his; it burned and tingled. 'It's all right. I promise. I've done this a hundred times over the years. Here we go.' Without warning, he pulled them close, scooped them up, one under each huge arm.

'Rob!'

He did not answer. He took two big steps, and then leaped forward. They were going to crash into the painting, probably explode right through the wall . . .

Only, they didn't.

The entire world rippled.

Rob landed on soft ground, let them both go, and they went rolling across the grass.

Grass . . .

Joe sprang up, looked around. The room was gone. He was standing upon the clifftop from the painting. Only now it was not a painting at all. It was real. There stood the little stone cottage, and beyond was a vast sea and a blue sky scattered with rolling white clouds. The stifling heat of Lake End had been replaced by a cool sea breeze that lapped over his face, refreshing him. The air was salty and mild and pleasant, and the smell of the swaying grass was every summer he could remember.

'Look!'

He swung around, saw Ivy, saw that she was pointing out over the grassy field behind the cottage. There was a window in the sky. Through it, Joe could see back into the bare, damp bedroom from which they'd come.

Joe was not a Witch, of course, but thanks to his experiences during the Evernight he had seen more powerful magic than most Westerly Witches in a lifetime. Even so, he never ceased to feel the wonder when he saw a great spell in action. And he fancied that this – jumping inside a painting – was one of the best spells he'd ever seen. It made those feelings of awe and wonderment bubble up in his stomach like a stew.

Ivy was looking up through that impossible sky-window, back into the bare room. 'If someone's standing out there looking at this painting, will they be able to spot us?'

'Nope.' Rob was smiling. 'I've seen it for myself. The painting looks just as it always does, no matter who's inside – and only a Westerly Witch and those he chooses can enter. You're safe here, Ivy. That, I promise. Now let's get some grub, eh? My belly's a-rumblin'.'

The cottage was cosy and comfortable, with a roaring fire and squishy chairs in the living room. There were three bedrooms – the number changed depending on how many people were staying in the safe house, Rob told them – and a kitchen with a wood-burning cooking range and a large wooden table and chairs.

Rob made a dinner of bean stew, which was so spicy it made Joe's nose run, and then it seemed that the drama and chaos of the past couple of days finally caught up with Ivy, and she went to her bedroom and fell dead asleep to the soothing sound of the ocean.

Back in the living room, Rob and Joe sat in the comfortable heat of the fire. Rob sipped from a silver flask. The first bristles of red hair were beginning to shadow his chin again.

'I think it's time,' he said, 'to tell you exactly why we've come south.'

Joe had been staring at the flames, transfixed, feeling tired, but he sat up and became alert.

Rob took another draught from his flask, and Joe could smell the stinging heat of whisky. 'Right. So, you know all about the Evernight Feast, yes?'

Joe nodded. 'It's happening in four days. The bleedin' king is throwing a great big party all over the Kingdom to celebrate the day we beat the Evernight – he's giving out free food, and he's brought half his army and navy to Lake End to march in a big parade. There'll be music and games, and it's all to make folk think he was the one who done it, not Lara! He upped and ran away and left the slum folk to die – including my granny. Makes me sick!'

'And you know the king has been living here in Lake End since the Evernight? That he'll be attending the celebration here?'

'Yeah. Coward. He's frightened of what the slum folk'll do to him if he goes back to King's Haven.' He paused. 'So, what we're doing here has something to do with the king?'

Rob smiled. 'Oh, yes, Joe Littlefoot. In fact, it has everything to do with the king.' He rubbed his chin absentmindedly, and the stubble scritch-scratched on his palm. 'You see, Joe, hundreds of thousands of folks are travelling to Lake End for the feast. It really will be the biggest party the Kingdom has ever seen. And among all the food and music and merriment, we'll have the chance to make our move.'

Joe leaned forward, hardly breathing. 'And what *is* our move?'

'We're going to snatch the king away!' Rob's voice had become an excited whisper. 'We're going to smuggle him back to Westerly Witch and make him stand trial for all the crimes he's committed, against Witches *and* against his own people. He'll spend the rest of his life behind bars, Joe.'

Joe could barely take this in. His chest rose and fell, and his heart drummed. He was here to help Rob kidnap the king! It was too huge a thing to get his head around at first, and when it did finally sink in, he was left troubled.

'Why me, Rob?'

'What?'

'Why me? I'm not even a Witch. There are a thousand others who are more qualified for this mission. So why choose me?'

Rob smiled warmly. 'Did you know they have an underground railway here?'

'What? No . . . I didn't know that, actually.'

'Well, they do. It's the first city in the Kingdom to have one. They say they'll build one in King's Haven soon.' He waved his hand. 'Anyway, there's a network of tunnels under Lake End, and the train moves through these tunnels, from station to station, on a constant loop. It's very clever. Took thousands of workers years to build. And, Joe, guess what we found out just very recently.'

Joe was leaning so far forward, he almost slipped off his chair. 'What?'

'We learned that while they were building those tunnels, the king had one made just for himself. He has his own secret railway under the ground, Joe! That's how we're going to get him. We'll find those secret tunnels and use them to get into the Red Fortress! If we can do that by the morning of the Evernight Feast, our job will be all the easier, because the king's guards will be so busy concentrating on the gathering crowds they won't ever suspect someone might walk right in through the back door!'

He sat back, took another swig from his flask, then turned it upside down and sighed when he realised it was empty. 'Nobody knows tunnels better than you, Joe. Nobody.

Not even Lara. All those years you spent toshing in the sewers under King's Haven. Finding secret ways, lost places. That's why you're here. You're going to help me find the king's railway tunnels. We're going to snatch the king. You and me, Joe, we're going to change the whole bleedin' world!'

THE INVESTIGATION BEGINS

The sun was just up, but already the roads were warm to the touch, and the air shimmered with heat. Lara's arms were wrapped tight around Ginny's waist as the horse galloped through this strange new city; with the wind in her hair and her heart hammering, she felt like yelling out in delight.

Through archways they galloped, between the tall red clay buildings, over walkways and bridges, passing the docks, hearing the cranes and the shouts, and smelling the spice cargoes. Then they were in the shaded backstreets, and Lara did not know it, but she was only a few streets away from the flat where Joe, Rob and Ivy were sleeping soundly in the cottage of their safe-house painting.

Ginny tied up her horse at a watering trough outside a coffee house, where a few early risers were already sipping from steaming cups. The tall blocks of apartment buildings were decorated with stone flourishes and gargoyles, and Lara could tell from the clean streets and quiet early morning atmosphere that this was quite an upscale neighbourhood.

'I thought Sprout's flat might have been in the slums,' she said. 'In King's Haven, Westerly Witches always stay in the slums. We can keep a low profile there, and it's easy to disappear into the crowds if need be.'

'I know how King's Haven works, thank you very much,' said Ginny, opening the door of one of the apartment buildings and ushering Lara into a neat hallway. 'I'm not some country Witch who's never been to the big city.'

'I didn't mean that . . .'

'It's different here in Lake End,' Ginny went on. 'Different in most of the south, matter of fact. This was the last part of the old continent to fall to the Silver Kingdom. Some people here still remember how it used to be, living alongside the Westerly Witches. The king can't make Lake Enders hate us, Lara, no matter how hard he tries. Don't get me wrong, there's always been an element that don't trust us, that would like to see us driven out, and technically it's illegal for us to be here, but mostly we can walk around freely – so long as we don't advertise the fact we're Witches. You understand?'

'I think so. I never imagined there were still places where we'd be welcome.'

'Not *welcome*,' said Ginny, holding up a finger. 'But not feared and despised either. Of course, there's some folks started to believe the rubbish the king is spouting about us – that we're Hags! Dangerous and wild and not to be trusted. People do forget easily, Lara. But I'd wager most folks in Lake End still respect Witchcraft. Hell's teeth, even the southern rangers regularly turn a blind eye to reports of magic. See, sometimes us Westerly Witches would work with the rangers back in the day, help out if there was dark magic about, or if some monster came out of the Veil Forest and they needed a hand to slay it.'

'So the rangers are sort of like Lake End's coppers?'

'I suppose so. Rangers work on horseback, though, and they're tough, and smart – much smarter than your average empty-headed King's Haven copper.'

Lara and Ginny were climbing the stairs, their footsteps echoing down the landings.

'Are the rangers investigating these murders?'

'I don't think so. There hasn't been a word in any newspaper about dark magic killings, just whispers on the streets – that's how I found out Sprout was dead to begin with. I think the rangers are hushing up these murders, probably on orders of the king. He won't want anything to spoil his precious Evernight party.'

They came to a black door, upon which there was a brass number: *72 f.* Ginny listened carefully to make sure they were alone in the stairway, then reached into her coat and brought out a spell bottle, the purplish spell inside twining and coiling against the thin glass. 'You ever used one of these? It's a lockpick spell.'

'No. Never.'

Ginny handed Lara the spell. 'It's a difficult one to get

right. Bernie could never master it – her version would always blow a door right off its hinges! If you do a good job today, I might show you how I write it later.'

Lara nodded, then reached into her waistband and brought out her wand. She spun the revolver, picked an empty chamber and loaded the spell bottle with a satisfying click. The spell glowed brightly, casting an eerie purple light all about the dim landing. 'Like this?' she pointed her wand at the lock and pulled the trigger.

The warmth of the spell travelled up the wand, into her hand and arm, and from the wand tip came a coil of incandescent spell smoke. The end of the coil of smoke became the shape of a key and entered the keyhole. There was a clunk from the lock. Lara let go of the trigger and the spell vanished as Ginny stepped forward and opened the door.

It was obvious to Lara as soon as she stepped through the door that there had been a struggle in this flat. Furniture was strewn about the place, and there were scorchmarks on the walls where spells had rebounded. A heavy, dank smell permeated the warm air, and Lara imagined something invisible and slick coating her skin, perhaps the echo of the terrible acts committed here.

'That's where the rangers found Sprout's body,' said Ginny, pointing to a patterned rug on the floor. There were dark reddish-brown stains on some of the colourful squares.

Lara stared at the bloodstains. 'What happened to him? I know you said it was dark magic, but what does that mean?'

'You ever heard of a reaper spell?'

'No. I don't think so.'

'You'd remember if you had. A reaper spell is the foulest bit of dark magic that was ever dreamed up. Worse than any other death spell.'

Lara inched towards Ginny. 'What does it *do*?'

'A Witch who uses a reaper spell to kill doesn't just end their victim's life. They *steal* it. As the victim is dying, Lara, the reaper spell takes all their life force and puts it in the murderous Witch who committed the crime. Makes 'em stronger. But there's a terrible price to pay for using such a spell. See, every time a Witch uses a reaper spell, it eats away at their insides a little bit more, makes their soul rot. And the more power they take, the more the spell makes them hungry, till it consumes them.'

'Hell's teeth!' Lara's voice was a whisper. 'And that's what's been happening here in Lake End?'

'Yup. Five killings in two lunar cycles that we know about, including in this flat with Sprout. And it's all been swept under the carpet to protect the king's party.'

Lara began to walk slowly around, taking in the room. 'So Double Eight stayed here with Sprout?'

Ginny pointed. 'That was his room. Come. I'll show you.'

The bedroom was small and neat. There was no sign of a struggle; the bed was made, and Double Eight's few possessions were neatly arranged on a desk. These included a picture in a wooden frame of Lara and Double Eight smiling widely. Lara's heart skipped a beat when she saw it, and she lifted it and stared at the happy faces looking out from behind the glass.

'I gave him this the day he left,' she said, and her throat was suddenly tight. 'I hope he's all right. But you don't think so, do you, ma'am?'

'I'm sorry to say I don't,' said Ginny. 'Look at this.' She picked up a book, handed it to Lara. It had a cover of old, cracked red leather, with a title in faded, curling silver letters.

Dark Magic Through the Ages
By Wilfred Twig

'Look where the bookmark is,' said Ginny.

Lara opened the book to the pages where someone – Double Eight, perhaps – had placed a leather bookmark. Her eyes bugged open. 'It's a chapter about the reaper spell! So he was finding out all about it?'

'Seems that way.'

Lara became aware that Ginny was watching her reaction with great interest. 'But this doesn't mean Double Eight is the killer, does it? Just because he was reading about the reaper spell doesn't mean he was thinking about using it.'

'What do *you* think it means?' asked Ginny.

'Well,' said Lara, 'what if the killer found out that Sprout and Double Eight were coming after him and he came here to get them first?'

'If that's the case,' said Ginny, 'why wasn't Double Eight's body here with Sprout's?'

Lara's brain was firing. 'Double Eight might have been out when the killer came to the flat. He might have come back and discovered Sprout's body and gone into hiding.'

One of Ginny's eyebrows shot up. 'You think he disappeared without so much as trying to contact his friends in Westerly Witch? Sounds like you're clutching at straws.'

Lara had to admit that was unlikely.

'Maybe your friend couldn't handle the pressure of being a Westerly Witch,' Ginny said. 'Or perhaps he had darkness in him the entire time and he was fighting to keep it hidden. Maybe the darkness in him grew too strong to hold back.'

'No,' said Lara. 'I don't believe that. I'll *prove* he didn't do this.'

Ginny sighed. 'Come. There's another thing to show you, this time outside the city.'

THE VEIL FOREST

Half an hour later, Lara and Ginny were on horseback, following a stony track by the lake under the baking sun, sparkling water on one side and a twisting, thorny forest on the other.

At last Lara heard Ginny yell, 'Whoa!' and the sleek black horse slowed and stopped. Ginny nipped down with ease, reached up and helped Lara to the ground. Lara watched as Ginny led the horse to the edge of the lake, where it began to drink. Ginny patted her horse and then unpacked several items from the saddlebag. 'I need breakfast. Collect some wood for a fire, will you? But don't go in the forest!'

Lara did as Ginny asked; there was no shortage of dry twigs and kindling on the edge of the trees. Ginny lit a small fire, and in an ancient frying pan she cooked up some red sausage marbled with white streaks. She mostly stayed quiet as she cooked. When the sausage was done, she cracked two eggs into the pan, and then plated everything up.

It was good. The sausage was spiced, and the heat made Lara's mouth tingle pleasantly.

'How long have you known Bernie?' she asked.

'Longer than I care to admit. We fought together when the king and Mrs Hester sent their armies to conquer the last of the free countries in the south.' She shook her head, gave a short laugh. It was, Lara thought, the first time she'd seen Ginny Adder smile. 'Bernie's a fine Witch, but I admit it still tangles my brain to think of her as *High* Witch.'

'I think it tangles her brain too,' Lara said. 'Bernie doesn't like to talk much about the Southern Wars, but I've read a bit about them in some history books in Westerly Witch. It sounds like a hellish time.'

There was quiet for a long moment. Then Ginny said, 'The Silver Kingdom came down from the north with their armies and navy and airships, and their White Witch magic, of course. Mrs Hester and the king at the time – he'd be the current king's father – they wanted more land and power. Us Westerly Witches were still allies with the Free Countries, see. Some of us lived down here in peace. We fought beside 'em to try to keep them free. But the king's armies were vast. They overran the Free Countries' defences, and pretty soon us Westerly Witches found ourselves trapped, and the Witch gates cut off.' She put down her plate, reached into her pockets and brought out the carving and the lock knife again, and started whittling away at the smiling little boy. 'We held out for a while. There were some hellish fights, girl. Some narrow escapes. We were always movin', always running, trying to find a way home. I saw friends killed beside me, stepped over their bodies on the battlefield.' She swallowed. 'Bernie was with me the day the king's armies finally surrounded us. We both made it out, of course, but we lost a great number of good Witches ... I lost my husband.' She stopped whittling, and Lara could see, as Ginny turned the carving over in her fingers, that her hands were trembling. 'And I lost my son.'

Lara was stunned. She felt her eyes filling up, her lips trembling. 'Is that him?' she asked gently, indicating the carving. 'Is that your son?'

'His name was Theo.' Ginny was staring into the carving's smiling face. 'He was eleven years old. I couldn't be with him when they attacked, see, because Bernie and me were on watch.'

'I'm so sorry.' Lara knew her words were useless, but she did not know what else to say.

'I've never been able to settle anywhere since then,' said Ginny. 'Always got to keep movin', keep busy, keep helping folks where I can.' She sniffed, putting the carving away. 'Anyway, we've got somewhere to be. Hurry up with that breakfast.'

Ginny's horse was quick, and soon they had gone far enough along the track beside the forest that the city had dropped out of sight behind its tall trees. Here the path was wild and stony, and when Lara looked into the forest and saw the deep, twisting blackness of it, her insides turned cold.

'Whoa, girl. That's it. Good girl.'

The horse came to rest, and Ginny and Lara dismounted. Ginny rubbed her horse's muzzle, kissing her between the eyes. The horse whinnied softly. 'Come,' she told Lara. 'This way.'

Lara peered into the darkness of the thorny trees. 'In *there*?'

Ginny gave Lara one of those piercing stares, when Lara thought the old Witch was looking inside her head. 'You feel it, don't you? The forest? Watching you as it's watched countless others over thousands of years. You're right to be wary. The Veil Forest is teeming with dark creatures. Monsters, some say. But we're Westerly Witches – afraid of no darkness. Stick close and you'll be fine.'

Lara took a long look back towards the sunlit lake before pushing into the overgrown tangle of roots and trees and shadows. 'It's so quiet.' She looked upwards, at the canopy of twisting branches. 'And dark.'

Ginny suddenly stopped, cursing under her breath.

Lara drew her wand, loaded spells aglow in their chambers. 'What is it? One of them monsters?'

Wild-eyed, Ginny ducked away from the tip of Lara's wand. 'Mother Earth's mushroom patch! Put that away! I've no wish to be blasted to the other side of the forest, thank you very much!'

'But I thought something was wrong.'

'I lost my trail for a minute, that's all. Put the wand away.'

They moved deeper into the Veil Forest, the trees seeming to close in around them with every step, until it was a struggle just to keep going. Somewhere nearby, the crack of a twig rang out, and both Lara and Ginny were still.

'Now it's time for the wand,' said Ginny. 'Just a light spell, mind. You got one loaded?'

Lara did; a light spell was one of the three lifesaver spells, along with the shield and stunning spells, that any Witch in the field should always keep loaded in the revolver chambers of her wand. Lara pulled the trigger and warm light spilled from her wand tip, forcing the darkness back. Bravery swelled in her chest.

'How much further?'

'Not far.'

Ginny's own light spell was silver-blue, the colour of the moon and dazzling in its brightness.

'I can feel things watching us,' said Lara, glancing out into the surrounding forest. '*Ow!* These hagging thorns!' The roots and branches seemed almost to be grabbing at them, holding them back at every step, as if the very forest was conspiring to stop them. Lara thought of her friends, wondering where they might be in the sprawling, dusty maze of the red city, and it all seemed so very far away. Another world.

'Stop,' said Ginny. 'We're here.' She made an awkward turn to face Lara, squeezing out of the reach of a jagged branch. 'You ever seen a dead body before, girl?'

Lara felt her throat tighten a bit. 'Once or twice in the sewers under King's Haven. I was a tosher there. And lots of people died during the Evernight fighting, but I didn't really look at 'em for long.'

This caught Ginny's interest. 'A tosher? Interesting work. You ever find anything good?'

Lara shrugged. 'A golden sovereign here and there. The odd bit of jewellery. Oh, and a golden clockwork bird with a spell inside that turned out to be the key to saving the world.'

Ginny's eyebrows shot up her forehead. 'The Doomsday Spell. Bernie never mentioned you found it in the sewer.' She shook her head like a dog shooing a fly. 'Anyway, the reason I mention dead bodies, is that's what we came here to see.'

'There's a body all the way out here?'

'There is. Another victim of the reaper spell killer. The most recent victim, in fact. From what I've been able to find out, the murder happened a bit away from here, near the edge of the lake, but the killer moved the body here to finish the reaper spell in a quiet place. This ain't a pretty sight. The animals have been at her. You better steel yourself. And if you need to be sick, don't get any on my boots.'

Lara took a breath and let it out slow. 'OK.'

The body lay in a tiny clearing beside a recently fallen tree. Mostly all that was left was the uniform of a southern ranger, ragged and torn where the animals had forced their way in to get to the rotting flesh and innards.

'I told you,' said Ginny. 'Not a pretty sight. Your belly holding up?'

Lara nodded, took another breath.

'Her name was Annalise Francco,' Ginny told her. 'Deputy third class, according to her badge. She and another ranger were on patrol along the Veil a week and a half ago. As you can see, Annalise didn't make it back.'

'Bernie told me about this,' said Lara, unable to tear her eyes from the remains. 'You mentioned that Ranger Francco had a partner?'

'Aye. Samuel Hushby.'

'And he was here when Annalise . . . when this happened?'

'From what I can gather, yes,' said Bernie. 'But finding him has been problematic. Seems the rangers are hiding him away. They're telling the story that poor Annalise here has deserted. Covering up the reaper spell killings, just as I said.'

'We have to speak with Hushby!' said Lara. 'If he's seen the killer, he'll be able to help us. And he could clear Double Eight's name!'

'Well, what a fine idea,' said Ginny, feigning surprised wonder. 'I'd never have thought of that on my own.' She shook her head. 'I brought you here first to show you what we're up against, what we must stop. This was a young woman with a bright future ahead of her. And someone took it away. Look here – you see those scratches on her jawbone? And how her neck looks scorched?'

'I do,' said Lara, feeling queasy. 'What does that mean?'

'That's the calling card of the reaper spell. The murderer takes blood – *life* – right from the artery in the neck. The heat of the spell is what leaves the burn marks.'

Before now, Lara had not really considered how she might feel if she saw one of the victims. But as she looked down upon the remains of Annalise Francco, southern ranger, she found that she was angry, and realised she was shaking. She could not stop her imagination running away, showing her terrible pictures of poor Double Eight meeting the same horrific fate as this ranger. She shivered. 'Can we get back to the light, please?'

'We will,' said Ginny. 'But first we should give Annalise a proper burial.'

Fifteen minutes later they stepped from the Veil Forest back into daylight. Lara shut her eyes and turned her face to the sky, letting the sun's rays warm her.

'Ginny?'

'Yes, girl?'

'If the rangers covered this up, how did you find out about it?'

'Good question. You've a decent mind, Lara. Could be very sharp if you learn to use it right. When you were a tosher, I imagine you found out all sorts of secrets and gossip just by walking the King's Haven streets and keeping your ears open. Am I right?'

'Yeah.'

'Well, it's the same here, you see? The rangers might want to keep these murders secret, but secrets are living things. They *want* to be told. There's always someone who lets something slip, in a pub after one too many beers or whatever. And once the secret has broken out, well, you know how it is on the streets. Information is power, ain't it? Information gets around. And if you know where to ask, you can find out pretty much anything. Once I knew there had been another reaper spell killing near the forest, I came a-lookin'. The reaper spell leaves a very strong aftershock, you see. Like an echo. I can trace that signal, and if I do it quick enough, before the echo fades, I can find the victim.'

Lara nodded. Her brain was ticking again. 'Isn't there a way to know as soon as a reaper spell is used? Then we could get there much sooner and maybe stand a better chance of catching the killer.'

Ginny gave Lara the sort of look that a teacher might give a student when they correctly answer an exceedingly difficult problem. 'Now that actually is a very good question. And as a matter of fact, I've been working on just such a spell. But it's very tough. Such a locator spell would need to be strong enough to cover the entire city, and that's not something I've done before. I reckon I'm getting close, though. C'mon. I'll show you back at camp.'

TUNNELS

That day, while Lara and Ginny were in the Veil Forest, Rob Nielsen and Joe Littlefoot were getting ready to make the first trip of their own mission under Lake End's streets.

'I'm sorry, Ivy,' said Rob, rechecking the many pockets of his Witch coat, making the spell bottles inside clink, 'but you'll have to stay here. I can't risk you coming along.'

Ivy Robin gave him a pleading look. 'But I haven't had an . . . *attack* since we got here. Please, Rob, let me come. I don't want to stay in this painting alone. What if you don't come back?'

'Why wouldn't we come back, Ivy?' said Joe kindly.

'I don't know. I have no clue what you're off to do. Anything could happen to you.'

Rob rubbed the scratchy shoots of stubble on his considerable chin. 'Nothing's going to happen to us, Ivy. I promise. We aren't going to be doing anything dangerous. It's just a scouting expedition.'

'Then why can't I come?' Ivy almost shouted. Those

now-familiar currents of pure magic began to leap between her fingertips in sparks of purplish light.

'Because of *that*,' said Rob, pointing to her hands. 'Ivy, I know you don't mean any harm, but if we do run into any bother, I can't risk you going off like a firework and drawing attention to us or turning a street into a crater. You understand?'

Ivy sighed. 'Yes. I understand.' She walked past Rob and Joe, and out of the front door of the cottage, letting in the pleasant sea breeze. A minute later, they heard her yell out in frustration, and a deafening bang split the air, making Rob and Joe duck down. Slowly, they went to the living room window and looked out towards the cliffs, where Ivy stood staring out to sea, the ground around her smoking.

Joe shook his head. 'I think she took that well, don't you?'

When the time came, stepping out of the painting was surprisingly easy. Rob went first, running towards the window in the sky. When he was close, he jumped, and Joe watched him suddenly grow huge in the sky and disappear through the window. A moment later his gigantic face appeared in the room on the other side.

'Well, that's the scariest thing I've seen in a while,' said Joe, pointing up at Rob.

Ivy actually smiled at this. 'Take care, Joe. Come back soon.'

'I will.' He gave her a grin, and then he shrugged and ran towards the window. When he was almost directly beneath the hole in the sky, he jumped. A pleasant feeling brushed over him, like stretching in bed when you wake up after a long sleep. Then, before he knew what was happening, he had landed on the bare floorboards of the apartment and was breathing the stifling southern air of Lake End. He peered back at the painting, amazed, seeing the little stone cottage and the clifftop and the rolling sea. There was no sign of Ivy though, and he felt bad about leaving her behind.

The streets of Lake End were busy. The late-morning sun baked the red stone buildings and the dusty streets. Coffee houses and pubs were crowded, their terraces filled with tourists, all buzzing about the upcoming Evernight Feast. Delicious smells of frying garlic and seafood drifted from the restaurants, and strings of many-coloured flags adorned the buildings.

'Blimey!' exclaimed Joe, coming to a sudden stop.

'What?' said Rob impatiently. 'What is it, boy?'

Mouth agape, Joe pointed past Rob to the row of shops and coffee houses. There, in many of the windows, was a large poster which read:

WANTED IN CONNECTION WITH WESTERLY
WITCH ACTIVITY.
LARGE REWARD FOR INFORMATION THAT
LEADS TO ARREST.

Below those shouting words was a huge close-up picture of Rob's face.

Rob stared at the posters seemingly in disbelief. Then he let out a bellowing laugh. 'Ha! I don't know who that poor bloke is,' he said, patting his newly-shaven chin. 'But I'm glad I don't look anything like him!' He gave Joe a conspiratorial wink, and Joe smiled.

Before long, they had reached the nearest underground railway station. The entrance was a gated stairway that led beneath the street, and as Joe descended the many stairs, the air took on a familiar, heavy feeling; it reminded him of the musky air of the sewers.

The stairs opened onto a wide, low tunnel, its polished terracotta tiles shining in the light of dragon-breath lamps. Rob bought two tickets from a man at a pay station in the wall, and then they went through a gate and down some more steps to the platform, where a number of people waited for the next train.

Joe went to the platform edge, looked over at the rails, and then followed them with his eyes, left and then right, until they disappeared at both ends into dark, circular tunnels. Looking into those black holes in the earth made his belly flutter with excitement.

A distant roar sounded the imminent arrival of a train, and the roar grew and grew until it was deafening, and a train came out of the dark and stopped at the platform. Joe had never seen anything like it. There was a sleek, silver engine with steam hissing from the many pipes and valves along its length. Behind it was a line of silver carriages.

When the carriage doors opened, a few people got out, and the ones who had been waiting on the platform got on. Rob grabbed Joe by the sleeve and guided him into one of the open carriages, where they sat on a wooden bench running the length of the car. Then the doors closed, and, with a loud hiss, the train moved off in a cloud of steam, into the tunnel.

Joe had spent much of his life underground, and yet these tunnels were a marvel to him. As the roaring train bulleted through the dark, he saw points of light streaking past the window where dragon-breath lamps lit the tunnel walls. The train moved at a terrific speed, and the carriage trembled and shook, until the screech of the brakes pierced Joe's ears and the blackness of the tunnel became the light of another underground station.

'We stay on,' Rob said as people departed and others came aboard. 'All the way to Fortress Park at the top of the city.'

There were seven more stops before they arrived at Fortress Park station and finally got off the train. Rob and Joe held back and watched as the doors closed again, and the train rumbled away into the darkness of the tunnel towards its next stop, leaving them alone on the platform.

'Come on,' said Rob, hopping down onto the track. 'Before someone sees us.'

Joe didn't move. 'Is it safe? What if another train comes?' He imagined what it might be like to see the lights of a train roaring towards him in the dark, and shivered.

Rob waved a hand dismissively. 'You think I'm an idiot? I've checked all that out. There's only one train on the track, looping around and around. It won't come back this way for an hour, and by that time we'll be long gone.'

Satisfied, and not wanting to cause bother on his first real mission, Joe jumped onto the tracks, feeling the warm, stale breath of the tunnel on his face, and followed Rob into the dark.

'Where are we now, d'you think?' Joe was walking behind Rob on the railway track, guided by the cold blueish glow of Rob's light spell.

'We should be somewhere near the Red Fortress,' said Rob.

Joe looked up, imagining an enormous red castle high above his head. 'How did you find out about the king's secret tunnel anyway?'

Rob raised his wand a little higher, examining the pipes running along the walls. 'I heard about it a few weeks ago from a runaway White Witch I helped to escape from King's Haven. She'd actually been to the Red Fortress, y'see. Just under a year ago, the king brought a group of White Witches south to reinforce the fortress's walls with magic. Apparently he's been terrified ever since the Evernight and he wanted extra security. Anyway, this White Witch and her group were taken to the fortress on the secret railway – but she couldn't tell me where the tunnel is, because the king made 'em all wear blindfolds so they wouldn't know.'

'How do you know she was tellin' the truth?' Joe asked.

'Because she agreed to let me use a truth spell on her.'

'Blimey. But if she couldn't tell you where the tunnel is, how are we supposed to find it?'

'She was able to tell me one thing,' said Rob. 'The king knows how badly the slum folk hate him since he abandoned them during the Evernight. He's become very paranoid that someone will try to kill him.'

'And with good reason,' said Joe. He pictured the king's smug face and clenched his teeth and his fists. Joe and his granny had been among the many folk the king had trapped in the slums, and Granny had died because Joe hadn't been able to escape to get her medicine. Every time he thought about it, his blood lit on fire with hatred.

Rob went on. 'Everything he eats or drinks or touches has to be thoroughly tested for poison. When his supplies are given the all-clear, they're taken to the Red Fortress on the secret railway line. It happens once a day, at noon. What time is it now, Joe?'

Joe took a small silver pocket watch out of his jacket. It had belonged to Granny, and it was his prize possession. He popped the watch open, looked at the shining face by the light of Rob's spell. 'It's almost noon!' He looked up at Rob, realisation dawning. 'We're going to use this tunnel to see if we can hear the king's train passing by! And follow the sound to the secret railway line!'

Rob smiled. 'And that, my boy, is why you're here. I fancy myself as a very decent Witch, and a hell of a ship's captain, but I don't know the first thing about tunnels. I'm counting on you, Joe, to lead the way. All those years you spent in the sewers under King's Haven! I bet you could hear a rat gnawing on a bone from a hundred yards away.'

Joe felt a swell of pride in his chest. 'I do have pretty sharp ears. Being a tosher means you have to learn to listen for animals and floods and footsteps, and all sorts of things that might bring danger. If the king's train passes anywhere near us, Rob, I'll know it.' Rob gave him such a tremendous pat on the back he almost fell over. Then Joe looked at Granny's old pocket watch again. 'If the king's supply train is on time, I guess we should hear it any minute.'

They fell quiet. Joe peered off up the tunnel, not really looking at anything but the darkness itself. How long had it been since he'd been beneath the earth? A year? Hell's teeth, could it really be that long? Before the Evernight, Joe could not have imagined a day passing when he did not leave the sunlight behind and venture into the subterranean world of the toshers. It was a life he missed, and longed for, and yet he knew that he could not go back, not while he had unfinished business with the king.

Something made Joe very still. A distant sound. Actually,

the more he concentrated on it, he realised it was more of a feeling than a sound, a tremulous rumble passing through the tunnels that he could sense in his bones. He crouched down, touched his hand to the tracks, felt the tiniest vibration thrum in his fingertips. 'You feel that?'

Rob copied Joe. His eyebrows knitted together. 'I don't feel anything.'

'It's there, and no mistake,' said Joe. 'And it's coming closer.'

The thrumming in the track grew, and Joe straightened up and went to the tunnel wall, putting his ear to the stone. The sound he heard made him imagine that there was a great creature somewhere nearby in the earth, waking up from a long sleep.

'I think I hear it now!' The light from Rob's wand pushed back the thick dark, casting his face in blueish light. 'Yes. I do!'

The rumble grew louder, and the thrum in the tunnel vibrated with more force. In just a few moments both Joe and Rob could feel it deep in their chests, as if the very world around them was trembling.

Then it faded, and became a whisper, and was gone.

'That was it,' said Joe. 'That has to have been it!'

Rob nodded, pointed to the tunnel wall to the east. 'It came from that way, right?'

'No.'

'No?'

'Sound,' said Joe, 'does funny things beneath the earth. It bounces here and there, tries to confuse you. It's sneaky. But I know where the sound came from, Rob. I'm sure of it.'

The tunnel was deathly still, and the darkness all around fought against Rob's light spell.

'Well?' Rob said. 'Are you going to tell me, boy?'

Joe crouched down again, smiled, tapped the track. 'It came from *beneath* us.'

Rob turned his light spell to the floor, illuminating the metal tracks and wooden sleepers. 'The secret tunnels are underneath these ones?'

'Yeah,' said Joe. 'And I'd wager there's something that connects them.'

'Really?'

'Think about it,' said Joe, going once again to the tunnel wall. He tapped one of the thick pipes, and drew back his hand because it was scalding hot. 'No matter how secret the tunnels might be, they still need pipes like these to function, to carry water and steam and such. I'll bet those pipes join these somewhere. And if they do, you can bet there'll be a way to get into the tunnels we're looking for. A secret service door or something.'

'Ha!' Rob gave him another mighty slap on the back. 'I knew you'd come through, boy. I knew it!'

'I haven't done anything yet,' said Joe. 'We still have to find . . .' The thought melted away and was replaced by something else. He crouched down to the track once more, put his hand to the ground. His heart froze. 'That can't be right.'

'What?' said Rob. 'What can't?'

Joe didn't answer at first. He wanted to be sure. Another thrum was coursing through the metal tracks, much more powerful than the last. 'There's a train coming.'

Rob frowned. 'But my information says there's only one train that runs to the fortress a day.'

Joe jumped up, adrenaline beginning to pump around his body, fear blazing through him. 'It's not coming from the king's secret railway line. There's a train in *this* tunnel, Rob! It's heading right for us!'

TRAPPED

Rob's eyes were bugging almost out their sockets, the whites of them seeming to glow in the wand light. 'That can't be,' he whispered. 'There's no train for another forty minutes. Hell's teeth, I'm sorry, Joe – they must have built a second train for all of the festival crowds!'

Joe felt the thrum on the tracks grow more intense. He straightened up, his chest tight with panic. Then the rumbling began to echo down the tunnel. 'Come on, we need to get out of here!' He grabbed Rob's sleeve, pulled, and Rob seemed to wake from a stupor.

They ran, gasping and panting, Rob's wand light bouncing about on the walls. The roar was catching them up.

'How far to the next station?' cried Joe.

Rob shook his head. 'Quarter of a mile. We won't make it. I thought we had time, Joe . . .'

Joe looked around wildly as they ran, the screaming roar of the chasing train growing and growing. His mind flashed back to the sewers under King's Haven. Once, when he'd been toshing near the river, one of the storm drains had burst, sending a wall of deadly water crashing through the nearby sewers. Joe had escaped by the skin of his teeth, making it back up to the surface just as the water reached him and fired him up into the street like a cannonball. But he had known those tunnels, every corner and twist and turn. Here, he was a stranger, and he could see no way out.

A piercing metallic screech made him swing around and look back down the track. The train came screaming around the corner, an iron monster that took up almost every inch of space, eating up the track at tremendous speed.

Before Joe knew what was happening, Rob had grabbed him by the coat, tossing him across to the wall. There he crouched, hoping that there was enough space between the train and the walls that it might shoot past without touching him. Then he saw Rob standing in the middle of the track, facing the onrushing engine, his wand pointed towards it. He shot a final glance towards Joe, a look that seemed to say, 'I'm sorry' and, 'Goodbye' and, 'Don't move' all at once. Then he looked back towards the train, steadied his wand hand, and pulled the trigger.

A stream of orange spell smoke erupted from the tip of the wand. As it thundered up the tracks, the spell became a gigantic man, filling up the tunnel, running powerfully towards the train. When the spell man collided with the train, a shockwave swept through the air, making Joe shield his face. A piercing, metallic roar filled the place, and when

Joe next looked, he saw the spell man's feet were planted on the tracks, that he was pushing against the train, slowing it down. Sparks were spraying from the engine's wheels, and the smell of hot metal was strong.

Among the flashes and roars and confusion, Joe heard Rob scream out, and he spun and saw his friend dropping to his knees on the tracks, his face screwed up in a grimace of extreme effort as he tried to hold the wand steady. But it seemed that the train was too big a thing, too powerful an object, for one Witch to stop. It continued to come, pushing the spell man back, until, with a final effort, Rob fell to the tracks, his wand spinning away, and the spell died, leaving only the lamps of the oncoming train to light the dark.

The engine was bearing down. Joe only had moments to act; he took a great breath and rushed out to the track, grabbing Rob, slapping his face to try to bring him properly around.

'Rob! Rob, you have to move!' He tried to drag him, but Rob was just too big. Then he looked up and saw the train was almost upon them.

He was out of time.

Joe closed his eyes, thought of Granny, of Lara and his friends.

BOOM!

Joe felt burning heat on his face, and the insides of his eyelids turned bright red. He opened his eyes a fraction to the dazzling light. Stunned, he looked up the tracks, and was amazed to see another spell person – a woman this time – pushing against the train. This spell seemed stronger than Rob's, because it was slowing the train down. The wheels screamed on the track, sparks flew, and a plume of steam engulfed the tunnel. The spell pushed and pushed, until, at last, the train stopped just a few metres away. Lying on the tracks at the spell woman's feet, Joe felt the immense heat of it, saw that the track had actually melted and buckled where its feet had dug in and finally brought the train to a stop.

The great spell woman flickered and was gone, leaving the tunnel in semi-darkness, the lamps of the train carriages emitting a soft glow from behind the huge engine. Not knowing what was happening, Joe shook Rob, slapped him again, and Rob sat up with a gasp, sucking in air.

'What happened? Did I stop it?'

'No,' said Joe. 'But someone did.'

Rob squeezed his eyes tightly shut, shaking away the cobwebs. 'Someone else? Who?'

Faltering footsteps echoed towards them from the dark. Then, into the light stepped Ivy Robin. She was shaking madly. Rob's wand was clutched in her hand. The effort of stopping the train had drained almost every bit of colour from her face, so that she looked like a walking corpse.

'Good thing I followed you, eh?' she said with a smile. A drop of scarlet blood ran from her nose.

Then she fell.

'Ivy!' Joe dashed to her, leaned over her. He called to Rob. 'She's breathing, but she looks in a bad way.'

Rob, still shaking off the effects of the spell, lumbered over and scooped Ivy up into his arms.

Voices called out from the train's cabin.

'Who's there?'

'What in the name of Lady Light happened?'

'Time to go,' said Rob. 'Judging by the state of the track, that train isn't going anywhere soon. C'mon.'

Five minutes later, the passengers waiting on the platform of the next station were quite amazed to see three people emerging from the tunnel. First came a boy, then a huge bear of a man carrying an unconscious young woman over his shoulder. They did not say a word as they climbed from the track and hurried up the steps to the world above ground, and soon they were gone.

A Familiar Face

When Ivy stopped the train, such was the power of the magic she unleashed that Witches all over Lake End could feel it.

Outside the city walls, in the hidden campsite, the hair on Lara's arms stood on end. Nearby, at the campfire, Ginny dropped a bowl of soup to the ground and stared off towards the distant red spires and tall buildings.

A great number of secret police agents and White Witches had travelled to Lake End for the king's Evernight Feast, and many of them sensed it too.

But there was one person above all else who felt the magic.

An hour after the event, that person stood in the shadows of the underground tunnel and watched as engineers huddled round the melted tracks and tried to figure out what had happened. The watcher sniffed the air. The place was thick with traces of leftover magic so strong it almost defied belief. This was interesting. Very interesting indeed.

They began to follow the trail; it was a skill very few Witches possessed. Sure, there were tracer spells, but you had to plant them on the person you wanted to follow. The art of tracking, of smelling out a particular magical trace, following it the way an animal follows its prey, was almost lost.

But not to this person.

Their nose took them away from the scene of the incident, to the next station, up the steps and into the daylight.

If Lara had been there, if she had seen them, she would have been overjoyed.

She would have run towards them and hugged them and told them how glad she was to see them alive.

But Lara was not there to see Double Eight. And so the killer disappeared into the crowds, the trail leading through the busy streets, where more colourful flags had been strung between buildings, and posters and children's drawings displayed in windows to celebrate a year since the Evernight was defeated. It took the killer to a quiet neighbourhood, into an apartment building, up several flights of stairs and into an apartment that seemed at first glance to be abandoned.

But it was not.

The trail led to a painting of a stone cottage on a pretty clifftop by the sea.

Led inside the painting.

The killer crept towards the cottage, ducked down, and

began to carefully look in through each of the windows. Through one window the killer saw two familiar faces and one strange. The first was Rob Nielsen. The killer had seen wanted posters up all over the city with Rob's face on, but he had shaved off his beard and wild hair and looked very different. The second was Joe Littlefoot. They were crouching over a third person, who lay on the floor, unconscious. This one was a young woman, and the sound of magic whispered all around her in crystalline waves. Without question, it had been *her* power that had left the trail to this spot.

Even in her current state, the killer could feel the power radiating from the girl. It was incredible. An unpleasant smile crept across Double Eight's face as the killer brought out a wand and pulled the trigger. In the wand's revolver chamber, one of the spell bottles burned bright, and from the wand tip came what looked like a large soap bubble. The bubble drifted towards the cottage window and passed through the glass, into the room. There it hovered right in front of Rob Nielsen and Joe Littlefoot, but neither of them could see it, or sense it.

Double Eight's eyes closed, and suddenly the killer was inside the bubble, in the room with Rob and Joe, looking out at them, listening to every word.

'Ivy?' Joe was saying. 'Ivy, can you hear me?'

So, her name is Ivy . . .

'Will she be all right, Rob?'

'I think so. She used a lot of energy. Hell's teeth, Joe,

I've never felt anything like what she did back in that tunnel. Wait . . . what was that? Did you hear something outside?'

Rob and Joe went to the window, saw nothing, and then Rob walked out the front door and checked all around the cottage. When he returned he looked troubled. 'Strange. I could've sworn I heard someone there. Must have been my imagination playing tricks on me after everything that's happened.'

Outside the painting, the killer left the apartment, closing the door gently, and smiled. It had been a risk coming here in person instead of using the spying spell, but it had been worth it. This had been the only way to feel the immense power crackling in the air around the girl . . . Ivy. And what power it was! Still smiling, the killer went back to the city.

SAM HUSHBY

Next morning, Lara and Ginny left camp and travelled to the southern ranger stables on the south-western tip of Lake End.

After speaking to Ginny, Lara had built up quite a picture in her mind of what a southern ranger should be. She imagined Sam Hushby would be tall and confident and immaculate. It was quite a shock, then, when she met him.

The ranger stables were a series of red stone buildings and open fields, where horsemen prepared the flesh-and-blood horses for duty. It was quite common, it seemed, for children to gather at the fences and watch the horses' training. Ginny and Lara secured Ginny's own horse outside the stables, and there they left her happily surrounded by kids, who fed her carrot ends and hay.

After all her experience of coppers and secret police in King's Haven, Lara was flabbergasted when she saw that the southern rangers kept the gate to their stables open and allowed visitors to wander freely in and out.

'Don't they worry about people stealing from 'em? In King's Haven, the horses would all be nicked and sold before the coppers were even properly out of the saddle.'

'It's different here,' said Ginny. 'Folks in Lake End love the southern rangers. Revere 'em. Rangers are quick to hand down justice. Even the most hardened criminal knows that messin' with the rangers is madness. Ah, there's our man.'

'Sam Hushby? Where?'

Ginny pointed. 'In that stable.'

'I can't see him. All I see is a stable boy.'

Ginny nodded. 'Didn't I tell you they're a-keeping him hidden away? Took me days of snoopin' to find him – and a well-placed memory moth in the ear of one of his superiors.'

'That's him?'

Ginny sauntered easily to the stable and leaned on the wooden fence. She removed her hat, took a breath of stable air: a humid, sweet and bitter mix of hay and horse manure. 'Mornin', ranger.'

He was shorter than Lara had imagined, and a little overweight. His baggy white shirt clung to his body with sweat as he shovelled up piles of horse dung.

'Yes. Morning.'

'Pardon me for asking,' said Ginny, 'but are you Sam Hushby?'

He stopped shovelling and looked up through the dark hair plastered to his forehead. 'Who wants to know?'

'A friend,' said Ginny.

He smiled, shook his head and went back to shovelling. 'I don't have any friends left.'

Ginny nodded to Lara, encouraging her to speak. Flustered, Lara thought hard about what to say, and eventually settled on, 'We believe you, Sam Hushby. We know your partner didn't run away.'

His head shot up, and his tired, startled eyes flicked between them. 'Who are you? What d'you want?'

'We want to find the truth, Sam,' said Ginny.

There was fear in his face. 'Is this a test? Did the chief send you to see if I'd talk? Because I won't!'

'It's not a test, Sam,' said Ginny, her voice low and calm. 'We found Annalise's body in the Veil.'

His eyes nearly popped out of his skull. He dropped his shovel and hurried over towards them. 'You *found* her?'

'We did. And we want to make sure whoever did this doesn't do it again. Will you tell us what happened?'

Sam Hushby's muddy green eyes had taken on a burning intensity. 'Why is this so important to you? What makes you think you can catch the killer?'

To Lara's surprise, Ginny pulled one side of her coat open, letting Sam catch a glimpse of her wand. His eyes stretched wide, and he took a half step back.

'You're Westerly Witches?' he whispered. 'You're not supposed to be here. The city's filled with secret police and White Witches for the celebration, and we've been told to arrest anyone suspicious on sight.'

'Are you goin' to arrest us, Sam?' Ginny asked. 'I don't think you will, because, deep down, I think you know we're on the same side. We all want justice for Annalise. And we want to catch the killer.'

Droplets of sweat were dripping from Sam's round face, from the end of his nose and his chin. His breathing was short and sharp, and his teeth worried his bottom lip. 'I can't talk here.'

Lara's heart was racing.

'Tonight, then,' said Ginny.

'Where?'

'The Church of Lady Light,' said Ginny. 'In the Gothica quarter. Eleven o'clock.'

He swallowed, gave a single nod and then, trembling, picked up his shovel and went back to work.

THE HUNTER ARRIVES

On the other side of Lake End, a large airship was touching down at the sky port. When the engines had died and the doors opened, Karl Younger, leader of the king's secret police, came down the steps and took a breath of warm southern air.

A carriage awaited him, and he climbed in, removing his hat and placing it on the seat beside him. As the ironhearts drove him through the city, he stared out of the windows at the red, arid streets. He did not like the south. It was too hot, and the people had more respect for their southern rangers than they did for the secret police. But he would change that soon enough.

Half an hour later, the carriage had navigated through a dozen neighbourhoods, from the grand archways and steeples of the Gothica quarter to the newer, northern-style buildings of the shopping boulevards near the centre, and at last to the vast circular Fortress Park, where the King would host the Evernight Feast, and up steep Fortress Hill to the walls of the king's Red Fortress.

He was escorted at last to a parlour where the walls were leafed with gold, and found the king sprawled on a couch while servants fanned him.

'Ah,' said the king, not sitting up. 'How was your journey?'

'Fine, Your Majesty. How go the preparations for the feast?'

The king waved a hand. 'I'm surrounded by idiots, Younger. You know how it is. But at least they've made a good job of my statue. It is, I think, a decent likeness of me.'

'Very good, sire. And how are the queen and the young princes? I trust they are well?'

He grunted. 'Away to the west, on the Gold Coast. The queen did not wish to be here for the feast. She does not encourage smiling or good cheer of any sort.' At this he let out a laugh and finally managed to sit up, his face flushing purple with the effort. 'Leave us,' he told the servants. Then, when he and Younger were alone, he said, 'Well? What's the latest?'

'I've just come via the town of Cobalt, Your Majesty.'

'Never heard of it,' said the king.

'It's not the sort of place that usually deserves your attention,' said Younger. 'Little mining town. Bit of a pockmark on the landscape. But it seems the Hag I'm chasing stopped there on his travels. He had the runaway Witch girl with him.'

The king sat forward. 'What happened?'

'The sheriff is an idiot,' said Younger. 'Went steaming in and frightened the Hags off. He gave chase down the river, but the runaway used her powers to block the way with a landslide.'

'And where are they now?'

'We found the steamer they had been using. Abandoned. But they may have taken another boat. I think they're coming here.'

'Here?' said the king. 'To Lake End?' The redness in his face deepened. 'I knew it. They're going to ruin my party! We can't let that happen, Younger. After the Evernight, I've already lost the support of the damn slum folk in King's Haven. This feast is supposed to remind my people that I led them out of the darkness, that they *need* me. Nothing can be allowed to go wrong.'

'I understand, sire,' said Younger. 'We've ten thousand troops in Lake End for the parade – not to mention hundreds of secret police on the lookout for trouble. The Hags don't stand a chance against those odds. I will find the Hags, Your Majesty. The Hags will get what they deserve.'

The king raised a finger. 'I don't want that runaway

Witch girl harmed, Younger. Remember that. Bring her in alive. We might be able to use her against the rest of the Hags.'

Younger supressed a sneer. 'As you wish,' he said.

In his head, however, he was trying to decide the best way to kill her.

THE TRUTH

That night, Lara held tight to Ginny Adder as her shining black horse swept through the Gothica quarter between steep canyons of red stone buildings adorned with spires and columns and statues. When they reached the church, they dismounted, and Ginny hitched her horse near a water trough by the side of the road.

The church spire reached high into the night sky, and it seemed to Lara, almost to the stars. The doors were open, welcoming light flooding down the steps. Inside, the place was empty, save for a few slumbering figures curled up on the uncomfortable pews. In the middle row to the right sat Sam Hushby. He was glancing around nervously, and when he spotted them, it seemed he did not quite know what to do. At first, he made to raise his hand in greeting, but he stopped himself and wiped the sweat from his brow. Lara and Ginny sat in the row behind him, close enough to speak in quiet voices.

'I wondered whether you'd show up,' said Ginny.

'I wondered that myself,' said Sam, not looking back. 'The city's crawling with secret police for the celebrations. If they caught me conspiring with Westerlys, they'd hang me. You understand that, don't you?'

'And yet, here you are,' said Ginny.

'Yes. Here I am.'

Ginny leaned forward. 'Tell us what happened, Sam. Don't leave anything out. You never know what might be important.'

'All right.' Sam took a breath, and seemed to be organising the facts in his head. 'It was my first proper night on patrol, and I'd just met Annalise for the first time. She made fun of me a little, but that's to be expected when you're a rookie. I thought she was pretty friendly otherwise.'

'And you were patrolling the Veil Forest?' said Ginny.

Still looking forward, his voice a low whisper, Sam said, 'That's right. It was a bit of a shock, actually. When I qualified, I had hoped they'd send me even further south, to the dust bowl to catch bandits. But they saw fit to assign me to the Veil Forest. That's why Annalise made fun of me. For being frightened.'

'Of the forest?' asked Lara.

'Of the things that might come out of the forest,' Sam corrected her. 'In any case, I was proved right, wasn't I?'

Ginny narrowed her sharp eyes. 'What happened that night, Sam?'

'Well, we were just starting our patrol and there was a sound. Annalise said it was probably just a fox, and she got down from her ironheart and went to check.'

'You didn't go along?'

He shook his head. 'Annalise told me to wait. I think she thought I might get spooked and fire my pistol in the dark. And she was probably right.'

'What then?' Lara could hear the urgency in Ginny's voice.

'I waited a little bit. It was all quiet. The Veil gets so quiet. Then there was a crashing sound, like a tree coming down, and Annalise called for me. I drew my gun and ran right in there without even thinkin' about it. It was so dark I could barely see anything. I called for her a few times, but she didn't answer. Then I heard these sounds . . . these *awful* sounds . . .'

He stopped. He was trembling all over. Ginny reached forward, placed a hand on his shoulder, and he flinched. 'It's all right, Sam. You're safe here. You're doin' just fine. Please go on.'

He took a shaky breath. 'I saw them on the ground. Annalise. And another person crouching over her. A boy, I think. Certainly not a full-grown man, but not a little boy either. I yelled at him to freeze, and I must've startled him, cos he looked up. And that's . . .' he choked. 'That's when I saw . . .'

Lara leaned forward, her heartbeat thudding in her

head, full of admiration and fear. 'What did you see, Sam?'

'It was like . . .' he shook his head in frustration, searching for the words. 'His face. It was like he wasn't a proper person. Like he was made of clay, or dough, and whoever made him stopped before he was finished. He was on top of me before I could get a proper aim. He was strong for a boy, but I managed to fight him off and get to my gun. By the time I got up, he was gone.'

He was quiet then. Lara could see that he was silently crying, his shoulders rising and falling. 'Now Annalise is out there all alone,' he sobbed. 'Just lying there. I can't stop imagining it. Can't get it out of my head.'

'But she's not, Sam,' said Ginny kindly. 'We buried her, Lara and me. Made sure she was at peace.'

Sam looked up. 'You did?'

Ginny nodded, and Sam wiped his eyes. 'Well that's something I suppose. Thank you.'

'Thank you, Sam,' said Ginny. 'You've been great. If you don't mind, there's one more thing you could help us with. Is that all right?'

Lara looked sideways at Ginny, wondering what she was going to ask of him.

'Fine,' said Sam, dabbing at his eyes. 'What is it?'

Ginny looked into Lara's eyes. 'That picture you found in Sprout's flat, the one of you and your friend, you have it with you?'

Lara frowned, and nodded. She had taken the picture out of the frame and kept it in her coat, in a pocket near her heart.

'Will you show it to Sam, Lara?'

Lara's heart began to beat very fast. She hesitated, and then she reached into her pocket and brought out the picture. Her own grinning face, along with Double Eight's, smiled up at her.

'Look at it, Sam,' said Ginny. 'You recognise the boy?'

Sam Hushby's attention flicked from Ginny to the picture. A moment passed, and then he took a sharp breath. His face changed. His gums drew back and his eyes became huge and fearful. Lara thought he might scream. His entire body was trembling. 'That's him . . .' he managed to croak.

'Who, Sam? *Who* is it?'

'The boy in the picture,' whispered Sam. 'He's the monster that killed Annalise! In the forest, his face looked like it had melted a bit, but that's him. I'd bet my life on it.' His eyes went to Lara, and she saw the fear in them become something else. Anger. He reached over the pew, grabbed at her, pulled her towards him. 'He's your friend? Where is he? I'll kill him!'

Lara wrenched herself free, breathless, shaken.

'Leave her be, Sam,' Ginny told him. Her wand was suddenly in her hand.

Sam saw it, stood up, panting, sobbing, looking all about. 'I have to go. I have to . . .'

And with that he stumbled out into the aisle, hurried to the door and disappeared out into the street, leaving Lara to stare through her tears at the picture of a smiling Double Eight.

The boy she thought she knew.

OLD TRICKS

Joe crept silently down the hall of the stone cottage safe house. His wax-coated canvas bag was slung over his shoulder and in one of his hands he clutched a note. He came to the room where Rob was sleeping. Gruff snorts and snores drifted out, making Joe smile as he pinned the note to the door.

The next room was Ivy's. As Joe passed, he stopped for a moment, opened the door a fraction and listened. He could hear the soft whisper of Ivy's breathing. It was a peaceful sound. In the time after the events in the underground railway, Ivy had regained some of her strength. She'd even eaten a little, which was good. Joe fancied that she was going to be just fine.

He left the cottage, closed the door, and set off up the hill behind the house towards the window in the sky. Before he left, he turned back and closed his eyes, letting the sun and the fresh sea breeze brush his face. Then he wheeled away, ran towards the window, and jumped.

The familiar, stifling warmth of Lake End air enveloped him, and he touched down upon the bare floorboards of the abandoned apartment. Then, wasting no time, he was away, out of the flat, down the stairs and into the streets.

It was early morning, but already there were people going about their business, opening coffee houses and bakeries, sitting in the early sun sipping coffee and eating sweet pastries. Joe moved swiftly, away from the wider boulevards and courts, looking for quiet, shaded places away from prying eyes.

After a short while, he happened upon a narrow delivery lane between a row of buildings, and began to explore. Steam billowed from coffee house kitchens, carrying the smell of coffee and toast into the alleyway, where it mixed with the stench of the overflowing bins. Joe stepped over one rubbish bag and disturbed a cat; it wailed and hissed at him, making him yelp and clutch his chest in fright. Then, on the ground, he saw what he'd come looking for.

A manhole cover.

The sight of it made his heart skip, made him feel light and giddy in a way he had not for the longest time. He stared at the metal disc in the ground, worrying his lip, going over the idea in his mind again, deciding if he was doing the right thing.

It would work, he was sure of it.

Some habits die hard. Joe had lived almost all of his days with his toshing bag slung over his shoulder. The life of a tosher meant that you had to be prepared for every eventuality. Joe had learned from Lara that a tosher was doomed if he wasn't always in tune with his surroundings, awake to the opportunities and the dangers that popped up every second of every minute of every day. The contents of Joe's bag had helped him out of more than a few scrapes; his crowbar had fought off packs of sewer rats and tripped up chasing coppers. His dragon-breath lamp had lit the way safely home countless times, had illuminated lost treasures in the darkest corners of the King's Haven sewers.

The toshing bag had, in short, been a loyal friend.

After the Evernight, when Granny had passed away and Joe had left his home and gone with Lara to Westerly Witch, he had taken only two things from the tiny attic flat he and Granny had shared – his toshing bag and Granny's silver pocket watch – and he kept them with him always.

Now he hoped the toshing bag would bring him luck once more. He brought it down from his shoulder, opened it, picked out the crowbar. Then he crouched by the cover, wedged it open and slid the heavy metal lid sideways. He could not help smiling as he worked; his body and mind had clicked instantly back into toshing mode, as if he had done this only yesterday.

Stowing the crowbar in the bag, he sat by the open drain, swung his legs in, found the ladder with his feet. Then, excitement building, Joe descended into the dark.

When his feet touched down on the sewer floor, he felt

instantly at home. The sound of the gurgling stream was cheery and musical. The smell, heavy and damp and not as unpleasant as your average person might imagine, wrapped around him like a warm hug. Reaching once again into his toshing bag, Joe produced his lamp. His fingers worked effortlessly in the dark, finding the dial, turning it and sparking a flame inside the glass to life. Familiar golden honey light pushed back the dark in a large sphere around him. The sewer was a simple construction; while the King's Haven tunnels were cathedrals of brick and mortar, it looked like these had been carved right out of the red stone of the land.

Joe did not have his wax-coated toshing boots with him, so the small stream splashed his feet as he went, but he didn't really notice because he was so happy to be back where he felt he belonged. As he went he wondered what treasures might lurk beneath the surface. Were there shining coins wedged in rocky fissures? Was he walking past sovereign rings tangled in ragged strips of clothing? Perhaps there was a diamond earring floating past him now . . .

He was sorely tempted to find out, to dip his hands into the water and brush the stone with his fingertips, and the thought of it made his belly bubble with excitement.

But no. He was not here to hunt for treasure, as much as his instincts were screaming otherwise. He was here because he and Rob had a job to do, and he, Joe, had woken in the night with a sudden bright idea flashing in his mind.

The labyrinth of sewer passages wound this way and that, and Joe used his instinct to guide him deeper and deeper, listening all the while for a particular sound. Then he turned a corner and became deathly still.

There it was. The *slosh-sloshing* of another pair of feet.

Creeping forward, Joe followed the sound, until he reached an intersection where a number of sewers met. He killed the light of his lamp, and let the darkness smother him. A warm glow was coming from one of the adjoining sewers. Joe made slowly for the entrance, peering around the corner with great care.

Twenty yards up the sewer stood a Lake End tosher. She looked to be around the same age as Joe, but she was taller than him. Her skin was very dark, her hair pulled tightly away from her face, which wore a familiar expression, one of great concentration, as she leaned over and peered into the sewer stream. Joe recognised that look: it was the spark of discovery.

The girl crouched down, reached into the water and felt around. Then, with a jerk, she pulled her hand back up, and held her palm open. Joe could see something small and gold glistening in the light of her lamp. She smiled to herself, showing a row of straight, bright teeth, and put the treasure into her toshing bag. Then she stood straight and walked off up the tunnel.

Joe followed, taking great care to hang back a fair distance, and to keep his feet as silent as he could. Again, he smiled at being back in this world, and at how he had not lost his touch. She had no clue he was even there. The tunnel reached a T-junction, and the tosher girl took the path to the left. When Joe reached the junction, he stopped, peeked around the corner, and frowned. Just a few feet away, the girl's lamp was lying on the sewer floor at the edge of the stream. Joe came out, walked slowly towards it, and when he reached it, bent to pick it up.

Before he could touch the lamp, a sound made Joe look up, just in time to see a dark shape dropping down from the ceiling. The tosher girl landed with a splash, and in one smooth movement she drove a knee, *ooooff*, into Joe's stomach. Then she pushed him back against the sewer wall, her forearm jammed against his throat.

'What you following me for?' she said. Her face was fierce, her big eyes filled with murderous intent. 'You thought I was an easy target, didn't you? A girl down here all alone. You thought taking my stuff would be easy!' She punched him hard in the gut, folding him over, and Joe could do nothing but drop to his hands and knees in the stream, hoping that he wasn't about to meet his end.

'I'm not a thief,' he managed to sputter. 'I don't want your stuff.'

'Ha! A likely story.'

'It's true! I'm a tosher as well. Look at my bag.'

Her eyes flicked toward his toshing bag and the lamp around his neck. Her stance was still that of a fighter, but her face relaxed a little. 'If you're a tosher, how come I've never seen you before?'

'I'm from King's Haven,' said Joe, still struggling to catch his breath.

'King's Haven? So what you doing down here? You moving in on my patch?'

'What? No! No way! I'm not even here to look for treasure, I swear. I'm lookin' for help. Can I get up, please?'

She remained in her fighter's stance, but she nodded and allowed him space to get to his feet. He wiped his hands off on his trousers, sucked in great gasps of air, and held his stomach. 'You punch like a heavyweight. I think you cracked one of my ribs.'

'If I had really wanted to hurt you,' said the girl, 'you'd know all about it.'

Joe grimaced. 'I don't doubt it. I'm sorry I spooked you. I just really need help.'

'What sort of help you expecting to find down here?'

'Info,' said Joe. 'The kind of info only a tosher would know. Look, can we start again, please? My name's Joe Littlefoot. Like I said, I'm here from King's Haven.' He held out a hand. 'And you are?'

She frowned. 'Not about to tell a stranger any secrets.'

Joe nodded. 'A fan of the king, are you?'

She looked at him like he'd just let out a stinking fart. 'You serious? I hate him.'

'We have more than toshing in common then,' said Joe.

'But I can tell you're not interested in helping me get one over on the king, so I'll go find someone else. Thanks anyway.'

He turned around, took a couple of steps.

'Wait,' said the girl.

Joe smiled to himself, then faced her, looking serious. 'Yes?'

'What do you mean "Get one over on him"?' Her eyes lit up. 'You gonna do something to his statue?'

Joe frowned. 'Statue?'

'Yeah. The idiot's unveiling a big statue of himself at the stupid feast he's throwing. It's supposed to be a secret, but mostly everyone knows. So? Is that it? You gonna paint a moustache on the statue or something?'

'It's better than that,' said Joe with a knowing smile. 'You'll find out soon enough – that is, if I can figure out how to get into the king's secret railway tunnel. That's why I came down here, see? In King's Haven, if you wanted to know a secret, you asked a tosher. Toshers see and hear things other people don't. They know secrets. I imagine it's the same here, right? Do you know secrets?'

For the first time, she relaxed out of her fighter's stance. 'Maybe I do. And maybe I don't.' She pointed towards his chest. 'That's a real nice lamp.'

Joe looked down at the dragon-breath lamp hanging around his neck. His stomach sank a little at the thought of giving it up. But there were bigger things to worry about.

'It's yours,' he said with a heavy heart. 'But only if you help me find what I'm lookin' for.'

She smiled. It was a radiant, glowing thing. 'The King's railway? That's easy. But I don't know why you'd ever want to go there. It's teeming with guards. You won't last ten minutes.'

'Leave that to me,' said Joe. 'You just worry about getting me there.'

GINNY'S BREAKTHROUGH

Since the moment Sam Hushby confirmed that Double Eight was the reaper spell killer, Lara had felt like she was trapped in a nightmare. Presently, it was a few hours after noon, and she lay on her comfortable bed in the tent, away from the searing sun.

'There you go,' said Ginny, coming into the tent. 'Seafood chowder. Get that down you.' She put the plate next to Lara's bed.

Lara continued to stare at the ceiling. 'Thanks.'

Ginny sighed impatiently. 'I know you're shaken up, girl, but you must come out of this fug. We've a job to do, and it won't get done with you mopin' around.'

Lara's gaze did not falter from the ceiling of the tent. 'I know. But I can't believe it. I just can't *believe* it. Part of me thinks Sam Hushby must be wrong. But his reaction when I showed him that picture . . . he was *frightened* of Double Eight. More than frightened.' She tried to choke back a mix of emotions, anger and sadness and betrayal. 'I don't understand. None of it fits. For the life of me, I can't imagine the sweet Witch I know doing those terrible things.'

Ginny folded her arms and tapped her foot on the floor. It seemed there was some toing and froing going on in her head. Then she seemed to decide on something, and she sat on Lara's bed, making the springs groan. 'Remember I told you how Bernie and me fought the king's armies when they invaded the south all those years ago? How a group of us Westerly Witches became trapped?'

Lara met Ginny's eye. 'Yeah.'

'Well,' Ginny continued, 'we spent days hiding, trying to find a way out. We enchanted our hiding place so the king's armies couldn't find us – not unless one of us told them where to look. Which was never going to happen, right?'

'Right,' said Lara.

Ginny gave a short, humourless laugh. Her lip curled into a slight sneer. 'That's what I thought too. What we all thought. What we didn't know was that there was a traitor among us.'

Lara sat up. 'What?'

'We found out afterwards that a Witch called Padme Wolfe turned her back on us and made a deal with Mrs Hester and the Kingdom. In return for a comfortable life, Wolfe told Mrs Hester where to find us. Because of Padme Wolfe, a lot of Westerly Witches died, including . . .' She swallowed hard and took a deep, calming breath. 'Including

227

my husband, and my son. I'd never have imagined Padme was capable of such a thing, just as you can't imagine Double Eight being a killer. You can never tell, Lara, what's inside a person, what struggles they're going through or what demons they're fighting. Sometimes the demons win. And sometimes the person you thought you knew turns out not to exist at all, but is just a mask.'

Ginny reached out, took Lara's hand, and squeezed. It was a small gesture, but one so unexpected that it took Lara's defences down; the tears came in a flood. Ginny said nothing, she just let Lara cry and cry, until there was nothing left. After that they sat in silence for a while, and Lara appreciated that Ginny did not feel the need to fill the quiet, to talk or ask questions or try to cheer her up. She was content simply to let Lara be, and that was the best gift she could have given her.

The hush was only broken when a tremendous *BOOM* rang out from the campfire, shaking the tent, making Lara jump out of bed and Ginny leap to her feet.

'Hell's teeth!' the old Witch yelled, 'It's ready!'

'What?'

'My latest try at a special locator spell. It's been a hard road, but I have a good feeling about this one. If I can crack it, the spell will lead us right to Double Eight next time he kills.'

Lara's stomach did a somersault. 'What happens when we catch him?'

'Well, that's why you're here. No matter what he's done, or how far along the path of darkness he's gone, I'm hoping there's still a little light in him, that seeing you, speaking to you, will wake him up and convince him to come quietly.'

'And if he doesn't?'

Ginny thought about this. Thick yellow smoke had begun to coil into the tent from her spell out by the fire. 'We'll worry about that if it happens.'

She turned to hurry away, but before she could go, Lara asked, 'Did you ever track down Padme Wolfe after she betrayed you?'

Ginny stopped, answered without turning around. 'Yes.'

'Did she come quietly?'

Ginny's shoulders slumped. 'No.'

'What happened to her, Ginny?'

Ginny did not answer. She simply left the tent without saying another word.

JOE'S NEWS

As Lara and Ginny were having a heart-to-heart in their hidden camp, the reaper spell killer sat in a dark room high over the city. Double Eight's face was a mask of concentration, the mouth thin, the eyes shut, the brow creased, watching, by means of the invisible spell bubble left there, events unfolding in Rob Nielsen's safe house, several neighbourhoods away . . .

In the field of long grass behind the clifftop stone cottage, Rob Nielsen stood with the girl – the one whose magical power trail had led the killer all the way from the underground railway across the city to the painting in the first place.

'Concentrate, Ivy!' Nielsen was barking. 'Listen to the sound of magic all around you. It's speaking to you.'

The girl, Ivy, stood twenty feet away, facing him, a wand in her quivering hand. From inside the invisible bubble, the killer was fascinated to see sparks of pure magic fizzing and jumping at the girl's fingertips.

'I'm *trying*.' The girl spoke through gritted teeth. 'I've

never been any good at using my wand. It's always fighting me. Oh!' One of her hands leaped off the wand, firing a jet of red smoke into the air like a rocket.

Rob Nielsen watched it go, his eyes like dinner plates. 'No,' he said. 'The wand isn't fighting you. *You're* fighting *it*. Hell's teeth, didn't they teach you anything in those White Witch factories?'

Ivy wrapped her hand around the wand again, so that both hands were grasping it, holding it out in front of her. 'We barely had use for wands! For years and years all I ever did was make the same spell from one of Mrs Hester's books!'

Rob shook his head. 'The wand is your friend, Ivy. It should feel like a part of you. Back in the railway tunnel, you picked up my wand and used it to save me from a speeding train, so what's different now?'

'I don't know. I guess I didn't have time to think about it then. I just did it.'

'Exactly. You're thinkin' on things too much. Doctor Vanderbill was a good man. The best. But he got it wrong when he kept you with him and didn't tell me about you. All that thinkin' he had you do, all that energy you spent trying to bury the great power in you, when you should have been embracing it, learning about it, feeling it out . . .'

'Rob! Rob!'

Inside the invisible spy bubble, Double Eight's face turned and looked out across the hillside, where Joe Littlefoot was galloping towards them.

'Rob!' Joe was running at such speed his foot caught on a rock and he fell, rolling three or four times, and then immediately got up and kept on.

Rob stared at him, agog. 'I've a bone to pick with you, boy! Sneaking off the way you did without permission!'

Joe reached him at last, but before he could speak he had to lean over and try to catch his breath. 'Sorry . . . ran all . . . the way from . . . the meat . . . packing . . . district . . .'

'The what?'

'Meatpacking district. I went into the sewers today, Rob. Sorry I snuck off, but I figured if anyone might know where to find the king's secret railway line, it would be the toshers and I'd be better off going alone. And boy, did they come through.'

Rob took another step towards Joe. 'What are you saying?'

Joe sucked in more air, smiled and nodded. 'I found it, Rob. I found the entrance to the tunnels. We're going to snatch us a king!'

It was almost dark by the time the killer finished listening. There had been much to take in, and it had all been most interesting.

From somewhere in the surrounding gloom came a muffled moan, and the sound of someone struggling against bindings. The killer turned around, burning evening light falling upon half of Double Eight's face. 'Shut up.'

The moaning and straining stopped.

Double Eight's face remained stony, but a great excitement was swirling in the murderous mind. A plan was forming. Without knowing it, Rob Nielsen had presented a golden opportunity.

As this new scheme blossomed in the killer's mind, it became clear that Nielsen's plot to kidnap the king during the Evernight celebration could not be allowed to happen. No. It was vital that the king be present to witness what the killer had in store. Rob Nielsen's interfering would have to be taken care of. But that would be easy, wouldn't it? Going by the wanted posters all over the city, the secret police would be very interested in where Nielsen and his friends were going to be tonight. So long as the girl, Ivy, remained unharmed.

Her magical power was awesome.

She was the key.

By the dying light, the smile on Double Eight's face widened. The killer sat down and wrote a short message on a sheet of witch paper, then tapped the paper with a wand and watched it fold into a bird and fly away.

That took care of one thing.

Now there was something else. One other loose end to tie up.

The killer was hungry, and it was feeding time.

Karl Younger stood on the ramparts of the Red Fortress, looking out across the sweeping view of the city. Beneath him, at the foot of the cliff on which the fortress was built, an army of organisers was putting the finishing touches to the preparations in Fortress Park. Many enormous tents had been pitched and filled with row upon row of long tables for the feast. Musical rehearsals played out, sending the distant sound of violin music out across the still park. The smell of cooking meat and curried vegetables drifted in the warm evening air, and the setting sun lit the surface of the lake on fire.

Tomorrow, hundreds of thousands of people would fill the park. A sea of beating hearts. The bearded Hag would be among them, Younger was sure of that. And with him would be the runaway. Younger clenched his fists. His blood boiled at the thought of them escaping him again. He would not let that happen. *Could* not.

A blazing flicker caught his eye, far off over the spires and rooftops. He watched it closely, his fingers hovering over his wand handle, ready to draw it from the holster on his hip. Witch paper birds were common, but he was on edge. He imagined that this one was meant for him, sent from the Hag, loaded with poison or an explosive spell.

He narrowed his eyes, tilting his head, following the paper bird as it flew out over Fortress Park, up towards the ramparts.

It *was* coming to him.

His fingers closed around his wand.

The bird landed on the rampart wall, ten feet from him. Younger drew his wand, held it out, aimed . . .

Before he could pull the trigger, the paper bird unfolded. Still ready to fire, Younger edged towards it, growing in confidence as he drew nearer and nearer and still nothing happened. By the time he was close enough to read the message, his trigger finger was not quite so ready to twitch.

Younger read the message on the paper. It was, as he had suspected, addressed to him. But it was not from the bearded Hag, or the runaway White Witch – at least that's how it seemed. The message was neatly written and claimed to be 'From a concerned citizen' who'd seen the wanted posters up all over Lake End. The author of the note claimed to have discovered the wanted Hag (who had shaved off his hair and beard to avoid detection) and overheard him making terrible plans in a pub the previous night.

Younger read it again. And again. And once more.

It could be a trap, of course. Or a prank. In fact, it almost certainly was.

But if it wasn't . . .

If it proved to be legitimate, this message went on to tell him exactly where he could find the bearded Hag and when. In spite of his doubts, Karl Younger smiled. He pulled the trigger of his wand, incinerated the paper, and watched its cinders float and spin out into the humid, darkening evening.

Maybe, just maybe, the hunt was back on track.

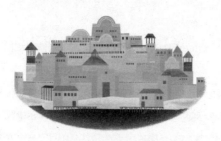

THE GHOST

In a pub near the docks a little later, the sound of an out-of-tune guitar and the laughter and cheer of drunken revellers washed over Sam Hushby. He had spent most of his day off here and was now quite drunk, but even in his inebriated state, the merriment all around him seemed foreign and cold. How could anyone be happy? How could people just go about their lives when poor Annalise's body was buried somewhere in the Veil Forest, and nobody was doing anything to catch the real killer?

Except maybe those Westerly Witches . . .

The tavern was filled with smoke and laughter and music; a man sat in the corner playing guitar, singing songs Sam vaguely recognised. Sam ordered another beer, drank it in three gulps. After that, he'd finally had enough.

Head spinning, he staggered out of the bar and across the street, feeling fuzzy and warm. As his drunken hands fumbled to free his horse from the hitch post, he realised that he was still thinking about Annalise. No amount of drink could take away the guilt, the feeling he'd let her down, that he should have done more.

After a few attempts he finally managed to climb into the saddle and turn his horse to face the right way. It was just as he was set to spur his mare into movement that he saw her.

She rode right by him on a black horse with a white mane, and as she passed him, she gave him a smile, tipped her hat and rode on.

Sam blinked. His heart was beating so fast he thought it might punch through his ribs. He watched her up the street, stunned.

'Annalise?'

He was drunk, he knew that, but not drunk enough that his eyes would deceive him so badly. It had been her. He was sure of it. 'Annalise!' He urged his horse on, and she galloped through the warm night air so fast he felt like he was flying. 'Annalise! Wait!'

She was moving at blazing speed, racing like a ghost through the city, low in the saddle, her coat tails flapping behind her. Sam did his best to keep up. 'C'mon, girl!' he told his horse as they wound and weaved between the alleyways and courts and narrow back streets, until, at last, he turned a corner to an abandoned, dead-end alley and there she was, at the other end of the alleyway, staring back at him.

'Annalise? Is that really you?' He dismounted, walked

towards her, staring up with tear-filled wonder. Her beautiful, stern face remained passive, expressionless.

'I've been watching you, Sam,' she said. 'You've been talking about me.'

Sam wasn't taking in anything she said. He stood by her horse, staring up with a dopey, puzzled expression. 'How? I saw . . . I saw you lying in the forest. That boy killed you!'

Annalise climbed down from her horse and stood face to face with him. It seemed they were a million miles from anywhere.

Sam was crying, sobbing and sniffing. 'They wouldn't believe me when I told them what happened. They made me go along with their story, that you ran away. I'm sorry. I should . . . should've done more to help . . .'

She reached up, took his face in one of her soft hands.

'It's going to be all right,' she told him.

And as he looked at her, her face changed, became doughy and soft and underdone.

Sam Hushby staggered back, his eyes huge with terror, and screamed.

Nobody heard him, and it was the last thing he ever did.

Follow the Trail

The night was warm and clear. Lara lay by the campfire, staring up at the immense southern sky, picking out scattered diamond constellations and breathing the sweet scent of the blooming flowers in the meadow beyond the camp.

Ginny was asleep on the other side of the fire, flat on her back with her mouth hanging open and a thread of drool hanging from her cheek. It was all very peaceful.

But the quiet didn't last for long.

A fizzing sound made Lara sit up, glance towards the fire. She stood, crept forward towards Ginny's cauldron, where thick yellow smoke drifted out over the camp in lazy curls from the locator spell within.

Fffffzzzzzzztt!

A blaze of yellow shot up into the sky like a rocket, making Lara jump back.

'Ginny! Ginny, wake up!'

'Whaa? Whassup?'

'The spell. It's doing something. Get up. Get UP!'

Ginny's eyes shot open. She bounced up like a spring and waddled around to Lara's side, peering into the cauldron with a mixture of wonder and shock. 'I think it's working,' she said, fetching her wand from her coat in such a hurry it got tangled up. 'Blasted thing!' Next she took a spell bottle, unstoppered it, and dipped it into the cauldron, her hand and forearm disappearing into the spell smoke. When she brought the bottle out, it was filled with swirling spell mist. Ginny's nimble, expert fingers placed the stopper back in the bottle, and she held it up.

'What happens now?' Lara whispered. The buttercup-yellow magic twining in the tiny bottle was bewitching.

'We put it in a wand and try it,' said Ginny. 'What else?'

'Is it safe?'

'I dunno. The others I tried blew up.'

'Blew up?'

'Not badly. Just singed my eyebrows a bit. Step back, girl. That's it.'

Lara fell back to the other side of the fire as Ginny loaded the spell bottle into the revolver chamber of her wand. She spun the revolver so that the spell was loaded and live, and it blazed like the midday sun. Ginny's eyes met Lara's, then went slowly back to the wand.

She pulled the trigger.

A ribbon of spell light jumped from the wand tip to the ground, swirled and warped and became a glowing yellow rat. The spell rat sat still, cleaned itself a little. Then its nose began to twitch, and it lowered its head to the ground and began to madly sniff about.

'Has this ever happened before?' Lara asked, transfixed.

'No. I think it's working.'

The spell rat raised its head, sniffing at the night air. It leaped up suddenly, leaped so high its eyes were level with Lara's, before landing softly, turning a few circles and scrabbling to Ginny. It ran around and around her feet, and then back the way it had come, stopping, looking back at them, whiskers twitching.

'Looks like it wants us to follow,' said Lara.

Ginny punched the air triumphantly. 'It must've picked up the reaper spell, Lara. It works! Oh, I'm good. Didn't I tell you I was good!'

'And this means Double Eight has killed someone else?' Lara asked, dread forming a heavy weight in her belly.

Ginny's expression hardened as her thoughts turned from her successful spell to the terrible act that must have triggered it. 'Yes, you're right. That's exactly what it means.'

Lara looked into the old Witch's eyes and knew there was no use in lying. 'I don't know if I'm ready for this, Ginny. Ready to face him. I don't know if I can.'

Ginny raised her eyebrows. 'Oh? And just how many more murders would you like to see happen, Lara?'

'What? None! Why would you even say that?'

'Because,' said Ginny, 'if you don't do everything in

your power to stop him – *everything* – you might as well put up a white flag and give him permission to go and kill as many people as he fancies. I'm not saying that facing down your friend isn't goin' to be hard. Course it is. But a Witch don't think about easy or hard. A Witch thinks about what's right. Ask yourself, what's the right thing to do?'

Lara stared into Ginny's eyes, so alive with fire and fight, and she knew what was right.

THE SLAUGHTERHOUSE

At precisely the moment Ginny's locator spell had begun to work, Joe Littlefoot was leading Rob Nielsen and Ivy Robin through the sewers beneath Lake End several miles away.

After trading away his dragon-breath lamp, Joe had to rely on the light from Rob's wand to guide him. He kept the pace slow and deliberate. If this had been King's Haven, it would have been a different matter, of course. But Lake End was strange to him, and even though he felt at home in the sewers, he did not know their hidden tricks and dangers, so he would treat the tunnels with the respect they deserved.

The sound of Rob's dry heaving every few minutes did not help Joe's concentration. 'It's not *that* bad,' he mumbled.

Rob's face had taken on a sickly greenish pallor. His eyes were red and watery from gagging, and he looked thoroughly miserable. 'Not that bad?' he said. 'We're walking in . . .'

'I think it's great,' said Ivy, her big eyes staring all about at these new surroundings.

Rob shot her a look sharp enough to pop a balloon. 'Don't make me regret bringing you along.'

'You couldn't come without me this time,' she said, waving his grumpiness away. 'I saved your bacon back in the underground railway. I'm your good luck charm.'

In spite of the tense situation, Joe smiled. The change in Ivy these past couple of days, since she'd followed Joe and Rob and, as she had put it, 'saved their bacon' was quite remarkable. It seemed to Joe that Ivy was, after a long struggle, perhaps beginning to come to terms with who she was, and what she was. Still, she was only at the beginning of her journey, and though accepting her magic had undoubtedly made her more stable, there were still moments, like now, where excitement or anger or fear would take over and those sparks would jump at her fingertips.

'Easy, Ivy,' he said. 'How about you keep that magic until we really need it?'

Ivy looked at her fingers, closed her hands, and the sparks died away. 'Sorry. Getting a bit nervous.'

'Me too,' said Joe. 'But there isn't long to wait now.'

He was right, of course. After a few more twists and turns, they arrived in the narrow sewer Joe had been aiming for. The stream gurgled at their feet, foaming a little, and Rob's spell light shimmered on the surface of the water and cast long shadows on the red rock walls.

'That's it,' said Joe, indicating a metal ladder that led up to the surface. 'Through the manhole cover up there we'll find the courtyard of the old slaughterhouse I told you about. When the tosher brought me here I didn't dare go up for a look myself because she said it's usually guarded by secret police.'

'Wise move,' said Rob. 'And the entrance to the king's railway tunnel is somewhere in the slaughterhouse?'

'Yeah. That's what she said. She was tellin' the truth, Rob. I'm sure of it.'

'All right.' Rob bit his bottom lip. His beard was beginning to grow back. 'We'll do exactly as we planned. I'll go up first and take care of the guards. Joe, once I'm up above ground, shut the cover and stay quiet.' He began to climb the ladder, then paused and looked over his shoulder. 'And what are you going to do, Ivy?'

She sighed. 'Stay here with Joe and wait for you to come get us.'

'And?'

Ivy rolled her eyes. 'Not blow anything up.'

Rob narrowed his eyes. 'Good.'

Rob climbed the ladder into the shaft leading to the surface; it was a tight space, especially for a man his size, and by the time he reached the cover he was barely able to raise his arms. He managed it, though, and in the darkened courtyard of the abandoned slaughterhouse, the manhole cover popped quietly out of place. Rob snuck his head out into the night, looked all about, then pulled himself out of the drain. The cobbled courtyard was wide and square, with a high-walled perimeter and a heavy set of metal gates. In the centre of the courtyard stood a large red stone building with three chimneys reaching up towards the sky. There were a number of smaller outbuildings too, and various types of carts and carriages parked up on the cobbles. Rob used these for cover as he began to move about, checking for security.

He found the first guard in one of the outbuildings, an abandoned stable.

As the guard walked the length of the place, checking each of the stalls, Rob nipped silently in behind him, snuck up and grabbed him, twisting his arm so that he dropped his wand, then clamping a huge hand over the guard's mouth, pulling him close and pressing the tip of his own wand to his throat.

The guard struggled for a moment, then seemed to realise Rob was so strong that it was pointless.

'That's it,' said Rob. 'Be smart. If you cooperate, you'll come out of this just fine. I know you're not the only guard here, so tell me: how many more are there in the courtyard? Nod your head to let me know the number.'

The guard nodded four times.

'Good. Now, how about inside the old slaughterhouse?'

Just one nod this time.

'And once I get into the railway tunnel? Will I find any trouble down there?'

The guard shook his head. Rob clamped his hand tighter over the man's mouth, jabbed the tip of his wand into his neck. 'You wouldn't be lyin', would you?'

The guard shook his head madly.

'All right,' said Rob in a gentle voice. 'All right, then.' He pulled the trigger on his wand. A spell ribbon burst out, wrapped around the guard's head and entered his right ear. Moments later, he became a dead weight in Rob's arms. Rob carried him to one of the horse stalls and lay him on the floor, sprawled and breathing the long, rhythmical breaths of someone who is in a deep, deep sleep.

He found the second guard walking the perimeter of the main building. Darting behind a cart piled with barrels, Rob waited for the guard to pass, and then snuck up behind him and despatched him in the same manner as the first.

The next two were a little trickier. Rob explored the perimeter and discovered a man and a woman standing together at what he assumed must be the front entrance to the slaughterhouse. He spun the revolver of his wand, loading another spell, pointed the wand towards the roof and fired. A rope of green light came lashing out, anchored onto the top edge of the building, and Rob used it to pull himself up the wall and onto the roof. From there he crept silently around to a spot directly over the remaining two outer guards.

'Can't believe we're missing the feast tomorrow to keep an eye on this place,' the man was saying. 'There's going to be curried goat. I *love* curried goat.'

Rob noted that both guards had their wands holstered. That was good.

'I'm glad of it,' the woman replied. 'Just imagine how busy Fortress Park is going to be. All those stinking little kids running around. I hate kids.' She shuddered. 'You're better off here, mate.'

Rob loaded a new sleeping spell, spun the revolver again. He aimed for the woman and pulled the trigger. It was over in just a few seconds. First, the sleeping spell whip-cracked out, hitting the woman, and she dropped to the ground.

'Here,' said the man, crouching over her. 'You all right?'

Rob dropped down from the roof and landed behind the guard. The guard spun around, his eyes popping wide when he saw Rob. He reached for his wand but Rob fired again, putting the man down.

'One to go,' he told himself. 'Nice and easy, Rob.'

He opened the door, walked through and found himself in a long, bare corridor lined with more doors, and lit sparingly with a few dragon-breath lamps. Rob moved swiftly and quietly from door to door, opening each one with great care, making sure each room was clear. Mostly they were old offices, scattered with yellowing sheets of newspaper. All were clear. It wasn't until Rob reached the end of the corridor and entered a huge chamber that he found the remaining guard.

The space was completely bare, with no windows, and lamps dotted around the wall in filthy, rusting sconces. Many large hooks hung from the high ceiling on thick chains. The coppery smell of blood lingered, and there were dark stains on the ground from long ago.

'Hey,' said the guard, spotting Rob, reaching for his wand. 'HEY!'

Rob spun the revolver of his wand again, aimed, fired.

The great grizzly bear came into being before him, made of spell light. He whipped his wand out towards the guard, who had drawn his own wand. The bear charged the guard, soaking up the desperate spells he shot at it, pounced, and pinned him to the ground, sending his wand spinning away to the shadows.

Rob approached calmly. The guard was struggling under the tremendous weight of the spell bear, gasping and swearing. Its enormous muzzle was right in his face, its lips drawn back over its teeth.

'None of your friends are coming to save you, if that's what you're hoping,' Rob said, his finger still squeezing the trigger of his wand, making sure the spell kept flowing. 'They're all taking a nap – and they won't wake up till this time tomorrow night.' He crouched down, staring into the furious, frightened eyes of the guard. 'Here's how it's going to work, pal. You've got one minute to tell me how to get into the hidden railway tunnel. If that minute goes by and you haven't spilled the beans, I'll let my friend here take over.' He nodded to the spell bear, and it expelled a low, rumbling growl. 'But be warned. He ain't as friendly as me.'

Ambush

'What's taking him so long?'

Joe and Ivy were waiting down in the sewer, Joe on the ladder directly beneath the manhole cover, and Ivy below him. Ivy was becoming agitated.

'Try to relax,' said Joe, glancing down at her, his eyes drawn to the sparks of magic fizzing between her fingertips. 'Rob knows what he's doing.'

Tap tap tap.

'What was that? Is it him?'

'*Sssh.* Let me check!'

Joe pushed upwards against the heavy metal cover, inching it out of place. Then the weight was gone from it, and it slid sideways, and Rob's face appeared in the hole, looking down at them with a serious expression.

'You're all right!' said Ivy.

'Course I am. I've taken care of the guards, so the way is clear.'

'You found the tunnel?' said Joe.

Rob offered a hand, pulling him effortlessly out into the warm night. He did the same with Ivy. 'One of the guards was kind enough to show me the way before he went for a beauty sleep,' he said. 'Come on.'

Rob led them across the courtyard, into the main building, and along to the large, open chamber.

'I don't like this place,' said Ivy, shivering.

'Me neither,' said Joe, casting wary glances around, trying not to look too long at the faded blood stains on the slaughterhouse floor, almost tripping on the sleeping guard. 'Where's the tunnel, Rob?'

Rob smiled. He looked up at the many large metal hooks hanging from the ceiling on their thick chains, and he began counting. 'Six along, twelve down . . . there we go. This one.' Reaching up, Rob grabbed one of the hooks, pulled it, and a deep rumble echoed around the chamber as part of the stone floor slid away, revealing a large, rectangular opening.

Ivy nodded at it. 'Down there?'

'Down there,' said Rob.

There were steps in the opening. Rob went first, his light spell showing the way. The steps were steep and roughly cut; they had to tread carefully, but even then it didn't take long to arrive at the foot and come out on a small railway platform lit by bright dragon-breath lamps. A silver engine sat on the line, gleaming in the lamplight. Behind it were three carriages: one was a plush-looking passenger carriage, while the other two looked to be for cargo.

'Are we going to take the train?' asked Ivy in a hushed voice.

Rob looked at her as if she'd just asked if the moon was made of fruit cake. 'While we're at it,' he said, 'why don't we announce our arrival at the fortress with a fanfare of trumpets, eh? Course we ain't takin' the train. Come on.'

He dropped down from the platform onto the tracks, and Joe suddenly flashed back to their near miss in another rail tunnel not too far away. His heart was banging, but he tried to stay calm as Ivy hopped down too, and together the three of them walked into the mouth of the waiting tunnel.

'Let's go over it again.' Rob was at the front of the group, leading the way along the track by the light of his wand.

'We've already been over it five times,' said Joe.

'And we still have half an hour's walk ahead of us,' said Rob. 'So, we can go over it another five. You can never be too prepared, Joe Littlefoot. Tell me, what are we going to do when we arrive at the platform under the Red Fortress?'

'Ivy and me are going to hang back and find somewhere safe to hide,' said Joe, trying to mask his exasperation.

'And you're going to clear the way like you did back at the slaughterhouse,' Ivy added.

'Very good. What then?'

Joe opened his mouth to answer, but Rob became still, held up a finger. 'Did you hear something?'

Joe and Ivy shook their heads.

Joe peered along the tunnel, his sharp ears suddenly hyper alert. 'Wait. Maybe I *do* hear . . .'

From somewhere up ahead, beyond the light of Rob's spell, a man's voice yelled, '*Now!*'

A wall of fire burst to sudden, violent life, encircling Joe, Rob and Ivy with flames ten feet high.

'Hell's teeth!' Rob drew his wand, instructing Ivy to do the same. 'Get down, Joe. Get out of the way.'

Joe was shielding his eyes from the light and heat of the flames. His insides twisted with panic. 'What's happening? Rob?'

But Rob's eyes were fixed on the fiery wall, and Joe suddenly saw why. Through the leaping flames, he caught glimpses of figures dressed in long black coats, a dozen of them. Secret police. They came forward, walking through the flames as if they were nothing, wands drawn, spells blazing.

Only one of them wore a hat, and he came closer than the others, and stood staring at Rob, and at Ivy, from beneath the wide brim.

'Well, well,' he said, his voice smooth and deep and echoing. 'Here we are, together at last.'

'It's him!' Ivy shouted. 'It's Karl Younger!' Her face became tortured, furious. 'You killed the doctor!'

'And now I'm going to finish the job I started,' said Younger.

Rob fired the first spell, a blaze of fiery magic that hit one of the surrounding agents in the chest, sending him flying away through the air to smash against the tunnel wall. After that, it seemed to Joe that the whole world had turned to flashes of light and screams and yells.

Rob and Ivy stood back-to-back. Rob fired his wand, and from the tip came a great grizzly bear. The grizzly, made of spell light, reared back, soaking up incoming spells, and then charged towards Younger.

Younger remained calm, even as the bear came within twenty feet, and fifteen, and ten . . .

He reloaded his own wand, pulled the trigger, and from the wand tip came an enormous sabre-toothed big cat, as large as Rob's bear. When the two spells crashed together, the sound was a clap of thunder, and the force of the magic gave off a powerful blast, knocking those closest to the ground.

Rob and Younger stood locked in battle, moving towards each other slowly, their wand arms shaking with effort as they each tried to gain the upper hand, and all the while magic was streaking overhead.

Nearby, Ivy dived out of the path of a spell light arrow, and it ricocheted off the wall, hit the roof and brought huge chunks of rock raining down. Seizing his chance, Joe darted behind one of the rocks for cover, while Ivy crouched behind another. In the centre of tunnel, Rob and Younger were very close to each other, their great spells battling.

But it was not a fair fight. The remaining agents had closed in around them, wands raised.

'Leave him!' yelled Younger. 'He's mine!'

Ivy peered over her rock, caught Joe's eye, and from his hiding place Joe stared back at her, his wide, desperate eyes begging her to do something.

Ivy, it seemed, decided that she could not just give up, could not stand by and watch Rob outnumbered. She came out from her sheltering place and smiled at Joe with tears in her eyes. Then, unarmed, she called out, 'Oi! Over here!'

'The girl!' Younger yelled. 'Get the girl!'

As one, the agents turned to face Ivy, distorted in the searing heat of Rob and Younger's duelling spells. They raised their wands and fired.

'Ivy!' yelled Joe.

Ten spells tore through the night towards her, screeching like firework rockets.

Ivy did not dive out of the way, or duck, or try in any way to avoid being hit.

Instead, she held up a hand.

When she opened her eyes, the converging spells were frozen in the air a few feet from her face, sparking and fizzing. Ivy closed her hand, watching as the spells did her bidding, joined together, growing. Trembling with effort, she raised her hand higher. The combined spells flew up into the air, and everyone watched, even Rob and Younger, as the magic came hurtling down and hit the tunnel floor like a comet. The ground trembled, cracking open, and the railway tracks buckled and bent. A ring of earth fell away beneath the feet of the agents, swallowing them up, casting them into an abyss.

Ivy fell to her knees, drained, exhausted.

Suddenly it was Younger who was outnumbered. His eyes grew wild, filled with rage. Still struggling against Rob, their spells roaring and clashing again and again, Younger backed away, but his feet found the edge of the ring where the earth had crumbled away around him. Realising that he was trapped on a circular island, he looked from Rob to Ivy, and then Joe.

What happened next unfolded almost in slow motion.

Younger swung around, pointed his wand at Joe, and his great sabre-toothed cat spell broke away from the fight, leaped over the fissure and bounded towards Joe.

'Joe!' Rob yelled.

But Joe was rooted to the spot. He watched the spell cat come at him, and the sight of it, both terrifying and beautiful, bewitched him.

Across the tunnel Rob tossed his wand from one hand to the other, spun, and sent his own spell after Younger's. The grizzly bear thundered across the ground, jumping to intercept the big cat just as it was about to hit Joe . . .

Joe flinched.

The big cat turned to smoke and vanished.

The grizzly went crashing and rolling along the ground.

And suddenly Joe realised what was happening. Younger had used him as a distraction. He spun around. 'Rob! Behind you!'

But it was too late. Younger's tactic had worked. He had already pointed his wand at Rob, who looked around in time to see him pull the trigger. A whip of angry red light lashed out from the tip of the wand, the end of it shaped like a scorpion's sting.

It struck Rob in the heart.

He fell, and the sound his body made when it hit the ground was sickening and final.

'Rob! No!' Joe ran to the edge of the ring, forgetting the danger all around. 'Rob, get up. Please get up!'

'He's not going to get up,' said Younger, his wand hand down by his side. He picked up his hat and placed it back on his head. 'Now it's time to finish the job.' Reaching into the pockets of his long coat, he brought out another spell, loaded it into his wand, and aimed at Ivy. 'When are you going to realise that you can't get away from me?' he asked.

Ivy was still on her knees, staring at the ground. She looked defeated.

'Everywhere you go,' Younger went on, 'people die. Doctor Vanderbill. The poor people who lived on his street. Now this Hag. How many more, Ivy? How many more innocents are you willing to see die for you? Let me finish it. Let me put you out of your misery.'

'Don't say his name.' Slowly, Ivy looked up, and when

258

she did, she was not crying any more. Her eyes seemed to burn with hatred. She struggled to her feet. 'How dare you say Doctor Vanderbill's name, after what you did to him!'

Younger's confident look faltered. 'Don't do anything rash. You're exhausted. You'll only prolong the inevitable. What's this—Wait! No!'

His feet left the ground, and his body grew rigid as he floated. Ivy walked towards him, her hand raised, magic flowing from her. Her eyes welled and spilled over. She clenched her fists. The ball of molten anger was white hot in her gut, and the heat of it was spreading through her, in her blood, her fingertips and toes, behind her eyes.

'Doctor Vanderbill didn't die because of me. Rob didn't die because of me. They died because of hatred. They died because people like *you* will never accept that people like me should be free.' Her hand was shaking, and she closed it slightly, imagining the air leaving Younger's lungs. He gasped, and gurgled, and reached out desperately.

There was a flash, bright and burning as lightning. Something hit Ivy on the back, and she fell to the tracks, releasing Younger, who dropped like a sack of coal, unconscious.

Dazzled by the light, Joe rubbed at his eyes, trying to see in the dark. 'Ivy! What was that? You all right?'

No answer came.

Something hit Joe hard on the back of the head. The pain was hot and stabbing, and he crumpled, trying to blink away the patterns that were blooming in his vision. Among those shifting shapes something appeared, a blurry face that was familiar . . . The face came closer. Joe squeezed his eyes tightly shut, opened them again, and saw a little better.

'Double Eight?'

Another shape came into his vision. Double Eight raised his foot and Joe was staring at the sole of his boot. Then it came crashing down on Joe's face, and with a sickening crack, everything was gone.

THE CHASE

In a back alley near the docklands, Lara leaned over the body of Sam Hushby and closed his eyes. 'Poor Sam. I know we only met him a couple of times, but he seemed to me like a good man.'

'He wanted justice for Annalise,' said Ginny, her head bowed. 'And he was willing to risk his own life to get it. This has to stop.'

It hurt Lara to look at Sam. His face had been contorted into a grimace of fear and pain, and there was a large, open wound on his neck. 'Is that where the killer . . . sucked out his life force?'

Ginny's eyes met hers. 'Yes. And we know the killer has a name now, don't we? This was Double Eight. Say it.'

Lara was shaking, her eyes brimming. 'It was Double Eight,' she repeated. Every word was a needle pushed into her heart. 'He did this to Sam. But why?'

Ginny nodded. 'When we bring him in you can ask him yourself.'

The locator spell rat was still sniffing here and there, and presently it squeaked and jumped up again, the way it had done back in camp when it first picked up the trail. It scurried to Ginny, ran between her feet, and then shot back down the alleyway towards the main streets.

'It's still on the trail,' said Ginny. 'The echo of the spell is sticking to Double Eight like a shadow. But it'll fade, so we must follow as quick as we can before he slithers back into the shadows.'

The spell rat scampered and twitched out of the alleyway, guiding them through a warren of dockland streets, between warehouses and factories. The night was thick with the smells of the fish markets and spice boats, alive with the sounds of the metalworks and shipyards. The rat led them at last to a high perimeter wall, and there it stopped, twitched its nose, looked back at Ginny and Lara, and finally took off through the wall.

Ginny and Lara stared at one another. Lara's heart thrummed, and even in the warm southern night her body became cold with dread. They checked all around the perimeter wall.

'Only one gate in and out,' she whispered. 'And we can hardly walk right through the front door when we don't know what's waiting. We'll have to go over. Here.' She rummaged in that many-pocketed coat of hers, produced two bottles filled with green spells and handed one to Lara.

'What is it?'

'Just watch me.' Ginny loaded her own spell, aimed, fired, and a rope of spell light shot out and attached itself to the top of the wall. Holding her wand tight in both hands, Ginny approached and, with the spell rope supporting her, walked up the wall, stopping at the top. 'Your turn,' she said, motioning for Lara to follow. 'Make sure you keep squeezing the trigger even when you get to the top.'

Lara nodded. She aimed her wand, her hand trembling, and pulled the trigger. The spell rope exploded up and anchored to a spot near Ginny's feet. Lara approached the wall, put one foot onto the stone, pushed up. She felt the spell rope take her weight immediately. She felt as if she weighed no more than a field mouse, and she found it easy to climb. Soon she stood beside Ginny, staring down at a cobbled courtyard dotted with coaches and outbuildings. In the centre of the courtyard stood a red stone building with three tall chimneys. It seemed the place was deserted.

Ginny nodded and went first, the spell holding her steady as she walked backwards down the other side of the wall to the cobbles. Lara came next. When she was down, Ginny led her to the nearest outbuilding, which turned out to be an abandoned stable. As Ginny checked the stalls, Lara was struck once again by how quick and quiet the older Witch was. Suddenly she stopped, stood stock-still and aimed her wand into one of the stalls. Then she seemed to relax. 'Lara. C'mere.'

Lara crept forward, looked in the horse stall. A man lay sprawled on the floor. She gasped. 'Is he dead?'

'No.' Ginny was crouching over him. 'Fast asleep, is all.' She gave his face a few slaps. 'Looks like someone's used a sleeping spell on him.' She spun the revolver of her wand, pulled the trigger, and the locator spell rat appeared again. It sniffed around the sleeping guard for a moment, lost interest, and left the stable for the courtyard. It scurried this way and that, and then popcorned up into the air and bolted off. 'It's got something!' said Ginny.

Halfway across the courtyard, Lara stopped. 'Ginny, look.'

'What, girl?'

'Here,' said Lara, crouching beside a circular hole in the ground. 'Someone's opened this sewer entrance.' She listened, heard the familiar, tempting sound of a sewer stream. 'I wonder if the killer . . . if Double Eight went into the sewers?'

Ginny shook her head. 'The rat says otherwise. Let's see where he takes us.'

As it turned out, the locator spell led them right to the front door of the largest building, where they discovered another two sleeping guards, a man and a woman.

'I don't get it,' Lara said. 'Why didn't he just kill them?'

The rat led them through the open door and along a lamplit corridor to a large chamber with dark stains on the floor and many metal hooks hanging from the ceiling on thick chains.

'Looks like it was a slaughterhouse,' said Ginny. 'And look here – another one of our sleeping beauties.'

The locator spell rat scurried over the sleeping man and flashed across the floor to a rectangular opening. It paused for a moment, sniffed at the air, and then disappeared into the gap. The opening revealed a steep stairway; Lara used a light spell to show the way as they descended the uneven stone steps until they found an underground platform, where an impressive silver engine and three carriages were stationed.

The spell rat sniffed again at the ground, and the air, and then sat up and stared back at Ginny. 'It's beginning to lose the trace,' she said. 'It must be fading.' No sooner had she said that, though, than the rat caught the scent again and went scampering off the platform and into the tunnel. Ginny glanced at Lara. Without a word, they followed.

Lara's light spell forced the darkness back as they moved along the railway tunnel, following the rat, which would stop every now and then and find the scent before dashing onward, the sound of its paws scritch-scratching on the sleepers and the metal track.

It occurred to Lara that she was suddenly much calmer, and she supposed that it must be because she was back underground, where she'd spent so much of her life. She had never been surer of herself than in those days, when she was the best tosher in the city, and she knew every trick and twist and turn of the sewers. It was as if the underground air had flicked a switch inside her, and that old confidence flowed again, even if a big part of her was dreading the moment they caught up to Double Eight.

They had been walking for some time, the spell rat losing the scent more and more, when something came into view at the edges of Lara's spell light, and she took a sharp breath and hurried forward, suddenly forgetting where she was, or why.

'Joe? Joe!'

Her friend was lying on the ground near the tracks, his legs splayed at awkward angles, his arms tangled beneath him. Lara's spell light reflected in a large puddle of dark blood at his head, and she called out. 'Ginny! Ginny, over here!'

Ginny rushed to her, kneeled beside Lara and began to examine poor Joe.

'Is he all right? Ginny? Is he dead?'

'Hell's teeth, let me work, girl. Give me some more light. That's it.'

Lara felt so helpless, so utterly hagging useless, as Ginny worked on Joe. First, she located the nasty gash on the back of his head and applied an ointment that smelled strongly of mint and seemed to stem the flow of blood. Then she gently examined his face; his nose was burst and broken, one of his eyes swollen shut. Ginny brought another bottle out of her coat, opened the lid and held it to Joe's nose. 'Smelling salts.'

Almost at once, Joe's head twitched, and his eyes rolled open. He coughed and spluttered, trying to sit up.

'No,' said Ginny, holding him down. 'No, boy. Stay down for now. You're hurt.'

'Ginny?' His eyes were glassy, rolling all over the place. 'Lara? Lara is that you?'

'It's me, Joe,' Lara smiled through her tears. 'I'm here.'

'Rob's here too!' Joe said. He was breathless, slurring a little. 'Oh . . . Rob! I think he's . . .'

'What happened, Joe?' Lara asked.

But he wasn't listening. He was confused, frightened. 'Ivy! Where's Ivy? Younger was here . . .'

'Younger?' Ginny looked around. 'Karl Younger?'

'It's all right,' said Joe, beginning to sound a little loopy. 'Ivy got him.' He frowned in a dazed sort of way. 'I saw Double Eight.'

Lara leaned in close. 'You did? Here, in this tunnel?'

'Yeah. He hit me. Why'd he do that, Lara?'

Lara's gaze met Ginny's.

'We have to wait, Lara,' said the old Witch. 'Sounds like Rob and Ivy are somewhere nearby, and they could be hurt.'

'We'll lose Double Eight!' said Lara. 'You said yourself the locator spell is fading.' She took a breath. 'Let me go after him.'

Ginny shook her head. 'I can't. Not alone. If anything happened to you, Bernie would never forgive me.'

Lara made a praying motion with her hands. 'Please, Ginny. You said yourself Westerly Witches always try to do what's right. And this is why you brought me here in the first place, isn't it? If anyone can get through to him, it's me. I don't think he'd ever hurt me. I won't be any use to you here – I haven't learned much about healing. We have to try, have to finish this. What if it's our only chance?'

Ginny's old eyes burned into Lara's, and she seemed to be having an internal struggle. Finally, she took her wand, removed the locator spell from the revolver chamber and handed it to Lara. 'Fine.' Lara smiled, made to take the spell, but Ginny grabbed her hand with such a tight grip, it was painful. 'Be careful, Lara. Don't do anything silly, you hear me? I'll follow on as quick as I can.'

Lara gave Ginny a grateful nod, took the spell bottle and loaded it into her own wand. When she pulled the trigger, the spell rat leaped out of her wand and onto the tracks, sniffed at the air for a long time and finally seemed to pick up the trace. It scurried off up the tunnel and Lara followed. As she went, she looked back, and saw that Ginny had cast a light spell and begun to search around the tunnel for Rob and Ivy.

Gathering her remaining courage and strength, Lara turned away, focused on the job at hand and went on alone.

SEEING DOUBLE

Lara hurried as best she could through the rail tunnel, but the faint glow of the spell rat was the only light anywhere at all, and she kept tripping and stumbling on the wooden sleepers.

After a while, she felt a change in the atmosphere, stopped and took a deep breath. There was fresh air coming into the tunnels. She carried on and saw a weak curtain of light cascading from the tunnel roof thirty metres ahead. Part of the tunnel ceiling had been blown away, and the light was coming from the streetlamps above ground.

Moving quickly, she spun the revolver of her wand with shaking fingers, selecting the spell that she and Ginny had used to scale the perimeter wall of the slaughterhouse. She fired the spell at the ragged hole in the tunnel ceiling, and it anchored above ground. Lara grabbed her wand handle tight, jumped up, wrapped her legs around the spell rope and began to climb. Half a minute later, her head broke the surface into the warm night air. The hour was late, and the street abandoned.

A scouting glance about told her she was in a backstreet of the Gothica quarter, with its tall, crooked, statue-covered buildings leaning one upon the other, all sitting in the shadow of nearby Fortress Hill, and the Red Fortress.

Spinning her revolver one more time, Lara loaded the locator spell. The rat leaped out of the wand, landing on the dusty road, but this time it sniffed at the air for a while and then simply turned and stared at Lara, its head tilted to one side.

'Go on,' she said. 'Find it!'

The rat did not move. It scratched and then began to clean itself.

Lara exhaled, looked to the heavens. 'Come on!' She kicked the spell rat gently, and it leaped up into the air and seemed at last to get the message, sniffing in random places until, at last, it picked up a scent and they were off again, winding through alleyways and streets, out into an open square and right to the door of a high clock tower. Then, without warning, the spell rat disappeared with a gentle *POP*, leaving nothing but a few wisps of spell smoke.

Lara stood at the door, staring at the spot where the rat had been. She took the spell bottle from her wand, examined it and saw that it was empty. The spell had run out.

Her mind racing, Lara took a step back, looked up and up and up to the top of the clock tower, which reached so high towards the sky that she thought it might pierce through the heavens.

Somehow, in her gut, she knew that this was it, *this* was the place she'd been looking for.

The heavy door was unbolted. Lara pushed it open, trying to be silent, but it creaked, and the hinges screamed, making her wince. After that, she stood at the foot of a narrow staircase, looking up, breathing deeply. Hands numb with fear, she brought stunning and shield spells out of her coat and loaded them into the revolver chamber beside the climbing spell. Then, when she had steadied her nerves as best she could, Lara started the long ascent.

The muscles in her legs were on fire by the time she reached the summit, but she did not dare stop for fear of losing her nerve. The tower smelled strongly of old wood and oil, and she breathed it deeply as she approached the door beyond the staircase. She found this one unbolted too. In one quick movement she pushed the door open and went through, her wand raised, ready to fire.

She saw no one at first, only a chamber filled with a great many enormous cogs and gears, all clicking and turning at a snail's pace, driving the hands of the clock. There was a frosted glass clockface on every wall, each twice the height of a man, and it was strange to look at the clocks from the wrong side, to see the second hands appear to tick in the wrong direction, as if time itself was running backwards.

Wand clutched tight, raised, ready to fire, Lara moved forward, among the cogs and gears, and found another staircase, this one even smaller and constructed from metal, leading to the belfry. The stairs shook as she climbed them, and she tried not to think about what would happen if they collapsed, sending her falling into the machinery.

Atop the staircase was all shadow, but she saw them at once, lying bundled on the floor next to each other.

'Don't move,' she said, shocked at the strength in her voice. She did not *feel* strong.

Soon she realised that they were not going to move, and she edged towards them. Ivy lay on the left, her eyes shut, breathing deeply.

Beside her was Double Eight.

He appeared to be asleep too. He was filthy, and his hair was matted and wild. A large, weeping wound on his neck had stained his shirt with blood and puss. Lara pointed her wand at him, trembling. 'I'm not falling for that one,' she said, giving him a kick. 'Get up. Get up and face me.'

His eyes cracked open the tiniest bit, and he turned his head slowly to see her. A spark lit in his eyes, and he gave her a weak smile. 'Lara?' His voice was barely there at all. 'Is that really you, or am I dreaming?'

'What do you mean?' Lara's wand was shaking in her hands, the spells blazing in their chambers. 'What are you talking about? Get up!'

His bleary eyes looked past her, and his face flooded with fear. 'Lara . . . Lara, look out . . .'

Still pointing her wand at him, she looked over her shoulder.

Her hands fell to her sides, wand forgotten. Her mouth dropped open.

She could not comprehend what she was seeing.

Double Eight was lying on the floor at her feet. But, impossibly, he was also standing at the top of the staircase, his wand raised, pointing it right at her heart.

Somehow, there were two of him.

Two Double Eights.

The Truth (Again)

'How?' Lara could not move, could not do anything but goggle at the Double Eight standing before her. 'How are there *two* of you?'

He smiled, but there was none of Double Eight's familiar warmth in it. 'Are you really that hagging stupid? Do you actually believe your little friend there could do the things I've done? You think he has the power? The mind for such greatness? No. No, girl, he does not.'

'You mean . . .' Lara felt slow, stupid as she tried to put the pieces together. 'You're not Double Eight?'

'I suppose you could say I'm many people,' said the Double Eight in front of her. 'If you don't like this face, how about I try another?'

What happened next was almost enough to drive Lara's mind over the edge. Double Eight's face *changed*. In moments, it had become soft and doughy, the features losing their shape, the nose disappearing, the eyes becoming black specks. Lara heard a moan of terror and realised that it was coming out of her own mouth. The thing that had been Double Eight continued to change, as if it were clay being shaped by invisible hands. The body swelled and grew. Dark locks of greasy hair sprouted from the soft, misshapen head, and finally the face began to resolve again, to form another set of features, the eyes closer together, the nose bigger and more pointed, the cheeks fuller.

The strength almost left Lara's legs completely. Where Double Eight had been standing, there was now someone else she recognised, someone she'd met, spoken with. Someone who was dead.

'Sam?' she managed to say, her voice tremulous, her eyes spilling over. 'Sam Hushby?'

Sam's face smiled like a knife. 'Or how about this one?'

Again, the face changed, became doughy, bubbled and lost shape, and after a torturous, long moment, Lara was staring at Annalise, Sam's poor ranger partner whose body Lara had seen in the Veil Forest. 'Or this?' said Annalise's beautiful face.

Another change, and this time Double Eight's late mentor, Krispin Sprout, stood across from her.

'Stop,' Lara whispered, her tears pattering down onto the ancient, dusty floorboards. 'Stop it. Who are you really?'

Sprout's face contorted into a sneering, vicious laugh. 'If I tell you that, I'll have to kill you.'

Lara returned his stare. She had never been more frightened, not even when she'd faced the Evernight. It had been so huge a thing, facing up to a primordial force from the era of the Old Gods, that she had not been able to fully understand it at the time. This creature was different. It felt evil and personal and wrong. Being near it felt like a violation, made the hairs on Lara's arms stand up with fear and revulsion.

And still she did not break. 'You're going to kill me anyway, aren't you? So why not tell me? Who are you?'

Sprout's face became very serious, his eyes boring into Lara. 'I've dreamed of this moment, you know. Dreamed of ending you, girl.' He grinned again. 'When I came to Lake End, I had one thing in mind: to kill the king. I never imagined I'd get the chance to kill you too.'

Lara shook her head. 'What? What does any of this have to do with me?'

'It has everything to do with you!' There was madness in Sprout's eyes now, and flecks of drool flew from his wet, purplish lips as he spoke. 'You cost me everything. You and your friends.' He pointed towards Double Eight. 'I couldn't believe my luck when I arrived here in Lake End and found him wandering about. He's quite a clever one, you know. There were a few killings before the ones that brought you here, and Double Eight picked up on them. He was on my trail, he and the first owner of this face.' The thing that had become Krispin Sprout stroked its own face and grinned horribly. 'I set out to kill them both before they began to cause me any real trouble. But after I got rid of Sprout, I had a better idea for Double Eight. I kept him, you see, because I knew that you would come looking for him, Lara Fox.' He spat Lara's name like it was something vile. 'I've used him as bait and he's done his job. Because here you are, right in front of me, like I've dreamed for a year.'

'Why?' Lara was yelling, her pulse pounding in her neck and her temples. 'What's so important about me? Show me who you really are – or are you scared?'

Sprout's face took on a look of disbelief. 'I. Am. Frightened. Of. Nobody.'

'Yeah? Then show me!'

Sprout's face melted. His skin fell away from his bones, became that malleable, waxy putty again, and when the next face formed, Lara knew that this one was not a mask. The strength went from her legs, and she let out an involuntary scream.

The woman standing across the belfry peered at her from beneath a greasy curtain of sparse white hair. Her tiny eyes were sunken, coated in membranous white film, her mouth a nightmarish cavity dotted with broken, rotten teeth. Her skin was waxy, her spine so warped and bent that she almost seemed to be bowing before Lara. But Lara knew that this Witch would never bow to anyone. Until the Evernight, she had been the most powerful White Witch in all the world, had helped the Kingdom invade and take over the entire continent with her army of White Witches.

'Did you miss me?' said Mrs Hester.

Lara could not speak.

'Don't be like that,' said Mrs Hester. Lara could smell the rot from her breath, and it turned her stomach. 'You *did* ask for the truth.' She pointed a twisted finger. 'You and your friends are the ones who did this to me!'

'You almost caused the end of everything!' said Lara, finding her voice.

'I had the Evernight under control!' Mrs Hester screamed. 'If you hadn't got involved, I'd be sitting on the throne right now, instead of the devious demon who has the gall to wear the crown. And what did he do after the Evernight, eh? What did the king do after you almost killed me? Did he send out his armies to look for his greatest servant? No! He forgot about me. He moved on! Nobody *forgets* me. Nobody. After I've killed you tonight, which will be oh so sweet, I'm going to take myself along to the Evernight Feast tomorrow, and I'm going to kill the king in front of his people.' She laughed. It was a dry, dead sound. 'You know, the Gods must really be on my side. For a year, ever since you reduced me to this –' she indicated her failing body – 'I've been working my way south to get to the king, using the reaper spell to build my strength. It hasn't just been Lake End, you know. Oh, no no no. There have been many victims all down the Kingdom, and every one of them is now in *here*.' She tapped her head, let out another dry, wheezing laugh. 'Even with all the lives I took, I still wasn't nearly as strong as I used to be. I knew getting to the king would be difficult. And then . . .' Mrs Hester pointed to Ivy, still out cold on the floor. 'Then the Gods saw fit to give me a gift. Led me right to that young lady.' She shook her head. 'Such power! And I'm going to use it. Maybe I'll show you now, eh? Give you a taste of what you'll be sadly missing tomorrow.'

Lara felt the faintest touch on her heel. Glancing down, she saw that Double Eight had tapped her foot with his own. A signal. Lara thought quick. Her arms were still by her sides, her wand in her right hand. Maybe there was a chance. Double Eight would need to be quick, and Lara could not be confident of that in his current state.

But did she have another choice?

As Mrs Hester pulled the trigger, Lara dropped her wand and dived to the side.

Mrs Hester let out a scream of rage, fired another spell, and another, both coming close enough that Lara felt the blazing heat as they roared past.

On the ground, Double Eight grabbed Lara's wand, aimed, fired. A whiplashing stunning spell erupted across the belfry, hitting the distracted Mrs Hester square in the chest and sending her tumbling over the railing and down into the tangle of machinery in the clock tower.

A terrible scream pierced the hush, and then the sickening sound of cracking bones.

Lara hurried to Double Eight. 'Can you stand?'

'I think so.'

She took his cold hands, helped him up, took back her wand. Then, together, they heaved Ivy off the dusty floor. With Lara taking most of the weight, they managed to carry her downstairs. As they passed, Lara could not bear to look at what was left of Mrs Hester between the clock's cogs and gears.

They had reached the doorway back to the staircase, were almost out, when the laughter began.

Trapped in the machinery, Mrs Hester's head snapped up, her eyes finding Lara and Double Eight. Her mad laughter reached fever pitch as her entire body seemed to become that dough-like material. She made a nightmarish, jerking, sideways movement, squeezing out from between the gears.

Lara and Double Eight were frozen, ice-water in their veins, the hand of fear gripping them tightly. They had no time to react as Mrs Hester, still hellishly crooked and broken, aimed her wand, shooting a lasso of burning light at them. The spell wrapped around them, making them drop Ivy. It brought them together, shoulder to shoulder, lifted them up and smashed them through one of the glass clockfaces. They screamed as they hung in the night, high above the street, knowing that death was coming for them.

Mrs Hester appeared in the broken clockface, a look of pleasure etched on her ancient face. 'I always win,' she said. 'And that's the last thing either of you will ever know.'

Lara reached for her wand, holding it unseen behind

her back. Then Mrs Hester released the trigger. The lasso of light disappeared.

For a moment, Lara and Double Eight seemed to hang impossibly in the air.

And then they fell.

A Final Parting

Just before Mrs Hester had let them drop, Lara had clicked her wand's revolver chamber around, knowing that there was a high chance she'd selected the wrong spell. Even if she hadn't, the chances of this working were slim, to say the least. As Mrs Hester had sent them to their death, Lara and Double Eight had embraced.

'Hold onto me,' she'd whispered. 'Until the end.'

Now they were falling, the wind tearing into their faces, the ground rushing towards them at unimaginable speed.

Lara pulled the trigger in desperation.

The rope spell fired out, anchored into the clock tower wall, and Lara's stomach lurched almost into her brain as they screamed to a halt and swung wildly into the wall, *ooofff*, knocking Lara loopy.

'Lara! Let go!'

But she couldn't. Her finger seemed to be welded to the trigger.

'It's all right, Lara.' That was Double Eight's voice,

echoing and distant. 'You did it. We've only a short way to the ground.'

The words reached her brain at last, and she released the trigger. They fell a short distance, landing hard on the street. There Lara lay for a while, on her back, staring up at the clear night sky, gasping for breath.

Double Eight's face appeared over her.

'Hello,' she said.

He smiled, helped her up and pulled her into a tight hug. 'I can't believe it's you. I can't believe you came for me.'

'Hell's teeth!'

Ginny had finally caught up, and she approached with her wand raised, pointing at Double Eight. 'You let her go, do you hear? Let her go now or I'll—'

'Ginny, it's all right.' Lara said. Her wits were returning, and she knew Double Eight was in serious trouble now. 'He's not the killer.'

'You've had a bang on the head,' said Ginny, her wand pointing right at Double Eight's head.

He raised his hands. 'What do you mean I'm not the killer?'

'See?' said Ginny. 'He's admitting it.'

'No, Ginny, he's not. Mrs Hester is the reaper spell killer.'

Ginny's hand wavered. 'You can't be serious. Mrs Hester is gone.'

'I thought so too,' said Lara. 'We all did. But she's back.

She's been using the reaper spell to gain some of her strength back – and she can wear the faces of all the people she's taken blood from. I saw it for myself, I saw Sprout and Annalise and poor Sam Hushby.'

The disbelief on Ginny's face was becoming something else. 'You *saw* it?'

'I did,' said Lara. 'Mrs Hester came to Lake End to kill the king, but when she came across Double Eight, she recognised him from the day we destroyed the Evernight and she snatched him. She's been planning on using him to get to me. She wants revenge on me for ruining her plans.'

Ginny looked at Double Eight. She lowered her wand.

Double Eight pulled at the neck of his shirt, revealing a scabbed-over bitemark. 'She took my blood too. That must be how she could use my face. I didn't know it was Mrs Hester. The entire time she kept me up there, I only ever saw the other faces she was using. There were *lots*.' He paused, turned to Lara. 'Did *you* think I was the killer?'

Lara did not know what to say. She opened her mouth to answer, but no words came.

Ginny stepped forward. 'Lara was the only one fighting for you. She never truly believed you were a killer, did you, girl?'

Lara blinked away a few tears. Double Eight took her hand, squeezed it. 'Thank you,' he said.

*

The first thing they did was climb back to the top of the tower, but, as Lara suspected, there was no sign of either Mrs Hester or Ivy.

'She's going to use Ivy to somehow get to the king at the feast tomorrow.'

'Ivy's the girl?' asked Double Eight.

Lara nodded. 'Ivy's power is frightening. If Mrs Hester taps into it, who knows what'll happen. There's going to be so many people there, too. We can't let her harm them. Did you find Rob in the tunnel? We could use him right about now!'

Ginny's face fell. 'Lara . . . there's something I need to tell you. Back in the railway tunnel . . .'

The sadness in her voice frightened Lara. 'What is it? Not Joe!'

Ginny looked at the floor. 'No, girl. Not Joe.'

Down in the tunnel, Lara and her friends gathered around Rob Nielsen's fallen body.

Lara thought, as hot, stinging tears rolled down her face, that he looked very peaceful. He could almost be asleep.

But he was not.

Rob Nielsen, a great bear of a man, the toughest Lara had ever known, was gone.

'The first time I ever met him,' she said through the sobs, 'I thought he was going to kill me. I snuck on his boat and found all these spells he was smuggling into King's Haven. I let one of 'em off by mistake – I didn't know I was a Witch then, see – and this spell made a forest grow inside his boat.' A ripple of soft laughter spread around her friends. 'Then I got to know him properly. He faced the Evernight with me, and he was loyal to his friends right to the end.' She kneeled, and looked at his peaceful face, and planted a gentle kiss on his forehead. 'Goodbye, Rob Nielsen. I'll remember you always.'

Lara went to Joe and Double Eight, and the three friends embraced and cried together.

'I'm sorry I ever doubted you,' Joe said to Double Eight. 'I'll never do it again.'

Double Eight nodded, and smiled, and hugged harder than ever.

'It's time,' said Ginny.

They stood back, watching Ginny bring a spell bottle from one of her countless pockets and load it. 'This is one spell I always pray I won't need.' Slowly, with reverence, she approached Rob's body, held out the wand and squeezed the trigger.

A drop of what looked like pure sunlight appeared at the wand tip. It fell, landing on Rob's chest, soaking into his clothes. Then the spot where the spell drop had landed glowed bright, and the golden light spread across Rob's chest, his arms and legs and head, until the light covered every part of him. More than that, Rob was *becoming* the light, burning brighter and brighter until Lara had no choice but to shield her eyes and watch through her fingers. She caught a glimpse of Ginny's face, all light and shadow, saw tears in the old Witch's eyes, and it occurred to her that perhaps Ginny had once, long ago, used this same spell when her own family had died.

Back on the floor, Rob's body, even his clothes and wand and jewellery, turned to spell smoke, and dispersed in elegant, twinkling curls. Lara watched the last of it go, and she fancied she heard Rob's booming laugh somewhere very far away.

Then all was silent.

The Covenant Spell

'Wakey, wakey.'

Ginny waved the smelling salts in front of Karl Younger's nose. His head snapped back, and he opened his eyes wide. When he realised where he was, he began to struggle wildly against the ropes of spell light that bound him tight.

'Fight all you want,' Ginny told him. 'But no matter how good you think you are, I'm better. There ain't no way you'll ever break those bonds, unless I say so.'

He stared up at her, and Lara could see the hatred and disgust in his eyes. 'You'll die for this, Hag. I promise you that.'

Ginny slapped him. Lara blinked, shocked.

'We don't have time to mess about,' said Ginny. 'I want you to listen very carefully to what I'm about to say. After everything you've done, there are a lot of people out there who'd like to get their hands on you. A lot of people who'd like to see you suffer. Now, personally, I won't have any hesitation delivering you to those people. Maybe I'll give you to one of the slum gangs in King's Haven. How does that sound?'

'Oh,' said Joe, 'I know for a fact there's an army of folk who'd like to get at him. The amount of poor innocent marked folk he's slaughtered. They all have families waiting for justice.'

Younger continued to stare, but Lara could see some of the steel was gone from his eyes.

Ginny held something up. Younger's wand. His eyes went to it. Ginny took the wand and snapped it over her knee. Karl Younger threw his head back and cried out in anguish and fury.

'On the other hand,' Ginny said, 'there's a lot going on. If you behave yourself, it would be easy for me to, say, take my eye off you for a moment. I'm sure that's all you'd need to escape.'

Lara, Joe and Double Eight exchanged shocked looks.

'Ginny,' said Lara, 'you're not talking about letting him go, are you?'

'Lara Fox,' said Ginny, her eyes flashing with dangerous fire, 'if you don't hush up, I'll put a binding spell on your tongue. It needs the rest.'

'What do you want?' Younger asked.

Ginny smiled and patted her white cloud of hair. 'I assume you don't know, Director Younger, that Mrs Hester is back. Not only that, but she has taken one of our very dear friends as a hostage – a girl for whom, I am led to believe, you have already caused a great deal of suffering. Mrs Hester intends to use the girl to kill the king during the feast tomorrow.'

Younger's calm expression faltered a little.

'Now, Director Younger, if there is one thing you are best at, it is hunting runaway Witches. I will give you credit where it is due. So, I want you to help me and my friends find Mrs Hester and stop whatever she has planned.'

Younger looked puzzled. 'You want to *save* the king?'

'No, Director Younger. We want to save our friend. As for the king? His days are numbered, and he knows it. His people are rising up against him. The whisper of revolution is in the air all over the Kingdom, and when it arrives, I think Westerly Witch will help drive him from power.' She smiled. 'So, what will it be? Will you help us and live? Or refuse and answer to the people whose lives you have ruined?'

The last of the fire went out of Karl Younger's eyes. His chin fell onto his chest. 'Fine. I'll do what you want.'

Lara could not keep quiet any longer. 'Ginny, no! We can't trust him. He'll double cross us the moment we're out in the open!'

Ginny rubbed her eyes wearily. 'It may shock you to know, Larabelle Fox, that I have done this sort of thing before. Now, where did I put that bottle?' Her hands began to search the lining of her coat again, feeling in pockets, making spell bottles clink together.

'How many spells has she got in there?' whispered Double Eight.

'Ah!' Ginny brought out a bottle containing a rose-coloured spell, held it up and swirled it around. 'You know what this is, Director Younger?'

Younger listened for a moment to the crystalline whisper coming from the bottle. 'It is a covenant spell, I think.'

Ginny nodded. 'You *are* good. It's a shame your talents have been wasted working as the king's lapdog.' She glanced at Lara. 'A covenant spell, Lara, is a spell that creates an unbreakable promise. If the Witch who makes that promise goes back on his word, he'll die a most painful death.' She turned her attention back to Karl Younger. 'Are you ready to make that promise?'

His mouth curled in disgust, and one of his eyes was twitching, but he gave a nod.

'Very well,' said Ginny. She raised her wand and began making funny shapes in the air. It took a moment for Lara to realise that she was writing. After the wand had formed the shape of each letter, that letter sparked to life in the air, burning iridescent pink like a firework, until an entire message was there for all to see, lighting even the darkest corners of the tunnel.

'Say those words, Director Younger.'

Lara watched him carefully. For a second she was sure he was going to change his mind, but then he opened his mouth and read the promise Ginny had written in fire:

'I, Karl Younger, bound by the power of this covenant, hereby swear that I will do everything in my power to help the Witches here present find their friend, Ivy Robin, and free her from the custody of Mrs Hester. I will not involve anyone else in this task. When the task is complete, I will grant the aforementioned Witches safe passage back to Westerly Witch.'

One at a time, every word he spoke burned brighter in the dark, then turned to smoke and drifted into Karl Younger's mouth. When he was done, he rolled his tongue around and looked like he had tasted something vile.

'It's done,' said Ginny, looking around at Lara and her friends. 'We leave at sunrise.'

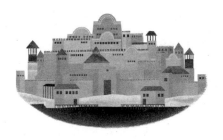

THE EVERNIGHT FEAST

Hundreds of thousands of people had gathered in the sprawling green spaces of Fortress Park in the shadow of the Red Fortress. There were clowns and fire-eaters, brass bands and stilt-walkers and contortionists, stalls handing out caramel apples and spiced sausage and candied fruits. There were enormous tents filled with countless rows of long tables where merry folk sat and guzzled all the free food their bellies could hold. The mood was jubilant; for months the people of the Silver Kingdom had lived under the cloud of violence, had been afraid of secret police raids, of accusations and hangings, but it seemed that they had decided to make the best of an opportunity to drink and cheer and be happy for a change.

Lara and her companions stood beneath a huge oak tree in the middle of the park, watching, waiting.

'Mrs Hester could be anyone,' Lara said. 'She could be walking past us right now and we'd never know.'

'Unlikely,' said Karl Younger.

Lara could barely bring herself to look at him. The fact they were relying on his help made her blood boil, but she supposed Ginny must know best. 'What did you say?'

Younger clenched his jaw; Lara could tell he was hating every minute of this, even more than she was, which cheered her a little. 'I *said*, it's unlikely she'll be down here among the crowds. Whatever she has planned, I'd wager she needs to be somewhere out of sight.'

'How long until the unveiling?' Ginny asked.

Joe checked Granny's old pocket watch. 'Ten minutes.'

The bandstand was in the centre of the park, in the great meadow. It was a tall, circular structure with a cone-shaped roof. By the time they made it to the meadow, midday was fast approaching. Lara could see, down the hill, that thousands of troops had gathered in regimented rows, standing to attention in the shadow of the gigantic covered statue that the king was to unveil to mark the occasion.

Lara and the others tried to weave towards the bandstand, but the crowd was dense and jostling, excited to see the marching bands.

'They're coming, mummy!'

'Lift me up, Grandad! I wanna see the soldiers!'

When they finally did push through to the front, they

saw that the king sat on a wooden throne on the bandstand, smiling falsely and waving to the masses while the bands marched by. As the parade went on, there was no sign of Mrs Hester, no hint of disruption, and soon the last of the marching bands had played and it was time for the king to take the stage. He stood before the mass of humanity, his body lost in folds of gaudy gold and purple silk, his arms outstretched. When he spoke his voice was magically amplified by the spell of a White Witch in the wings.

'My loyal subjects,' he said, his voice strained and eyes bugging from the sockets. 'One year ago, we faced the greatest threat this Kingdom has ever seen: the Evernight! But as darkness rolled over the land, as it threatened to snuff out our very way of life, we did not wither. We stood together!'

At this there were some boos from the crowd.

'What about the poor!' came a shout.

'You left the people in the slums to die!' yelled Joe.

Lara smacked him. 'Joe! Shut it!'

'Traitor!' came the yells.

'Scum!'

The king ignored these shouts, and his secret police began wading into the audience to silence the hecklers. He went on. 'Leading you, my people, through such a test was the greatest challenge I have ever faced. But I am proud to say that I did not shirk from the job at hand. I stood tall, and I led by example, and together we showed that no power in this world can come close to the might of the Silver Kingdom!'

Many in the crowd cheered. The king stretched out his arms. 'Now, to commemorate our victory, and to make sure it is never forgotten, it is my great pleasure to unveil this statue: *The Torch Bearer*!'

He motioned to the towering structure, and the coverings fell away. There were gasps and cheers from the crowd. There was also laughter, and booing. The statue, one hundred feet high, was of the king. Only this version of the king was slim and handsome. He was looking to the sky, holding aloft a great torch to push back the dark.

The Silver King stood before his people, oblivious to their laughter and scorn, and raised his hands in triumph.

And that is when the giant statue began to move.

Screaming.

Yells of shock and fear.

The sound of children crying.

All around Lara, the park became a blur of panic, of stampeding people and crushing crowds.

High above, the gigantic statue's head moved, and it seemed to look down upon the people. With a great rumble, it broke free from its base and reached down, swiping its torch, gouging it deep into the earth, shaking the ground, leaving a hole fifty feet deep.

Lara and Double Eight turned around and began to run, almost tripping over an elderly lady.

'Run!' Lara yelled, helping the woman up. 'Get out of here!' She spun to face the others. 'Where is Mrs Hester? She must be close by. She must be doing this!' Some distance away, the great statue ripped a tree from the ground and tossed it at the fleeing crowd. People were charging for the food tents, taking futile shelter under the long dining tables. 'We have to help them!' Lara screamed.

'We can't beat that thing,' said Ginny. 'We need to cut it off at the source!'

Karl Younger was quiet. Lara noticed that the Witch Hunter was taking no notice of the statue, or the carnage it was causing, but gazing up instead towards the Red Fortress, high on its rocky ledge. He pointed to the fortress battlements, hundreds and hundreds of feet above.

'There,' he said. 'She's up there.'

Meanwhile, the Silver King slipped, snake-like, to his carriage by the bandstand and struggled in, wheezing and whimpering and spitting. 'Protect me!' he was yelling to his guards, spitting. 'Protect your king!'

The driver urged the ironhearts on. They galloped through the park, up the great driveway of Fortress Hill and into the Red Fortress.

'Close the gates!' yelled the king.

'Your Majesty,' called one of the guards. 'There are

people coming up the hill. Should we give them shelter? The fortress is protected by enchantments, they will have a better chance here.'

'Let them look after themselves!' shouted the king.

Moments later, the huge gates of the Red Fortress began to close.

Face-off

'They're shutting the gates!'

Lara and her companions hurried up the hill towards the Red Fortress, surrounded by people who had the same idea, sure their king would shelter them. But it appeared they were mistaken.

'Hurry!' yelled Joe.

Pushing among the crowd as the enormous doors slowly shut, they made it to the gates just in time. Great numbers of people were overwhelming the guards, trampling them, and Lara and the others only just made it through, the gates shutting with a final bang behind them.

'This way,' Karl Younger called. 'Follow me.'

Through the sea of panic they pushed, past the sounds of crying children and screaming men and women, and all the while thunderous crashes and rumbles came from beyond the walls. They reached a heavy, bolted door, and Younger pounded on it with his fist.

'It's Director Younger! Let me in at once!'

The door opened. Younger led the way once more, climbing up and up staircase after staircase, passing servants and guards who paid them no attention as they watched the gigantic statue approach the fortress and start to batter on the walls.

After what seemed like hours, they reached the ramparts, where they could see out over the entire city, right down to the sparkling Giant's Foot Lake and the Veil Forest. Along the ramparts they dashed, the fortress shaking with every blow from the giant statue, until they rounded a corner and skidded to a stop.

'Don't come any closer!'

Mrs Hester stood over Ivy's prone body, a fine golden thread of light connecting them at the heart. She looked unmistakably younger. Her crooked bones had straightened, and her skin had new lustre.

'You leave her alone!' said Joe. 'If you hurt her, I swear I'll—'

Mrs Hester laughed. 'You'll what?'

Ginny stepped between her friends and Mrs Hester. 'Stay back. She's taking power from Ivy.'

'The reaper spell?' Lara asked.

'No, she's not taking life, not yet. Just transferring magic from Ivy to herself, by the look of it. She's using Ivy's power to bring the statue to life.'

'You shouldn't have come here,' said Mrs Hester. 'With Ivy's magic running through my veins, you'll be no match for me.' Her eyes found Lara, and a look of shock passed over her face, followed swiftly by rage. 'Don't you know how to die, girl? Everywhere I look, you're there! I'll save you for last, I think, and I'll make sure of it this time. You'll *welcome* death when I'm through with you.'

A flash of orange, and a smoking bolt of magic whizzed past Mrs Hester's face.

'I won't listen to any more,' said Ginny. 'It's time to end this.'

The castle shook as the giant statue pounded the walls again, and Mrs Hester used the distraction to cast a blanket of thick rolling smoke across the ramparts. Lara could not make anything out, save numerous flashes of light.

'That all you've got?' she heard Ginny say. 'I thought you'd be better than this, Hester!'

The sound of Mrs Hester's angry growl pierced the thick smoke, then she heard Ginny again. 'No, Joe! Stay back from her!'

All became quiet on the rampart, and in the smoke, the sounds of the city in chaos seemed very distant.

'Ginny? Joe? Someone answer! Let me know you're not hurt!'

'Watch out, Lara!' called Ginny. 'She has me bound up!'

'Lara?' That was Double Eight.

'I can't see!' This time Joe.

A lump of fear rose up in Lara's throat as Mrs Hester emerged from the smoke. Lara tried to cast a spell, but before she could pull the trigger, her wand was ripped from her hand and went spinning away.

'Maybe I won't leave you until last, after all,' said Mrs Hester. 'Your friend was right: it is time to end this.'

She aimed her wand at Lara, and from the tip blossomed a huge, glowing python. It came forward, struck at Lara and wrapped around her. She tried to breathe, tried to move, but the snake was immensely powerful. As it coiled tighter and tighter, she felt the air leave her lungs, felt the pressure build behind her eyes. Her vision blurred, darkened at the edges, and she knew that it was over.

Somewhere in the smoke, Joe Littlefoot crawled on his belly, right past Mrs Hester's feet, and found the spot where Ivy was lying.

'Ivy,' he whispered, taking her face in his hands. 'Ivy, wake up, please!' When she didn't move, Joe continued to try. 'You've got to fight, Ivy. Whatever spell she's got you under, you're strong enough to break it, you hear me? We need you. Your friends need you. Your *family*, Ivy.' He took her hand and kissed it. 'Please. Please wake up.'

She stirred. 'Joe?'

Joe wiped his eyes, smiling down at her.

'Where am I, Joe? What's happening?'

'Mrs Hester is back, Ivy,' said Joe. 'Lara's in trouble. The whole world will be in danger if we don't stop her.'

*

302

Mrs Hester stared into Lara's eyes and laughed. 'I'm going to enjoy watching the last twinkle of life leaving your eyes, girl. You cost me once with the Evernight. You won't do it again.'

The snake coiled tighter still, and Lara flitted in and out of wakefulness. The smoke was clearing, and in the moments that she was conscious, she could see that Ginny and Double Eight were tied up with binding spells.

Mrs Hester lifted her free hand, and Lara's friends floated off the ramparts and spun in the air, their eyes wide with fear. 'You see the power I have?' she said. 'You see why you could never stop me? Before you die, girl, I want you to know that I am going to take every bit of power in your little friend's body. I am going to go to Westerly Witch and kill Bernie Whitecrow and take my throne. I want you to go into the next life knowing that you failed to stop me . . .'

She took a sudden, sharp breath and looked down at the golden thread of light that was connecting her to Ivy. It was burning brighter and brighter, as dazzling as the sun. 'Yes!' she yelled. 'I've never felt such power!' Her eyes were blazing orange marbles. Her fingertips seemed to be on fire.

She laughed, and, raising a hand, sent a shockwave of magic out from her fingers that ripped part of the rampart away, sending it tumbling down the side of the fortress. Her entire body was on fire with spell light. The air around her crackled and sparked and spat.

She threw up her arms in triumph. 'I'm going to bring the entire city crumbling down! I'm going to make sure—'

Suddenly, she lunged forward, eyes wide, holding onto her belly. Then she clutched her head in her skeletal hands.

'No. NO!' She staggered back, and Lara could see that her flesh was burning, cracking open. Through the cracks Mrs Hester's rotten insides were aflame.

The spell snake around Lara turned to smoke and vanished. She reached for her throat, so thankful to have air in her lungs again, sucking it in. Ginny and Double Eight were freed too, and Ginny picked up Lara's wand and tossed it to Lara. 'Look, girl,' she yelled, pointing. 'Look!'

Ivy was awake and walking across the rampart towards Mrs Hester, her furious gaze fixed upon her.

'You want my magic?' she shouted. 'Take it. Take as much as I can give. Here!'

The golden thread connecting them turned to flame. Mrs Hester stared at her hands, her arms, watching in horror as the spidery cracks crept all over her flesh, opening wider. The cracks reached her neck, her face, joining up until there was no flesh left, only burning muscle and sinew and bone.

Then, with a final, terrible scream, Mrs Hester exploded in a blinding, searing flash that knocked everyone to the ground, where they lay until their senses began to return.

Ivy stood tall, staring out over the ruins of Fortress Park like she'd just woken from a dream. She looked over at Lara, at Ginny and Joe too, and her smile was dazzling.

Bang.

A pistol shot rang out over the ramparts.

Ivy's smile vanished. She clutched her upper arm and looked down. Blood was gushing out through her fingers.

Lara drew her wand as she ran, and she and her companions caught Ivy as she fell and lay her gently down.

Across the rampart, Karl Younger watched them, a smoking pistol in his hand.

'What have you done?' Ginny screamed. Her hands were busy trying to stem the flow of blood. 'You broke the covenant!'

Younger smiled. 'I promised to help you find your friend, and to free her, and to grant you safe passage home. At no point did your covenant specify that she had to be *alive* in the end.'

The hatred in Lara was seething. She aimed her wand.

'Don't try anything, any of you,' he said. 'I'm a lethal shot and I could drop the four of you before you blink.'

'Why did you do that?' said Joe, looking tormented, tears flowing freely down his face. 'You didn't need to!'

'If my career is coming to an end, as I think it might be by the sound of the baying crowd down there, I want to go out on a high.' He indicated Ivy. 'She's the most powerful Hag in generations. But *I'll* always be remembered as the one who put her down like a dog.' He shook his head smugly. 'Now, if you'll excuse me, I think this place might be about to burn to the ground.'

He backed away, ducked through a door and was gone. Lara stared after him, until Ginny's voice brought her round.

'Never mind him!' She was breathless, sobbing a little. 'There'll be plenty of time for that. Right now, I need help with this.' She took Ivy's face in her hands, and Lara noticed how pale Ivy had become. 'Stay with me, Ivy. Stay with me. I won't lose another one. I won't!'

Ivy opened her eyes, looking around at them all. 'It's all right. I'm not afraid. I'm with family.'

Then she was unconscious.

REVOLUTION

Outside the walls of the Red Fortress, the gigantic statue of the king fell, shattering as it hit the ground.

As the dust settled an enormous crowd gathered at the gates. And, as their fear subsided, their mood became poisonous.

'Let us in!' they yelled. They banged on the gates, pushing and scratching.

'The king abandoned us!'

'He left us to die, just like he did the slum folk in King's Haven!'

'He locked the gates!'

'Looked after himself and left us to die!'

'He has to pay for this!'

'He's a coward!'

'A traitor!'

'Open the gates!'

'Storm the gates! They can't stop us all!'

'Down with the king!'

'Down with the king!'

'Down with the king!'

They roared and pushed and hammered, and under the sheer weight, the combined strength, one of the gates began to give.

There were soldiers on the outside, but many of them were just as angry as the people – the king had left them to die too, after all – and so very few of them tried to defend the Red Fortress, and those who did were soon swept aside.

From his room atop the tallest tower, the king looked on in horror.

'Do something!' he yelled at his guards. But they only looked at each other. They knew, as the king truly realised in his heart, fighting this many people would be like trying to hold back a tidal wave armed with nothing but a dustbin lid.

He realised that these would be his last moments as king, and he thought of all the others who had come before him: his father and grandfather and the many generations who had fought to make the Silver Kingdom great. And *he* was the one who was going to lose it all.

But whose fault was all of this, really? Mrs Hester, the conniving Hag. If she hadn't brought the Evernight back, none of this would have happened. If he, the Silver King, had not listened to her . . .

But he had. Just as he now listened to the people who were storming the fortress. The people who were about to begin a revolution.

And so they came. And just like that, the Silver King's reign was over.

THE TRAVELLER

One week after the events of the Evernight Feast, Karl Younger sat in a plush private carriage on the Dustbowl Steamer and watched the southern desert streaking by his window. The train was taking him to the southernmost tip of the continent. Once there, he'd find one of those two-bit fishing villages far from the centre of the revolution and make a comfortable base for himself before deciding his next move. Money was not a problem. He had taken as much gold as he could carry from one of the White Witch vaults before he left King's Haven.

He did not look like the Karl Younger of a week ago. He had used a spell to grow his hair, and his face was mostly hidden behind a beard. He no longer wore the uniform of the secret police, dressing instead in an expensive cotton suit, and was going by the name Kristopher Yarrow.

He leaned his head against the window and closed his eyes. His hand went into his suit jacket and found the new wand he'd robbed from a Hag a few days before. There were six killing spells loaded in the revolver chamber. When he fell asleep, he dreamed of using those spells on Larabelle Fox and her friends.

Later, in the opulent dining car, Younger ate a dinner of chilli pepper stuffed with curried rice. It was quite delicious. At one point during his meal, an apple-cheeked woman came into the dining car. When she passed Younger's table, her scarf fell to the floor.

Staying in the character of Kristopher Yarrow, Younger leaned over to pick it up. 'Excuse me.' He held out the scarf, and the woman turned and smiled at him.

'Oh, gosh. Thank you, sir.'

Younger nodded, went back to his dinner and thought no more about it. But he should have.

The steamer arrived in the city of Port Carlos the following afternoon. The air was searing hot when Younger stepped onto the station platform, the smells of baking sand and saltwater carried on the warm sea breeze. By the time he collected his case from the luggage car, he was sweating profusely.

'Excuse me, sir. Would you be kind enough to help a lady in distress?'

Younger turned, saw the same woman whose scarf he'd returned in the dining car. She grinned. 'I'm travelling alone, and my trunk is awfully heavy. I don't suppose you'd help me get it to a taxi? After that I'll leave you alone, I promise.' She stepped aside, revealing her travelling trunk.

Younger's heart almost stopped.

It was the very same trunk he'd first discovered in the attic of the opera house in King's Haven, the one the Hags had used to escape him. Stunned, he took a slow step towards it. The ever-present, twinkling lullaby of magic in the air fell silent, and his insides became cold. He stepped back, and made to reach for his wand.

'Don't be stupid,' said a girl's voice from behind him. He felt the tip of a wand dig into his ribs, and he knew then that it was over.

'Turn around,' a second girl's voice said. He did as she ordered, and came face to face with the two of them, their faces hidden under long hoods. Together, they lowered their hoods, and he saw them.

The first was Larabelle Fox. It was she whose wand pointed at him. The second – how could this be? – the second was Ivy Robin, the runaway Hag he'd shot on the battlements of the Red Fortress. Her left arm was in a sling, her face pale. A satisfied smile played at the corners of her mouth. 'Surprised to see me? Hand over your wand.'

He did.

'You know who I am?' said the older Witch, the one with the travelling trunk.

Younger shook his head.

'My name is Bernie Whitecrow. I'm the High Witch,

leader of all the free Witches in the world. Now, I don't usually make a habit these days of going out in the field. But you, Director Younger, caught my attention, you see, when you murdered my best friend in a tunnel under Lake End. Rob Nielsen was worth a hundred of you any day of the week, and you're going to pay for what you did. Now, get in.'

The station platform was now deserted. Bernie Whitecrow opened the trunk, revealing a ladder leading down to what looked like a jail cell far below. Again, Younger did as he was told, climbing into the trunk, down the ladder, into the cell. There he sat on the stone floor, sighed and stared up. The faces of Bernie Whitecrow, Lara Fox and Ivy Robin looked down upon him, framed in a rectangle of blue southern sky.

'See you in Westerly Witch, Karl Younger,' said Bernie. Then the lid was shut.

AFTERMATH

In the future, they would refer to the day of the Evernight Feast as the Awakening. The entire Kingdom, under the spell of kings and queens for centuries, had finally stirred from slumber, its people ready to take their country back.

In the days and weeks and months that followed, news of the revolution spread around the Silver Kingdom. Not only was the king in custody, but Karl Younger, his most feared deputy, was no longer prowling the streets. This emboldened the people, and with the help of Bernie Whitecrow's Westerly Witches, the revolution grew stronger every day. There were still battles to be won, of course, still adventures to be had, but those are stories for another day.

The king stood trial in King's Haven, and had it not been for a last-minute intervention from Bernie Whitecrow, he would have been hanged in Reaper's Square.

Instead, the king lived out the rest of his life behind bars in Westerly Witch.

Karl Younger spent the rest of *his* life two cells along

from the king, and they passed most of their time bickering through the walls, blaming each other for the fall of a once-proud empire.

The night after the trial, Lara gathered with her friends at the foot of the Mother Tree, and there they paid tribute to Rob Nielsen.

They each lit a candle and placed it on a great leaf from the tree, then pushed the leaves out into the bay. As Rob's candles drifted towards the open waters of the Pewter Sea, the sun was falling over the horizon, its evening rays streaking the sky with crimson brushstrokes.

'We're going to miss you, Rob Nielsen,' said Bernie Whitecrow. 'Happy sailing.'

That night, there were feasts all around Westerly Witch to celebrate Rob's memory. In the palace, Lara sat at the top table with Bernie, Double Eight, Ivy and Ginny.

'How are you feeling?' Lara asked Ivy as she bit into a juicy roast chicken leg.

Ivy smiled. 'Better. The wound is almost healed now. And listen to this, Lara: ever since what happened on the roof of the Red Fortress with Mrs Hester, I haven't had a single "incident".' She held out her pale hand, and there was no sign of magical sparks at her fingertips. 'Bernie thinks maybe I gave up a lot of my power for good when I fought off Mrs Hester.'

'Blimey,' said Lara. 'How d'you feel about that?'

'I hope it turns out to be true,' said Ivy. 'But even if it doesn't, I'm with people now who can help me figure things out. I'm not frightened any more.'

Lara smiled, raised her glass. 'Here's to not being frightened.' She looked around the table, saw Double Eight laughing with Bernie, and she wished that Joe had come back with them to Westerly Witch. Then she noticed Ginny's seat was lying empty. 'Bernie, where's Ginny?'

Bernie looked up from her plate, and Lara knew at once what had happened. Ginny had left. 'She didn't want a fuss, Lara,' said Bernie. 'You'll know how she is by now, I suppose. But she did leave you something. Here.'

Bernie reached under the table and brought out a small, oddly shaped brown paper package. Lara went to her, took the package, and unwrapped it. When the last of the paper was gone, she was left holding the wooden carving Ginny had been making of her son. She had finished it at last. It was beautifully detailed and coated in shining varnish. Lara held it gently, her throat feeling like it might close up.

'Can I still catch her, Bernie?'

'I think so, love. If you hurry.'

Ginny Adder was finishing up packing her modest belongings onto a small boat when Lara made it down to the jetty.

'What do you think you're doing?'

Ginny started and turned around, looking sheepish. 'Oh, Lara. You all right?'

Lara walked towards her. 'Don't give me that. You were going to leave just like that? Without saying goodbye?'

'I didn't want no fuss,' said Ginny.

'I thought you might stay for a while,' Lara said. 'I hoped you would.'

Ginny looked up at the Mother Tree, all aglow with lamplight and spell smoke. The crystal music of the Blossom danced with the wind, breathing magic into the world. 'It's beautiful here, Lara. But it isn't home. Home for me wasn't a particular place, y'see. Home was always just wherever my family were. My husband and my boy. But they're gone now.' Tears spilled from her old eyes, and she wiped them away and took a steadying breath. 'No. I'll keep movin', Lara. There's lots of people out there who could do with my help.'

Lara held out the carving. 'I can't take this, Ginny. It's special.'

'That's why I want you to have it, girl. Go on.'

Lara took back the carving, turning it in her hands.

'Remember me by it,' said Ginny.

Then Lara rushed forward and wrapped her arms around the old Witch, hugging her tight. 'Thank you.'

Ginny boarded the boat, unmoored it, and it began to drift out. 'You're going to be a good Witch, Lara Fox. Keep working hard, and maybe look me up one day.'

'I promise,' Lara said. The boat's engine started, and it picked up speed. Lara ran along the wooden jetty, waving, until she could go no further, and then she watched Ginny Adder until the boat was swallowed by the dark.

Alone now, she sat on the edge of the jetty, her feet dangling, and stared up at the countless twinkling stars.

Another adventure had come to an end. The world was changing. She, Lara, was changing too, and that was all right. That was how a person grew. If you always stayed the same, she supposed, then it meant you hadn't learned a thing.

She was looking forward to returning to her studies, of seeing more of the world and becoming the best Witch she could.

But before that, there was one more trip to make.

One Last Time

A few days later, Joe Littlefoot stood knee deep in the bubbling sewer stream under the streets of King's Haven, the rich yellow light from his new dragon-breath lamp glistening on the water, casting shadows on the circular brick walls. His face was set in deep concentration, his eyes searching all about for the right spot.

Around a corner, and he was there: a narrow tunnel under Hangman's Row. Nervous excitement fluttered in his belly. He sloshed forwards and got to work, reaching low into the water, his fingertips searching about the scum-covered bricks beneath the stream, until he felt a deep crack in the mortar between the brickwork. His heart leaped. Something was lodged in there!

Joe's fingers were dextrous, nimble, and they worked the stuck thing free in moments. He stood up, shaking the water away, and held his hand open to the lamplight. He laughed and punched the air.

A golden coin nestled in his palm.

'Nice find.'

Joe almost dropped the coin in fright. He spun around, his fists clenched, ready to defend his loot. His angry expression turned to surprise, and then to delight. 'Lara! What are you doing here?'

Lara had been hanging back in the shadows, watching, and now she came properly into the light, grinning widely at the sight of her oldest friend. 'Thought I'd drop in, is all. How you been?'

He took the coin he'd found, stowed it away in his toshing bag. 'Good. I moved into your old place in the opera house. Thanks for letting me have it.'

'I don't need it any more, do I?' she said, and a surprising pang of sadness hit her. 'We miss you in Westerly Witch, Joe. You sure you won't come back?'

He stared into her eyes, and she knew his answer before he started to speak. 'Thank you, Lara, but you know how it is. I don't belong there. As much as I love Bernie and Double Eight, and you, of course, I'll never feel like Westerly Witch is where I ought to be.' He motioned all around him. '*This* is my home, Lara. This is where I'm happy, and content, and free. You understand?'

Lara did understand. Of course she did. She had searched most of her life for a place to belong, had found it among the Witches, even if part of her missed the simple life of a tosher terribly. If Joe was happy, then what right did she have to try to take him away from that happiness?

'What will you do now?' he asked her.

'Me? I'll learn. Get better. Try to take it easy for a while, instead of fighting to stop the end of the world.'

Joe chuckled. 'We both know taking it easy isn't your style, Lara.'

'Nah. You're probably right.'

A mischievous look suddenly leaped onto Joe's face. 'Say, you fancy a challenge?'

Lara raised one eyebrow. 'What sort of challenge?'

'A straight shoot-out,' said Joe. 'Two hours in the sewers, whoever finds the most loot, wins. Loser buys dinner.'

'You sure?' Lara asked. 'Remember who you're dealing with here, Joe Littlefoot.'

He jokingly waved her away. 'You might have taught me how to be a tosher, Lara, but you're about to learn that the apprentice has become the master.'

Lara laughed, rolling up her sleeves. 'Oh, fighting talk, is it? We'll see.'

And with that, off they went, into the tunnels in their little island of honey-coloured light, together one last time like the old days. Two best friends, hunting for treasure.

ACKNOWLEDGEMENTS

As always, I owe a great debt of gratitude to a great many people for helping make this book a reality.

Firstly, to Charlie, Chloe, Paul and everyone else at Andersen Press, I can only say thank you for your guidance and advice every step of the way. It's a joy to work with you all.

Stephanie Thwaites and Isobel Gahan, you are truly the Dynamic Duo among literary agents. I'm more grateful than I can express for everything you do on my behalf.

Thanks to Mum and Dad for the encouragement and support you've always shown me.

To Aileen, Selina and Mollie: I love you. Thank you for putting up with my grumpy editing moods and constant daydreaming. You are my sunshine.

And to the readers and librarians and teachers who continue to seek out my books, and to invite me to schools and festivals, I can only say a million thank yous. I am in a constant state of stunned amazement that people find pleasure in the stories that spill from my head!

EVERNIGHT

ROSS MACKENZIE

THE EVERNIGHT
HAS BEEN UNLEASHED ...

As far back as she can remember, orphan Larabelle Fox has
scraped together a living treasure-hunting in the sewers. In
a city where emotionless White Witches march through the
streets and fear of Hag magic is rife, Lara keeps her head
down. But when she stumbles upon a mysterious little box in
the sewers, Lara finds herself catapulted into a world of wild
magic – facing adventure, mortal danger and a man who
casts no shadow.

'Epic good-versus-evil fantasy'
Guardian

'Beautifully cinematic, *Evernight*
is a spellbinding tale'
The Scotsman

PATRICK
NEATE

SMALL
TOWN
HERO

Ever since his dad died in a shock accident, thirteen-year-old Gabe's world has been turned upside-down and back to front. Literally: Gabe has discovered the ability to tell stories which take him into the past, or imagine an impossible version of the present or future that seems as real as real. Gabe has no clue what is going on. But the answers may lie with his mysterious uncle Jesse, an online game called *Small Town Hero* which seems to mirror Gabe's own life, a long-lost grandmother, and the very fabric of time and the universe.

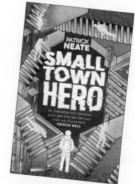

'An irresistible lead character and a plot that will melt your brain out of your ears (in the best way)'
Patrick Ness

'Gripping'
Guardian

SAM GAYTON

Pia lives in a zoo with her parents (both ghosts), several old and cranky genies, a devil, and two young angels. She spends her days trimming genie-beards, trying to avoid being tricked into selling her soul, and waiting for the angels to make a miracle big enough to save the world.

Then the angels go missing. Can she solve the riddles of the mysterious haloes the angels have left behind? Is the zoo's devil really trying to help her? And what does this all have to do with her best friends, the Rekkers? Pia needs to solve the mystery fast, because everything around her seems to be ending: her friendships, her childhood, and maybe even the world itself.

'An incredible fantasy fiction book full of humour' *The Sun*

'Mind-stretching, moving and explosive' *TLS*